DESTINY'S IRE

Howard Scott Shuford

Copyright © 2021 Howard Scott Shuford

All rights reserved

The characters and events portrayed in this book are fictitious. Any similarity to real persons, living or dead, is coincidental and not intended by the author.

No part of this book may be reproduced, or stored in a retrieval system, or transmitted in any form or by any means, electronic, mechanical, photocopying, recording, or otherwise, without express written permission of the publisher.

ISBN-13: 9798415178681

Cover design by: Art Painter
Library of Congress Control Number: 2018675309
Printed in the United States of America

For Amanda
Little sister, dear friend, inspiration, guide

CONTENTS

Title Page

Copyright

Dedication

Prologue

Chapter One: Worth Lost   6

Chapter Two: Worth Found   19

Chapter Three: In the Court of King Phyllaman the Foolish   27

Chapter Four: The Banquet   39

Chapter Five: The Council Breaks   67

Chapter Six: Tragedies Abound   75

Chapter Seven: The Raid   101

Chapter Eight: Destiny's Agent   128

Chapter Nine: More Tragedies   136

Chapter Ten: Flight   151

Chapter Eleven: The Second Kingdom Revisited   169

Chapter Twelve: A Reunion, and a Fateful Flight   175

Chapter Thirteen: The Mountains   183

Chapter Fourteen: Girding for War   202

Chapter Fifteen: Three Spells Cast   208

Chapter Sixteen: The Land Goes to War   212

Chapter Seventeen: Closing the Gap   218

Chapter Eighteen: The Council's Decision. 222
Chapter Nineteen: Answers at Last 225
ABOUT THE AUTHOR 231

PROLOGUE

It is said that the best way to live one's life is to live without ever looking back. Unfortunately, His Majesty the King disobeyed the rule.

Where there was silver, he saw smoke; where there was gold, he saw splatters of blood. It was in this way he saw his castle: an abode of doom. There was that castle: an abode of doom. There was that little spot on the wall in the throne room; that spot that everyone else had forgotten but he couldn't. The spot was small—miniscule really—but no amount of polishing or looking away could make it vanish.

One fateful evening, the King walked the halls of his castle. Dressed in the heavy finery of brocade and linen that suited his position, he bore a package beneath the outer layer of his tunic.

The voice of his wife echoed through the hallway, where the stones had been covered with the gold and silver of his kingdom.

The Queen tore from the nearby throne room, its great wooden doors colliding with the walls producing and a terrible din. "There you are!" she spat.

The King sighed; his queen had obviously grown weary of waiting and sought him out like a crow searching for a worm. One of her young and beautiful chambermaids followed, quaking from fear. So fussy was the queen that she required assistance in all her endeavors, especially complaining.

"You must speak to Edwin immediately," the Queen said, her dark eyes flaring in anger. "I tell you that boy is absolute terror." She extended her hands from beneath her own brocade finery and clasped them in front of her. Her pose and demeanor required action.

The King clasped his hands behind his back in a pose that indicated his patience. There was no sense in arguing; he had learned long ago not to question his wife when she was in one of her moods. "Where is the boy?" he asked.

"In his chambers," she replied. "I've confined him there until further notice."

"Confined him? He's a little old for that."

The gaze the King earned by his disapproval of her judgment would have been enough to make the servants fall on their faces and kiss her feet. He chose to keep the conversation moving rather than let the queen's bile boil. "And what will be the subject of the lecture?" he asked.

"Someone told him about his forthcoming engagement to Princess Allannah of the Seventh Kingdom," she snapped. "That wouldn't be you, would it?"

"Me?" the King asked quietly. "No."

The Queen regarded him with suspicion. "Edwin says that he will not accept her hand. Do you know how long I fostered our relationship with King Roland? Do you know how many banquets I've thrown, how much time I've spent with that drooling boob and his dullard wife? Edwin is not going to ruin this for me. You will see to that."

She whirled away from him, with her long skirt following a moment behind. The chambermaid jumped with a start and took her place behind her feared mistress, trembling with the knowledge that the entirety of the Queen's fury had not yet been vented. Now it was on to some other part of the castle and new prey.

The King watched her go, shaking his head. If anyone in the kingdom was incorrigible it was his wife, not her son. Such was a noble marriage.

*** *** ***

Edwin was sitting on his favorite chair, gazing out the window at the stables. The chair was special; it was carved of dark, rare wood from the forests at the edge of the mineral flats. The back of the chair was carved with the image of a dragon; its small arms extending out and grasping the arm rests with its terrible talons. It was a man's chair, a symbol of potency and power. Edwin secretly feared that he possessed neither of those qualities.

Edwin was not aware that the king had entered and did not notice the package that his father was carrying behind his back.

The King closed the door behind him and cleared his throat. Only then did Edwin turn away from the window. "I'm in trouble," he said.

"I thought I told you not to tell your mother that you knew about Princess Allannah."

Edwin turned from the window. "Sorry Father," he said sheepishly. "It—it slipped out. Mother was going on and on about my birthday and what I was going to do and when and I–"

The King raised a hand in mercy, cutting the boy off. "It's over with now; there's nothing you or I can do."

Thin and pale, Edwin rolled his blue eyes, something his father did often in his youth. Edwin said, "You're the king. You can do whatever you want."

The King slowly sat on the great, high bed, wincing at the pain in his bad leg. "If I was to do as I pleased, we would probably be fighting a war right now," he said. "Come over here and sit with me."

The Prince obeyed. There was to be yet another father/son talk precipitated by the mother.

The King produced the hidden package. It was wrapped carefully in yellowing parchment sealed with wax that bore the royal seal.

"I wasn't going to give this to you until it was officially your birthday," the King began, "but I feel that it might do you some good now." He extended the package to the boy.

"What is it?"

"A book."

Edwin rolled his eyes again, dropping the book into his lap.

"Gods!" the Prince exclaimed. "Another book? I've read so many in the past year that the very thought of the stinking paper makes me sick."

The King smiled. "Ah, but this book is different."

"You mean it's even more boring than the others?"

"No, I mean that I wrote it."

Edwin suddenly found interest. "You? You hate books! Why would you write one?"

"I don't hate books; I hate the lies within them. This book, yes, I wrote for the future king of this realm and no other. I command that you do not show it to anyone. I don't want you to even breathe a word of its existence. If your mother ever found out there would be no explaining. She would fly into a rage that would consume us all. When you are finished with it, then remit it to me personally. Understand?"

Edwin could not stop staring at the package. "Yes, Father," he managed to say.

"I love you, Edwin."

"I love you too."

*** *** ***

Edwin wedged cloth in the gap between the door and the floor; neither the Queen nor anyone in the castle must have an inkling that the tale was finally being told to eager ears.

And so in the flickering light of an oil lamp, Edwin broke the seal.

The binding cracked ominously as Edwin opened the tome. The pages were old and delicate, the inking steady, learned, and undeniably that of his father:

Dear Son,

If we ask ourselves, "What is truth?" we cannot answer without deceiving ourselves. We think we "know" things, when everything is relative and dependent on other truths, which may not be true at all.

Everything you've ever been told, everything you've ever read, is a lie.

At the time of this writing I do not know your name, nor do I know if you will ever exist. However, the contents are such that I cannot bear them alone. Someone must know the truth. I cannot live the rest of my life with the burden of truth weighing so heavily upon me, and so I now choose to lay it upon you.

I know by now that you've the histories of our kingdom and of the terrible Banderwallian wars. Forget all that, for those books are what we back on the farm call bull waste. Darius, like all historians, has a way of twisting things. And for you, my son? For you, I shall set the record straight, and you will know the price peace costs.

I swear on the Golden Oracle that the words contained herein are true. I know some of it is hard to believe, but son, I was there. The Litanies proclaim that naught produces naught, and together the universe gives the right to be. I tell you this is true.

Your Father.

Edwin turned the page, and, in the light that flickered like the ephemeral truth, began to read.

*** *** ***

CHAPTER ONE: WORTH LOST

Sing, O ye people of the Land
Of a farm boy lowly
Whose noble deeds
Would make the land holy
-The History of the Second Banderwallian War, verse 1

My father was always trying to strangle me.

He was a kind and patient man, but on the day, I was born I made it clear that I was the one child out of ten who was to test his limits as a father.

From what I am told, I was born in my parent's bedroom on their farm along the outskirts of the Second Kingdom. My parents were diligent workers who toiled in the fields to make a better way of living for themselves and their children. Father was tall, sturdy, and strong, and mother was lithe and willowy, but mind you, she had a strong back.

Our farm started out slowly, being built by new plantings everywhere, until it blossomed into a pastoral scene, I have never seen the likes of. From the porch of the main house there was the breathtaking view of the multicolored fields that stretched as far as one could see, all the way to the mineral flats that lay at the base of the mountains. Rows of houses with smoking chimneys rimmed the fields; this was where father's many hands lived their lives. It was a quiet, peaceful existence.

Back to the story about my father's desire to choke me. Mother says that I kicked so hard trying to get out of her that she bled profusely and that Sissy (the farm's cook and midwife, as the need frequently arose) feared for my mother's life. Exhausted, Mother lapsed into unconsciousness. I was clear of her body, and apparently father thought I had killed her, and so he proceeded to wrap his rough hands around my neck and throttle me. I never quite understood what he hoped to achieve by my death; perhaps it would have been a small comfort in the face of losing his wife of twenty years.

Sissy hit Father over the head with a chamber pot, and by the time he came to my face was no longer blue and Mother was awake again, wondering what had happened. As far as I know, no one told her about this first attempt on my life.

As a boy I did house chores, which were not considered work. I had a habit of dropping everything fragile, and mother was forever picking up behind me. No one needed to tell me that I was not helping.

When I turned eight, I was taken to the farmhands, and I was thrust out into the fields with my older siblings. Funny, all my siblings left the farm as soon as they were able. I can't tell if they were bored, did not like being under the thumb of my father, or if they feared the idea of working with me.

On that first day one of the hired hands gave me a hoe and a bag of seed. Father claims that I insisted on using the wrong end of the hoe to do my digging, although the rest of the family disputes that account.

Regardless of which end of what implement I used, everything I planted came up withered and stumpy, and so I was soon moved from the production end of the operation to the refining end.

I overheard a conversation. My diminutive, submissive mother said, "Perhaps he could thresh the wheat instead."

"Threshing is too complicated for him," Father snapped while tugging on his graying beard. He shifted his massive, burly bulk on his stool, blowing smoke from a pipe up the chimney. "Knowing Kyle, he'd throw out the grain and keep the husks!"

Mother cringed at the derision; my self-esteem was

obviously fragile at this point, and Father's irritation with my performance hampered her every attempt at offering me encouragement.

Mother, dear Mother, persisted. "Guylak, there has to be *something* Kyle can do."

"He's small and weak. He can't and never will be able to keep up with the hands. The boy is a walking disaster." He spat into the fire.

That revelation gave him an idea.

The next day, I was given two curious black stones and a task. I was told that they were flints and had special powers. If I struck them together, a spark would fly. Flints in hand, I was instructed to go out into the fields and burn the useless stalks the wheat kernels had been removed from. What could go wrong? I was effective in destroying things around the house, so why not about the farm?

The field hands had been careful to confine the stalks to an area far from fields still waiting for harvest, lest the fire somehow get out of hand.

I found the golden, dry field rubbish at the edge of the mineral flats that marked the limits of the farm's arable land. I saw at the edge of the flats the basket of grain intended as an offering to the Soda People. Even at such a young age I was convinced that my parents' belief in something as silly as invisible gnomes that consume the salts that encrust the flats were not only unfounded, but ridiculous as well. If the Soda People were invisible, how could they be sure that they were living in the flats? Did they leave tiny footprints behind on the strange, orange soil as they made their way from clump of salt to clump of salt? None that I ever saw.

Shaking my head at such foolishness, I turned to the task at hand. I found a suitable place amongst the debris of the farm and took the flints to it, attempting to light the wheat stalks.

Click, click, click, and no spark came.

Click, click, click, and still no spark. Was it that I was too weak, as father implied? I did not want to face that possibility.

In my childish mind I reasoned the flint had somehow burned itself out. (Flints never wear out, of course, but I didn't know that at the time.) In a typically boyish gesture, I sought to discard one of them by throwing it as far as I could. I watched as the stone flew all the way into the ripening squash field at the edge of the oak forest—not a bad throw for a slight boy of only eight!

I found the second flint more effective in starting a fire when I struck it against a common rock, and as most of the stalks caught flame, I sat upon the ground to admire my work in progress.

A short time later, I heard a commotion coming from the direction of the farmhands' cottages. It was an uproar. I assumed that one of those rogues had been caught cheating at their gambling games and thought nothing of it. Curiously though, a pack of men were charging my way—and it was not until the smell of wet, green smoke reached my nostrils that I realized what had happened: the squash patch was ablaze, set aflame by the flying flint.

Horrified, I took to my feet to alert my father, but he was on his way with buckets of dirt to smother the flames, as the hands were.

"You idiot!" Father screamed as he ran. "Can't you do anything right? Gods, what did I do to deserve such a child?"

Afraid that any inactivity on my part would only incur more anger from him, I grabbed a handful of mineral dirt and ran for the squash patch. The fire had spread rapidly along the drying vines from the rock that the discarded flint had struck, and even though my feeble handful of soil was some help in smothering the flames, Father was not appreciative of my effort. Before I knew it he dove for me, hands seeking my throat. Not only did he wish to extinguish the fire, but my pitiful life as well.

Perhaps I am too harsh. My father was an impulsive man and I feel sure he regretted his rash mishandling of me, even though it took three men to pry his hands from my throat. Even so, he did not apologize. Held back by two burly hands, he continued to rant with his chest heaving: "Kyle, you idiot! What are you trying to do, ruin us? Get to the house this instant! It's women's work for you from now on–forever! Do you understand?"

I nodded. I was all too aware of my fate.

Humiliated beyond description, I hung my head and made my way back past the hands and others that had been roused by the commotion. Even though I could not bear to look at their scornful faces I knew they were looking at me. I could feel the caustic effects of their disdainful gazes on my very soul. In that moment I wished that the tales of the Soda People were true. O, that I could roust their anger by stomping on their salt crystals and that they would then rise from the mineral flats and singe me with their hot breaths so that I would no longer suffer the miserable fate that Destiny had confined me to!

Alas, the Soda People could not oblige due to their being but a fable. And yet there was another fire beginning to smolder in my head; a fire that forced my eyes from the ground to stare into its flame: *she* was standing at the edge of the field, having forsaken the churning of butter out of curiosity over the emergency activity.

Her name was Sariah, and of out of all those that lived with and worked for my family in those days, I think of her the most.

Sariah was not a blood relative of anyone on the farm. My mother had found her wrapped in a blanket on the porch one morning. She and father decided that such a cruel gesture as abandonment called for a good deed. Sariah was adopted into the family. She lived and worked on of the farm families. No one knew where she came from, but we all loved her just the same.

Sariah was a year younger than me, but even at that age her stunning beauty was apparent. Her skin was as pale as cream, hair long and golden, eyes wide and blue. At that age I could not explain nor understand what it was I felt inside me when I looked at her, but as usual, joy was tarnished with shame that day.

"Ooops," I heard myself say as I walked past her. She followed me with those deep eyes; in them was not the scorn the hands had dispensed but that unspoken sympathy that children hold for one another.

When I crept into the kitchen (the nearest entrance to the fields, and at the far corner of the house), I was surprised to see that Sissy had not come outside with the others. She was standing in front of the fireplace, ladling stew into a bowl.

"This is for you," she said as I tried to sneak past. I tell you that woman had some sort of queer sense that told her what was going on behind her; some of the folks in town swore she was a sorceress, but I of course, did not believe that. No one in those days was foolish enough to dabble in magick.

My desire to bury myself under a quilt in the sleeping loft was overridden by hunger. I sat down at the table, which, incidentally, my father had fashioned with his own two hands, yet another testament to his many skills.

Sissy put the bowl in front of me without as much as commenting on my bungling of my chores. I ate, countering her silence with that of my own.

Out of all the people I came to know in my early years, Sissy was and forever will be the dearest to me—no wait—I just assigned that lofty position to Sariah. It is a king's prerogative and folly to change their mind. I will forever hold their memory in my heart.

I always thought of Sissy as incredibly ancient; to my knowledge no one knew exactly how old she was, and she certainly wasn't about to tell. Even through the cloud of soot that hung about her as she prepared the meals for everyone associated with the farm, it was not hard for me to imagine that in her time she had been a great beauty. Time and hard work had taken its toll; her face was brown and deeply wrinkled, her figure hunched and paunchy. However, her eyes remained soft and clear with a glint of something that I could not find a suitable word for until I was older: nobility. Not the type of nobility that is traced through bloodlines, but the true nobility of a kind, compassionate heart that had taken what others would see as a life of hardship and made it into a test of spirit and passed. My son, as your father and King, I tell you that if every you should meet such a soul, take them into your court and heart. Today, such wisdom is badly needed to rule many a kingdom and yet is so hard to find.

Back to the story.

Even while I finished my meal Sissy did not speak, but I could feel her eyes on me, and they spoke louder than any voice. A long moment passed between us before I had the courage to meet those eyes with my own.

"I set the squash patch on fire," I said meekly.

"So?"

"So?" I echoed, amazed by her lack of concern. "I burned the crop!" My eyes fell to the empty bowl. "Father is furious about losing the squash…and it was only a *few* squashes! The patch isn't—I mean *wasn't* that big."

"Yes, I imagine he is angry. After all, the squash wasn't meant for the marketplace; it was to be his offering to the Golden Oracle. He has a right to be upset."

The Golden Oracle indeed! More superstition. I would have fared better in the matter if I had burned produce marked for sale in the city. The Second Kingdom had dedicated itself to the Golden Oracle over a hundred years ago as tribute to victory over the barbarians who had come across the Great Sea looking for plunder. Anyone who studied the Histories could tell that the victory was due to Phyllaman the First's leadership and not some giant eagle that spouted soporific rhymes. Even my father had fallen for the silly religion and took a portion of the farm's produce to the shrine so it could rot. Now Father undoubtedly saw my accident-prone nature and its repercussions with the squash as a threat to prosperity in the kingdom. It wasn't enough to offer other produce; the very production of it had to be dedicated for the sole purpose of tribute. Perhaps the Gods would have been appeased if the hands had offered them my blood.

Sissy seemed to read my thoughts. "You were careless, Kyle. No being is destructive by nature. I want you to understand this so you will better understand your parents' concern."

"But I can't do *anything* right! I've tried to raise everything from corn to chickens and all I get is weeds or runts."

Sissy sighed; her wrinkles slumped into a frown. "Perhaps you did your best, perhaps you didn't. Only you know that. And if you did, well, perhaps Destiny has something in mind for you other than farming."

"Destiny!" I scoffed. "You're just as dumb as everyone else is. There are no gods, Sissy."

"Oh? I don't suppose you believe in dragons, either?"

"No," I said flatly.

Sissy smiled and leaned back in her chair. "I had a great grandfather who ran into a dragon once. It singed all the hair from his head, and his scalp was so burned that his hair never grew back."

"Sure," I said. "And if dragons are real, then where are they? Why haven't I seen them?"

"They left the Land long ago. Men can't get along with each other, so how can you expect them to get along with something as grand as dragons? They were wise in moving on. Just because you haven't seen something doesn't mean it's not there."

Dragons and lofty gods! What rubbish. No one had seen hide or hair of either in recent history; all their deeds were confined to moldy parchment and old people's imaginations. If Sissy was trying to comfort me by explaining my Father's behavior or by second-guessing so-called Destiny, then she had failed. I went up to the loft and closed the door.

*** *** ***

By the time I was sixteen, the farm had swollen to such a size that my parents had seventy-five hands working for them. The economy of the Second Kingdom was booming, and King Phyllaman the Second (now referred to as Phyllaman the Foolish, although I have other, more harsh names for him) was promoting open travel with neighboring kingdoms. This was a time of benevolence and growth that would be fondly remembered in the turbulent years that followed.

At that time, the King's city was known as Rind. Yes, it was a very stupid name. As was the custom when a new king ascends the throne, Phyllaman was allowed to re-name the city, as he desired. As the story goes, Phyllaman was eating a melon at the time his Chamberlin pressed him to bequeath the city a new identity, thus the vegetable moniker.

The public market that flanked the castle was the largest of its kind in the Thirteen Kingdoms. It was a colorful place of street vendors and entertainers, rogues, nobility, and common folk. Everyone tried to make their stall more colorful than its neighbors, using gaily dyed pavilions of fabric in hopes of attracting a customer.

I am proud to say my family had a hand in the market's growth, for as the most productive farmers in the region they sold their wares exclusively in Rind, and soon other farmers and craftsmen moved into the city to profit from the traffic our stall produced.

True to his word, my Father turned me over to my mother to help with her chores, which consisted of selling the produce the men produced. It was honorable but demeaning work; though many young men worked in the marketplace I figured they did so because they were good at it, and not because they couldn't do anything else right. Still, I was consoled because *she* often worked beside me.

By now I had matured to the point where those odd feelings I felt when I beheld Sariah's beauty were no longer a mystery to me. Her proximity was maddening; often she would walk past me and the ruffle of her skirt or the bare of her arm would brush me and then the roar of the crowd in the marketplace would swallow me and I would be falling, falling, falling in love for the first time in my life. As the day grew long and activity in the square began to wane, my mind would turn to fanciful tales of courtly love.

In my favorite fantasy Sariah was a princess promised by her greedy father to the evil god Baluck in exchange for fabulous wealth—*incredible* wealth, for so great was the princess' beauty that she fetched an enormous price. In addition, on her eighteenth birthday she would be carried resolutely to the ruins of the temple on the edge of the Great Desert and be chained to the horrible sacrificial stone that bore Baluck's terrible mark. The king and his men would wait and wait…and then the terrible and awesome god would rise from the sands, breathing fire from his nostrils and with venom dripping from his forked tongue. The king would cover, and his knights flee from the sight lest they go mad. And then there was me, the lonely mercenary who watched from the bluffs and came tearing into the scene on his noble steed to snatch the maiden from the fiend's cruel talons only seconds before its wretched drool could befoul the princess' gorgeous hair-

"Kyle? Kyle!"

"Huh?"

I snapped out of my daydream to see my mother standing before me, clutching her stomach. "Gods, but you were so far away!" she exclaimed, not knowing how right she was. In the dim afternoon light I could have sworn that her pallor had taken on several shades of green.

"I need you to go to the farm and retrieve some herbs from Sissy," she continued. I feel…I feel *sick*."

"It's those green peralokcs," I said. "Sissy warned you about eating too many."

"I asked you to retrieve some medicine, not to give me a lecture," she snapped.

"Wouldn't it be simpler if I went to the herbalist and-"

"And what? Pay good money for something we have at home? If your father and I threw our coins around in such a reckless fashion, we wouldn't be where we are today!"

Mother's logic seemed sensible to me, but all the same I couldn't help but think that, knowing my clumsiness, she didn't trust me with the money. That was far more valuable to them than any herb.

"You're a man now," she explained to me, as if sensing my doubt. "I know you can make it home all right. Just keep telling yourself "I can, I can, I can…"

Oh gods, the cart! I would have to drive the cart all the way home because of her stinginess and her distrust of anyone else but Sissy with her innards. So be it.

Gripping the reins tightly, I managed to maneuver the cart through the crowded city streets with a minimum of difficulty. I passed the many-colored pavilions of the wood workers, the herbalists, the entertainers, and everyone who sought to get you to part with your money. Yes, the market was like a carnival, but I never enjoyed it.

I breathed easily once the cart pulled into the open countryside between Rind and the town where the farm was located. Yes, I was a man, and this was a simple chore. I would see it through.

I urged the horses down the road, past the great oaks that lined. It was said that the Gods wanted the trees in their geometric placement, which neatly flanked the road toward the clearing and into the forest beyond. I had not come up with an idea as how they got there.

The trees were not on my mind.

A league from town the trees thinned, allowing a view of the Great Mountains to the south. To my knowledge, no one had ventured into that cold, desolate place, for there was the dwelling place of the Nevermen, yet another superstition. The Nevermen were said to skulk down from the mountains under the cover of night and snatch incorrigible boys from their beds, leaving a rock behind as payment. Such children then became terrible Nevermen themselves, whose countenance was said to cause death from fright, should the unwary traveler happen upon them. I knew such stories were but myth, for if the Nevermen existed, they would have surely claimed me by now. My Father would have seen to it.

And so my mind began to wander back to my fantasies

and them into the mountains. I look back on them now and recognize the contradiction they represented, for if I did not believe in the gods or the Nevermen, why did I daydream of them so? I tell you it was Sariah; she bewitched me to the point where I'd believe *anything* if she was a part of it.

...The Nevermen came down from the mountains to claim the misbehaving children-

-and then one of them, peering through a window with their bulging blue eyes, saw the beautiful Sariah lying asleep in her bed and could not resist...

Lost in thought, I did not see the boulder at the edge of the road. Before I knew what was happening the cart pitched over on its side, sending me headfirst into a narrow, rocky drainage ditch. The last thing I remembered before blacking out was the light of the sun being blocked by the cart as it followed my path and landed on top of me.

When I came to, Mother, Father, Sissy, and a man I did not recognize were standing over me, concern glazing their faces.

"The leg won't have to come off, but it won't be much good when it heals," the doctor said.

Leg? What happened to my leg? I didn't care; all I could think of was the cart and how it I had most certainly destroyed it. Though my head was spinning from Sissy's pain medication, I struggled to beg my Father not to choke me.

"Rest easy, son," he said, taking my hand into his. "Everything's going to be all right."

I remember thinking that perhaps my Father didn't hate me after all, and then fell back to sleep.

Sleep was merciful but did not last. When I woke, I knew that I would be no good around the farm or the market now. I was a total liability at the age of sixteen.

Now son, I know that you heard my leg was crushed when I fell from my horse during battle, and as I wrote this manuscript, I debated upon whether I should tell you the truth. There are two important lessons to be learned here: first, sometimes the Gods throw you against a wall just to see if you'll bounce back. Second, and more importantly, don't believe everything you hear or read.

*** *** ***

CHAPTER TWO: WORTH FOUND

Lame and rejected, the boy did linger,
Before he felt the God's hot finger
-The History of the Second Banderwallian War, verse 47

It seemed at first as if there were benefits to being lame. One exceptional morning I woke to find Sariah sitting next to my bed, holding a warm bowl of gruel.

"Um, I brought your breakfast."

Immediately my tongue was seized in my mouth, caught in passion's cruel vise. I could hardly mutter my thanks, nor swallow my food.

"Does it hurt bad?"

"Not much," I managed to say. I cannot tell you what a clod I felt like; here was the opportunity of a lifetime and I could not take advantage of it because of my own accursed timidity.

Still she sat, her doe eyes fixed on my pitiful, worthless countenance. Neither of us said anything further but that did not matter to me. Sariah's asking if I was in pain was tantamount to a most eloquent expression of concern.

After what seemed like years in bed, I felt I was ready to walk again. I did not make a big affair of it; Father was in the loft visiting with me and I made a simple statement: "I think I'm going to try to walk."

My father suddenly jumped to his feet and dashed down the stairs. "Wait a moment!" he called as he dashed past the bed, and but a few seconds later he was back.

"For you."

In his hands he held an ornate cane. He did not have to tell me that he had fashioned it himself, for its artistry and beauty spoke of the time he had spent working on it. It was lacquered black with a beautifully carved shaft depicting the roots and branches of a tree. The handle was the crest of the tree, bursting into blossom. The knob at the top was one of a fruit, an apple. I tell you no gift ever meant more to me than that cane.

Oddly enough, neither of us said anything further; we lapsed into that same strange silence that haunted Sariah and me. Then again, I suppose that in that instance we needed no words; my appreciation of my father and the cane was as evident as his caring for me.

I grasped the knob of the cane in my left hand and swung my left leg out of the bed. *That* was the easy part; next came my gnarled, lumpy right leg. The bones knit just as the doctor said they would (even though I didn't believe they would) but they had been so badly crushed that they could only reform a vague semblance of the former appendage. Nervously I leaned on the cane—yes, I *could* stand after all! In addition, walk? Well, I was so much slower than I used to be, but each step came quicker than the last.

"Are you sure you want to try going downstairs?"

"It's nothing, nothing at all," I insisted. "All I have to do is lower the left leg down first-"

Suddenly, images from the fall off the cart came flooding back to mind. Luckily for me my father was there to catch me and help me down the rest of the way.

Mother was downstairs, and how her eyes lit up when she saw me moving about on my own! She might have cooed and cooed over me had I not made for the door, wanting to finally be outside in the fresh air, instead of upstairs where all the hot vapors collected.

Cool air splashed on my face as the wooden door swung open to reveal the outside world. My spirit, bound by the many days inside the dark loft, immediately began to soar as I stepped out onto the porch. And then it shriveled, losing shape and determination as it crawled back into a dark crevice in my mind. For *she* was standing there, and even though her back was to me I could feel the weight of her soul issuing from her eyes. I knew that when they beheld me in my inability to walk that all hope would be lost. All those fantasies that had been beyond my means were now truly out of my grasp, for even if the Gods existed and Baluck was real, I could not offer him battle. I skulked back into the house, feeling more miserable and sorry for myself than ever before.

*** *** ***

During the next two years, I did whatever I could to ease the burden my family bore because of the accident. Since I could not do heavy work, my parents decided that I should be educated, and hired tutors from Rind to school me in history and philosophy, for the sake of bettering my mind. What dandies those men were in their elegant clothes and strange hats! My favorite was old Bryson, who was so learned that he had almost forgotten his own name. Still, I couldn't help with indoor or outdoor chores very effectively. My tutors, who were supposed to help me find a useful role in life, did nothing to help the situation. Both insisted that I be schooled in the superstitious Litany that had been passed down from the ages by court storytellers; I often found myself dwelling on a certain passage: *That which is not useful is waste, and wasteful is He who is not of use.*

As my eighteenth birthday approached, I began to grow even more morose. The day that I was finally to be considered an adult was near, but I felt considerably less than such.

Exactly seven days before my birthday, I sat outside the kitchen watching the hands work the fields. Uselessness' cloying presence was drawn tight about me just then.

"Hello, Kyle," a sweet voice intoned.

Tearing my sorrowful eyes away from the fields I beheld Sariah. She was finished with her morning chores and had taken the pause to sit next to *me,* of all people.

Fair Sariah approached. By now I knew that truth: I knew that Sariah knew much hardship. Even with her great beauty, with no Father to bequeath a dowry she was hardly a choice for marriage.

"Hi," I said morosely.

Ever so perceptive, Sariah's beautiful faced glowed with sympathy. "Is anything the matter?"

"Is anything the matter?" I asked in stuptification, unconsciously lashing out at the object of my affections. "I'm crippled, that's what's the matter. I'll be a beggar for the rest of my life."

Sariah thought for a moment. "You're not a beggar now. What makes you think you'll become one in the future?"

"Because I would rather be a beggar than make my parents and the rest of you support me," I snapped.

"Oh Kyle," she said softly, "Don't be so glum. What about your schooling? That is certainly worth something. You may not be able to man the plow or even shovel manure, but you can read and write, and that is more than anyone else at this farm can say. Have you ever thought about becoming a tutor yourself?"

"Oh wonderful. We've finally found something I'm useful for. What good is learning? My mother and father have been fine without it."

Her voice took on another tone; I think it was irritation. "You're going to have to change that attitude if you're ever going to be happy," she said.

Horror set in as I theorized that I had offended her; I did not consider that her sharp words had been born of concern rather than ire.

Floundering for the proper words to find favor with, I looked at my leg. Even through the heavy fabric of my trousers I could see the knots and lumps of bone that had refused to knit properly. Happy? I was sure that happy was something I would never be.

Suddenly I felt cold, as if someone had slipped a shard of ice down the back of my blouse. A terrible look must have dawned on my face, for Sariah's deep blue eyes grew wide with worry.

"Kyle, are you all right?"

No, I wasn't all right. "I—I feel sick," I said, clutching my stomach. "I think I'm going to vomit."

In the distance I heard Sariah tell me to stay put as she went for help. Darkness swirled around me as fever crept into my veins.

The next few days were akin to those immediately after the accident that robbed me of the ability to walk unassisted. I drifted in and out of feverish sleep, groaning and mumbling to myself all the while. During the short periods that I was awake, I was conscious enough to understand that not only was my illness serious, but mysterious as well. The doctor was concerned by the sudden nature of the fever that had gripped me, and I heard talk of bewitching or a hex. Hogwash, I remember saying aloud to an empty room.

On the eve of my birthday, the fever still had not abated. Mother sat beside my bed in an all-night vigil, as if she could force the sickness from my body by sheer will. Exhausted, at some point she fell asleep, and that was when it happened. Delirious from the affliction that racked my body, I got out of bed and stumbled out of the house unnoticed, without so much as stockings on my feet.

The night was moonless and dark, yet for me it was alive with mysterious, swirling color that led me away from the farm and into the countryside. It is hard to describe that which is beyond our ken, but that colorful aura had a voice that rang in my head as clear as day: *Come and see, Kyle. Come and see what Destiny has in store for you! Come see, come see…*

At some point I stumbled from the main road that parted the farm and onto a trail I did not recognize. The woods closed in around me; the magickal colors filtered in through the branches, lighting my way. Steps appeared beneath my feet, stones that led me deeper into the colorful forest. I collapsed to the ground, unconscious.

*** *** ***

I woke from my swoon to the warm morning sun on my face. I was vaguely aware that my back was sore—and then I realized that I was not in the loft, but outside! Still dizzy, I lay on the ground for a few moments, wondering what had happened. Dappled light filtered through the trees, and it gave me a serene feeling.

It was then that I heard voices, and this time they were those of men.

"Look! This is my son's cloak! He came this way! He came this way!"

I instantly recognized my father's low bellow. Knowing he would be worried that I had left the house without warning them (Gods know I was worried, having not warned myself) I tried to sit up, but my aching head would not allow it.

The sound of footsteps pounding down the forest path reached my ears, and in a moment their owners were upon me.

"Kyle! O Kyle, my son!" my father cried. He bent over me, his hand going to my temple. When I saw that it came away bloody, I nearly fainted anew, having a weak stomach for such things. Other men (presumably drawn from the town and the hands) ran up behind him, peering over his shoulder.

I struggled to speak. "I'm all right, and I think the fever's broke."

And then a grizzled old man behind my father pointed at me and shouted: "His hand! Look at his hand! Gods be praised be praised! Your son has been Claimed!"

The crowd drew in a sharp breath and took a step backwards down the steps. Steps? I craned my neck to see that I had collapsed in front of the town's shrine to the Golden Oracle. The rickety thing had been knocked askew by some force: me when I fell against it.

My Father gently lifted my right hand into the sunlight. In my fall I had scraped it on the edge of the small, box-like shrine; flesh had caught on the rough, gold gilded edge and torn from the back of my hand. "Gods!" my father exclaimed, and then he too backed away from me.

Curious as to what had frightened everyone so, I lifted my hand so I could inspect the wound. It was not all that deep and wasn't bleeding anymore, though there was a bit of gold under the skin. What was the commotion about?

"It's only a scratch," I said.

The old man saw it differently. "It's the Golden Mark! It's the mark of the Oracle! A prophet! A seer! Gods be praised!" He then prostrated himself at the foot of the steps and began to wail in the most unseemly manner. Soon *everyone* was wailing, much to my chagrin.

Golden mark?

"Don't be ridiculous!" I said. "It's only a cut! And look, the gold comes right off..."

It was too late: before I knew it, the men had borne me upon their shoulders and were carrying me. One of them broke from the crowd and ran on ahead of the group, shouting all the way: "A seer! A seer! The first in ten generations!"

"And remember, he's my son!" my father called after him. Was that pride I detected in my progenitor's voice?

The men rushed me back to the farmhouse and laid me into bed, whether I wanted to sleep or not.

"Please, I'm fine!" I protested and tried to get up, but my Father placed a rough hand on my chest and pushed me back into bed.

"Save your strength!" he said. Wide-eyed Sissy was at the side of the bed in no time, examining my hand.

"I'm so glad you're here," I sighed. "You're the most sensible one on the farm. Go on, tell them it's only a cut!"

Sissy took my injured hand in hers and examined it closely. "Why, it *does* look like an eagle!" she said in awe. "And the gold! Kyle, you been *Claimed!*"

I knew that there was little hope of convincing these people that their beliefs were unfounded and that gripped with fever I had come across the shrine by blind luck.

"And his fever is gone, too!" I heard my mother exclaim to

some unknown party downstairs.

"It's a miracle!" I heard the other party shouted. Muted voices mumbled in agreement.

Gods, what a predicament!

Father began to yak with Sissy, and I suddenly found myself in the company of the grizzled man who started the hysteria. "I'm Jezzidiah; I own a farm not a league from here. I've known you since you were a boy. You remember me, don't you, Kyle—er, Your Grace?"

"Yes," I groaned. I didn't, but why argue?

Jezzidiah leaned closer. "We've been having problems with the well, you see. Sometimes the bucket comes up dry and other times the water is putrid. What I'm asking is where do we dig a new one?"

"In the ground," I spat.

Jezzidiah's forehead wrinkled. "Er, yes Your Grace, in the ground. But which part of the ground?"

Gods! How in the hells was I supposed to know?

"Next to the barn," I said. I couldn't care where he dug the well if he left me alone. "Now go away! I'm tired.

Jezzidiah backed away, nodding, and bowing, nodding and bowing. He would have fallen down the steps if Father hadn't alerted him that they were there.

I looked at the timbers of the ceiling and sighed. What a cruel fate I had found!

*** *** ***

CHAPTER THREE: IN THE COURT OF KING PHYLLAMAN THE FOOLISH

And so the boy becomes a man
And the Oracle Claims by the mark on that hand
-The History of the Second Banderwallian War, verse 96

    The next morning I woke with a clearer head and the knowledge that there was a crowd outside. Even through the walls of the loft I could hear my parent's voices as they spoke with the crowd.

    "No, he isn't up yet. No, he hasn't said anything at all about next season's harvest! For Gods' sake, he was only claimed yesterday!"

    I rolled over in my cot and groaned. The events of the past day were not a nightmare. I had slept through the day to escape the assertions that I was a prophet, but when I woke, they were still there to haunt me.

    I got dressed and went downstairs to get something to eat. Sissy smiled when she saw me and curtsied slightly.

    "Cut it out," I complained, and sat down at the table. "I'm still the same person I was a two days ago."

    "If you say so," she said, dishing out a bowl of gruel. She brought the food to me and sat down across the table, that same stupid smile plastered on her face.

"What?" I asked, knowing she was about to say something.

"Do you still think that the Gods are only a legend?" she asked.

"Yes," I replied curtly. "And I always will."

Sissy laughed. It was the deep, warm laugh of a woman who had encountered many a skeptic in her time, only to see them change their minds. She was old enough to know how it worked; it could be read in the deep lines in her face and the roundness of her belly. Very well. Sissy would wait an awfully long time before I did the same.

She returned to the fire, moving the pot of gruel aside in order to begin lunch for the hands. "I think you should know that Jezzidiah uncorked a spring next to his barn yesterday afternoon."

I nearly bit the bowl off my spoon in horror; gruel lodged thick in my throat. I was only kidding about where Jezzidiah should dig the well. What a horrid coincidence! It was clear to me that if I did not want to further my reputation as a seer, I had better keep my mouth shut.

Suddenly the door to the kitchen burst open. In rushed my mother, who had been driven into frenzy by some unknown occurrence. "Men from the castle!" she shouted, lines of worry drawn on her ruddy face. "Knights, in full armor! The King has summoned you, Kyle!"

The gruel that had lodged in my throat was met with that which had previously been in my stomach. A Royal Summons! One of the idiot townspeople had undoubtedly run to the castle with news of my being "Claimed."

"Up, quickly!" my mother urged, pulling my chair out from under me. "You must go—*now!*"

Why me? I asked silently. Was I being punished for doubting the God's very existence? Was this the hell they had fashioned for me in anger?

Both women pushed me out of the kitchen and into the

28

morning sun. A fair-sized crowd had gathered about the farm, and was being held back by several frustrated, skeptical knights. A burly one, made even larger by the armor he bore, approached me. He bowed nervously, and then spoke: "Are you Kyle, son of Guylak, Claimed of the Golden Oracle?"

"I guess."

"I have a summons for you to appear in the Court of His Majesty, King Phyllaman the Second."

My eyes shifted to my father, who was beaming with pride. What was I to say to them? That I was not the seer I was professed to be? Such denial would surely bring scorn upon my family and townspeople, branding them as hysterics and myself as a charlatan. I had no choice but to accept.

"Very well," I sighed.

The knight led me through the crowd toward a carriage that had been prepared for my journey. As I passed through the crowd, people shouted questions at me, wanting to know if trouble was brewing over the Great Sea, wondering why the Oracle had chosen to claim one as Her own after a hundred years of silence. One woman even shoved a cow's liver in my face which to divine her child's future.

I ignored the shouts and did not dare so much as to breath until the knights had helped me into the carriage and the crowd was behind us. My trusty cane in my lap, I contemplated using it to sconce the next person who asked for a prophecy.

I sighed as the carriage began to move, and as the fields began to move past the window my eyes were drawn outside, toward the figure at the edge of the squash patch. I looked away before I consciously realized that it was Sariah, who was regarding me with such befuddlement. The door to the romance of my dreams clanged shut with a terrible thud. I was *sacred*. There was no chance of winning her hand now.

*** *** ***

The carriage was fine, upholstered in velvet and woven fabrics of golden thread. It was the finest vehicle I had ever seen, fashioned out of dark wood from the outer terraces near the Great Sea. And as that ridiculously elegant carriage drove me away from the farm, we passed the trailhead that led to the Golden Oracle's shrine. "Stop the carriage!" I shouted.

The driver did so; a moment later a knight stuck his head in the window. "Is something wrong, Lord Seer?" he asked.

"I need a moment to commune with the Oracle," I said hastily.

The knight assisted my disembarking and I trod off down the trail.

The woods looked much different in the daylight. Gone were the swirling colors of fever and the voices of delirium.

The shrine was a sight to behold. It had been righted again, and new gold gilded the image of the Oracle that stood on its pedestal. Gifts of produce, woven goods and carpentry had been heaped about the steps as thanks for my calling. I wondered what would become of the offerings. Those less honest members of society would undoubtedly carry them off.

I mounted the steps that were still spotted with blood—*my* blood—and stood in front of the shrine.

The Oracle was a golden eagle, wings spread as if in flight across the future. I looked into the eagle's bejeweled eyes and spoke loudly: "If you are indeed real and can hear me, then I demand that you appear to me in the light of day and claim me as your own."

A cow mooed in the distance.

Ha! I knew the Gods and the Oracle were a hoax! Satisfied but distressed, I returned to the carriage.

*** *** ***

The castle that King Phyllaman the First had built in his honor was opulent, but his son had seen to it that there was no other castle in the Thirteen Kingdoms that could challenge its beauty and luxury. The stones that comprised its towering walls had been completely gilded with silver and gold; in the autumn sun the glare from the structure was enough to blind the unwary traveler who looked at it without shielding his eyes.

Oh, but the gilding made for a terrible sight! The weird,

spiraling parapets and curved windows looked very bizarre in metal. They may have been elegant in stone, but in their current state they were a horror.

The carriage clacked over the drawbridge and came to a halt. The great, metal covered doors to the courtyard opened, and the carriage was ferried inside. Stopping at the main entrance to the abominable castle, the burly knight offered his hand to help me down from the carriage. "It's been a long time since a Seer was Claimed," he said. "You don't—you don't see anything about me, do you?"

"And if I did, would you really want to know what it was?" I asked. "I have a feeling that if most men knew what their fate was, they would try to fight it—but if there is an Oracle and I am truly Claimed, then it's useless. So why don't you just relax and let things take their course?"

Even though his helmet shaded his eyes, I saw the knight blink. If there was one thing I had learned from my philosophy lessons, it was to answer unanswerable question with another question.

"There you are, Lord Seer!"

I turned to see a squat, little gray man bedecked in fine linens and jewels walking toward me. "I am Chamberlin Bule," he said, bowing his head.

Was I supposed to bow in return? I didn't.

Bule, incredibly short and prissy, stood for a while, as if eyeing me. He looked over my simple peasant clothing that though not cheap, were not regal. "We *can't* have you seeing the king in such clothing," he declared. "Wherever did you get such crude things?"

"I'm a peasant, you lordship," I replied.

"Not anymore."

Bule took me by the hand and led me out of the courtyard and into the castle proper. His gate was quick and mincing, and his grip limp and damp. He moved so quickly that I had to struggle to keep up.

"Come on, come on!" Bule urged. "We mustn't keep the

King waiting!"

"I am crippled, you know." I said.

Bule stopped in his tracks and looked at my cane and lumpy right leg. "So you are! Why didn't you tell me?"

"You didn't ask," I said, surprised that there had been a need to tell him.

We did not use the main entrance, instead the Chamberlin ushered me into a side door.

Just inside the hall there was a musty old room filled with trunks and cabinets. An old man in a bizarre costume sat on a stool, dozing.

"Priory!" the Chamberlin shouted.

The old man woke with a start, nearly falling from his perch. He emitted a choked sound that I assumed was an acknowledgement of the Chamberlin's words.

"Sleeping on the job again, eh?" Bule asked. He then introduced me with a flourish. "This young man is the Seer I told you about. He was just Claimed two nights ago."

Priory's sleepy eyes came to life. He shambled across the marble floor, eyes watering and lips quivering. "Gods be praised!" he said, taking my marked right hand in both of his. "Oh young Seer, I have the most delightful costume for you! Tell me, what is your name?

"I am Kyle, son of Guylak."

"Guylak?" Bule said. "What an ugly name. We must discard it."

Before he could say anything more, Priory released my hand and began to rummage through his trunks and cabinets, producing various garments.

The outfit Priory assembled for me was ridiculous: billowing black pantaloons, a black and gold blouse, a flowing cape with a hood, and pointy slippers.

"No," I said. "I won't wear it. I'll look like a sorcerer in all that black."

A disappointed slackness washed over Bule's face. "Oh but Lord Seer," he said, "you *must* have a costume that suits the role.

Oh, please wear it. Please? The King will be thrilled."

I sighed and went behind a screen to don my clothing. In the glass I looked ridiculous; all I need to complete the ensemble was a pointy cap with runes on it, which Priory could not find, thankfully.

"How do I look?"

Priory clapped his hands together. "Splendid, but it's missing something." He turned and dug into yet another chest, from which he produced a leather band. I turned it over in my hands for a moment before I realized what it was.

"Not an eye patch!" I exclaimed.

"Seers are supposed to look old and grizzled," Priory exclaimed.

I rolled my eyes. "Isn't my bad leg grizzled enough?"

"Yes," Bule conceded, "but we can't have you running around in your undergarments to show it off, now can we? Please put on the eye patch, kind Seer. *Please?*"

I groaned and slid the patch over my forehead. "Where's my cane?" I asked.

Priory produced a cane that served the costume better. It was of some shiny blue material with an onyx knob on the top. It was garish and ugly. I was nervous about that cane since I was so destructive. Who knew what might happen to it?

"Where's my old one?" I demanded.

"It clashes with the outfit."

"My father made that cane for me. Where is it?"

Bule cocked his head in a gesture of sympathy and patted me on the back. "Now don't worry, young Seer. We'll put your cane in your chamber. Now we must go see the King."

Chamberlain Bule led me into a marble hallway that was lined with portraits of people I did not recognize. Portraits gave way to tapestry; from my studies I surmised that these scenes depicted the exploits of Phyllaman the First against the barbarians.

The castle was as big as any building I figured I'd ever been in. Chamber after chamber opened from that great hall. I could have sworn that we passed at least seven kitchens on the way to the throne room.

Our route took us to the end of the hall. In front of me stood two great wooden doors, flanked by guards in full dress. In a moment the doors were opened, the fanfare began, and I was led down the intricately woven carpet that ended at the king's throne. Here, gilded marble had given way to imposing granite. Lords and ladies in all manner of finery watched speechless as I limped into the room. Chatter began as I passed on the red carpet; I was relieved that I could not hear what they were saying, for their conversation was surely like that of the crowd that flanked the farmhouse back in town. People are the same wherever you go.

The King had not yet taken notice of me. Perched in his throne, he had a giggling, pregnant maid on his lap with whom he joshed and tittered—not a very dignified sight. Seated to his left were his three other wives (two of whom looked pregnant) and to his right were his six daughters—a dour sight indeed. None of them followed their mothers' good looks.

The Chamberlin stopped short of the dais. "Wait here," he said to me, and addressed the King: "O most noble King of the Second Kingdom, sovereign Lord of thy dominion and bearer of the staff of the city of Rind, and Executor of The Will of the Gods, I present to you Lord Kyle, Claimed of the Golden Oracle."

Bule motioned for me to step forward and bow.

I won a glance at the man who ruled over the kingdom. His "costume" was worse than mine. The crushed red velvet of the strange tunic the king wore was a bizarre sight. He was pale, and seemed to be fragile, like a pane of glass. I was disappointed.

The King looked past his maiden's bosom at me. "Huh? Oh. Come closer, Lord Seer."

Not impressed, I bravely stepped onto the dais.

Phyllaman, foppish and effeminate, regarded me with pity. "My dear young man," he said, "Whatever happened to your eye?"

In time of doubt, my tutors instructed me to always tell

the truth. "Er, nothing, Your Highness," I replied.

"Then what are you wearing that silly eye patch for?"

I turned and looked at the Chamberlin, who shrugged. And then to the King I said: "Priory bade me to wear the patch, Your Majesty."

King Phyllaman burst into high, screeching laughter that nearly shook his golden locks from his head. Around me, the Lords and Ladies of the court echoed his merry giggles with sycophant laughter of their own.

"Oh grand, grand!" the King said. "Lord Chamberlin, tell Priory that his job is well done! What a good sport the king's Seer is! Ha, ha!"

Disgust boiled up within me. If I was to be dubbed a Seer, then I would play along with their game—and so it was time to lay down the rules. "I may be your subject, Your Highness," I said, "but I am not *your* seer. As Claimed of the Golden Oracle, I answer to Her and Her alone."

My words put Phyllaman in his place. His laughter ceased immediately. He composed himself and swept his hair from his face in an effeminate gesture. "I see," he said meekly. Was this the man with whom the Lords and the peasants entrusted their lives to? His behavior was less kingly than it was manly. "I am so very sorry," he continued. "And do you have anything in the way of a prophecy for me—I mean, for us?"

I quickly thought of something meaningful to say: "I see nothing but woe in the future if such foolishness continues."

The Court drew in a quick, stunned breath. What I had said was true and useful, but it came out more harshly than I had intended. However, I felt no need to apologize or water-down my "prophecy"; I felt sure that without a serious king there would soon be serious trouble.

Phyllaman finally found words. "Oh. How dreadful. It has been suggested to me that you accompany the Court at the Council of Thirteen, which this season, shall be meeting in the Third Kingdom. Considering such dire prophecy, I would say the suggestion is well founded, wouldn't you?"

I nodded my head in agreement. I had always wondered what went on when the Kings of the Thirteen Kingdoms gathered, and here was a chance to discover the answer fist hand. It was a decision with many future ramifications.

"Splendid," Phyllaman said. "We leave tomorrow." He then leaned closer. "Tell me," he said, patting the bloated stomach of the woman on his lap. "Is this one a boy?"

How was I supposed to know? Judging from past births, the odds seemed slim. "No," I responded. There were even chances that I was right.

Phyllaman's gay visage saddened considerably. "Damn," he muttered. "Maybe I should take another wife."

A waltz began then, played by an orchestra I had not previously noticed. Chamberlin Bule tugged at my cape, signaling that my brief audience was over.

"Come with me," he said. "There is much to discuss."

*** *** ***

Chamberlin Bule led me deeper into the castle and up several laborious flights of stairs. He then ushered me into a chamber. "These are your quarters," he said, closing the door behind him.

"My quarters?" I asked. "With all due respect, Chamberlin Bule, I'm not staying here."

Bule sighed. "I don't blame you for wanting to go back to your home and family, but if you'll just stay tonight After the Council meets you can return to your home. Your stay is a token gesture, you might say. With all due respect to His Majesty, I must say that we often find ourselves having to humor him. You will stay the night, won't you?"

"Very well," I said. "You must send a messenger to the farm immediately. My parents will be concerned if I have not returned by supper."

Bule smiled. "I surely will. You're a sensible man, as I had hoped." He sat upon the bed, a bed unlike any I have seen before —it was quite luxurious in construction. It was a finely carved thing, and it made me nervous to think that clumsy me would be sleeping on it.

I watched as Bule's expression become grave. "I have a confession to make: When I heard that the Oracle had Claimed a Seer, I myself suggested to the King that you accompany us to King Clayton's court for the Council meeting. Having been around the Thirteen Kings many years—I must always accompany Phyllaman for no one else has the patience it takes to see he is well served-I've learned that they are fickle, proud men who are not given to listening to one another. I hoped that, given the prestige of your position, you might be able to warn them of the coming strife. Indeed, you have warned King Phyllaman already, but see how he scoffed?"

A chill ran up my spine. The Chamberlin saw strife in the works, and my words had confirmed his fears. I had to learn to keep my mouth shut if I was ever to be free of the mark of the Seer.

"What strife is that?" I asked.

Bule raised an eyebrow. "You mean you don't know? You haven't seen it?"

I had to think fast to get out of this one. "I am a Seer, not a mind reader," I replied. "My power is not my own; I cannot call upon it at will. Now what about the strife you speak of?"

The Chamberlin glanced about the room, as if to confirm that we were alone. "I have heard tales of devilry in the Third Kingdom," he whispered. "A cousin of mine was born there and found himself in debt to King Clayton's tax collector. He is presently working off the debt in the castle's kitchen. My cousin has spoken of magick potions, and of strange sounds at night coming from the woods surrounding the castle. Clayton is dabbling in magick!"

The chill spread from my spine and to the rest of my body. Magick had been abolished before I was born, after some fool broke down the barrier between this world and the next and let the dread Banderwallian Demons through.

"Magick?" I exclaimed. "Why would Clayton—or anyone, for that matter—take up such wretched practices?"

Bule looked about the room once more, and this time when he spoke, his words were hardly audible: "*Conquest!* Clayton is devising some scheme to extend his kingdom beyond its boundaries."

Conquest? To the north of the Thirteen Kingdoms lay the Great Desert, useless land at best. In another direction lay the mountains and the Nevermen, and to the other sides, the Great Seas. If Clayton was seeking to increase the size of his kingdom, he would have to attack neighboring kingdoms—and the Second Kingdom was the only land that bordered Clayton's.

I cannot describe the feeling of dread that assailed me then. The Thirteen Kingdoms had been at peace with one another since long before the barbarians invaded. Why would a king seek to destroy something as precious as peace?

"All I ask you to do is to warn the kings so that they are on guard when the trouble comes. Please, Lord Seer. The fate of all the kingdoms in The Land could hinge on your powers of persuasion."

My head was spinning on my neck. How was I, a lowly peasant, thrust into such maddening circumstances?

After Bule left, I lay in my bed contemplating his words. Even I had heard rumors concerning Clayton's nasty disposition, but could it be true that he was evil in intention?

After a while I wandered the halls of the castle, looking for something to do. I happened upon the royal library, from which I snatched a few enticing volumes. I returned to my chamber and read for the remainder of the day.

At some point a maid fetched me some water, and it was utterly foul. It had a charred taint that I didn't understand, but I drank it anyway.

*** *** ***

CHAPTER FOUR: THE BANQUET

*Brave was the Seer who stepped into the fire
And thus incurred Destiny's ire.
-The History of the Second Banderwallian
War, verse 306*

    I do not know exactly what time it was when I woke the next morning, but by the angle of sunlight that streamed through my chamber's window, I surmised that it was well into the morning. Confused as to why I had not been wakened for breakfast, I donned my Seer's costume (Priory had not seen fit to put my old clothing in the cabinet) and searched for my old cane. My head swimmed as I sat up. The cane was not in my room as had been promised; I sighed and took the more elaborate one. The gold on the knob was little comfort; the cane Father had made for me had sentimental value that no amount of gold could compensate for.

    Leaving the eye patch behind, I went in search of the Chamberlin. Having no idea as to where he might be found, I stopped a maiden in the hall and asked where Bule was.

"He has gone, Lord Seer," the girl said, averting her eyes.

"Gone?" I asked. "Gone where?"

"Why, to the Third Kingdom, for the Council meeting."

"*What?*"

    I left the girl; she had no way of knowing why I had been left behind. I angrily stomped down to the courtyard and inquired of the guard at the stables, who was busily shoveling manure—and from the way he looked, he wasn't very good at it.

"Why was I not alerted as to the caravan's departure?"

The guard shrugged.

"Was a carriage prepared for me for the journey to the Third Kingdom?"

The guard shrugged again.

My vexation grew. Was this man mute? If not, it was rude not to answer.

Deciding to wield the power of my position I sternly made a demand: "Prepare me a coach!"

The guard shook his head. "I'm afraid I can't do that, your honor," he said, finally finding the tongue in his head. "That would require the stable master's permission."

"Then find the stable master and ask him!" I shouted.

"He's gone. He went with the caravan to the Third Kingdom."

I shook my cane in his face. "Now see here! There must be someone who can authorize a coach! Who is second to the stable master?"

"I am," the guard replied, "but I cannot requisition a carriage without the stable master's seal. Formalities, you understand. Say, I have a sister in the family that I'm afraid is going to be an old maid. Will she ever find a husband?"

The urge to clobber this dolt was supplanted by my desire to attend the Council meeting. I could not shake the feeling that someone had intentionally allowed me to sleep late, therefore blocking by participation in the caravan. I could not resist, however, giving the guard food for thought: "Yes, your sister will be wed—but not before the flesh is picked from your bones by a hungry Demon," I snapped.

The guard's eyes widened in terror as I turned away. There was little chance of *that* prophecy coming true, but it would surely cause the guard to lose several nights' sleep. As for me, by the malaise I felt, I was sure that the foul water was tainted.

Frustrated, I hobbled across the courtyard, heading for

the drawbridge and the market beyond. My family would have their stall in operation, and I could surely arrange for someone to transport me into the Third Kingdom via the family cart.

As I crossed the drawbridge, I remembered with dismay that today was the first day of the new season—and therefore the market was closed. I was stranded.

The clack of hooves reached my ears. As I stood wondering how I was to get to the Third Kingdom, a Forest Troglodyte pulled his wagon onto the street that flanked the castle. Knowing how greedy Trogs are, I quickly came up with a plan.

As the Trog passed, I held up my hand. In the sunlight the wound that had been inflicted by my fall against the shrine must have been painfully clear, for the Trog immediately covered his huge, knobby ears. "Don't tell me!" he screeched. "If you see anything about me, I don't want to know what it is!"

"I'll give you ten gold pieces if you'll drive me to the Third Kingdom."

The Trog's warty hands flew from his ears to the reigns; his eyes widened with desire at the prospect of earning such a costly fare. "Ten gold pieces!" he exclaimed. "Climb aboard, young sir, climb aboard!"

I hastily did as he suggested, and the journey was underway.

*** *** ***

I had never spent any time in the company of a Trog; my parents forbade me from associating with such types, having been told that any creature with as many warts as a Trog was unclean. It was also rumored that their bulbous eyes had evolved specifically for the task of peeping at ladies through keyholes. Such musing may or may not be the case, but one thing was clear: Trogs were extremely loquacious.

"So anyhow," the Trog continued, "My grandfather saw a mystic at a moon festival and was told he was going to be squashed by a boulder. And do you know what happened? *Splat!* Just as the mystic said, he was crushed by a stone that had loosed from the castle parapet! Isn't that terrible?"

I agreed. If only the poor denizens of The Land could see that the mystic merely got lucky.

We were hardly an hour from Rind by that time; at this rate I wouldn't reach the Third Kingdom until nightfall. For all I knew that could be too late.

"Erdo, can't this horse travel any faster?" I asked.

"Yes, my lord. The problem doesn't lie with the horse; it's in the wagon. I'm afraid that if we go too fast, it might fall to pieces. I had a cousin who drove such a cart for most of his life, and the Gods know he was a patient man, but one day he went to fast as he crossed Gallman's Bridge and wound up in the drink—as far as we know. All we found was the cart toppled over in the middle of the river."

Gods! All I asked was a simple question; if I had wanted a family history, I would have asked for it.

Sometime later, Gallman's Bridge finally came into view. I sighed with relief; here at last was the boundary between the Second and Third Kingdoms.

As we crossed the bridge, I realized why it was as dangerous as Erdo's tale of his hapless grandfather suggested. Someone–Gallman I presumed–had taken the time to pave the wooden bridge with flat stones, many of which had been lost because of the enormous amount of traffic the bridge saw. Alas, no one saw fit to replace said stones, leaving the surface pitted with ruts. Even at our slow pace I had to hold onto the seat to keep myself from being thrown into the raging currents of the Great River below.

Erdo was visibly relieved when we reached the far bank. "Now that wasn't so bad, was it?" he said.

Then there came a sharp cracking noise. The cart lurched; my heart flew into my throat as the sensation of falling gripped my body, a feeling not unlike the one I had when the accident that took the use of my leg occurred.

The sensation was brief; the cart came to rest at a steep angle. Erdo's nag bayed in frustration as its harness held it back.

"That damn wheel!" Erdo exclaimed, immediately recognizing what had happened. He dumped his stumpy body off the bench (of which his side was higher in the air than mine) and trotted to the back of the cart. I turned to see him kick the left rear wheel, of which a spoke had shattered.

"Gods!" he said to me, inspecting the damage. "Weren't you aware this was going to happen?"

I answered with the same excuse I gave Bule: "My power is not my own. I can only see what the Oracle wills me to see."

Erdo was visibly disappointed. "Ten gold pieces blown to hells!" he moaned. "There's no repairing this damn thing; I'll have to get a new one. I *knew* I should have replaced that wheel when I first saw the cracks in the spokes!"

I looked to his horse, thinking it might offer transportation. Alas, its back was so slacked and bowed that it would hardly support Erdo's weight, much less my own.

What was I to do? I had no idea exactly how far it was to Clayton's castle, but it couldn't be *that* far; none of the Thirteen Kingdoms were very large. The thought of walking did not appeal to me; but it was better than giving up. Perhaps another cart would pass by, and I could hire a ride.

Still trembling from the surprise of the mishap, I climbed of the cart and neatened my clothing. "I will walk from here," I said, and began to take my leave before the abominable Trog decided to tag along.

"But what about my wages?" he complained. "I brought you this far; that must be worth at least five gold pieces."

I cringed. I had no gold pieces, of course. I was expecting Chamberlin Bule to come up with them. All the same, I did not want to seem ungracious or gain a reputation as disreputable. Being called a Seer was bad enough.

"Well..." I said reluctantly, "I'll give you seventeen if you keep me company."

Erdo's mood improved considerably. "Seventeen gold pieces?" He turned his bulbous eyes to the sky, calculating in his head. That will buy fifty wheels—no, fifty new carts *and* fifty horses! It's a deal."

The Trog promptly set the horse free; it ran off into the countryside at a speed I would not have thought it capable of.

Erdo decided to leave the cart stranded in the middle of the road, reasoning that someone would come upon it and either break it up for fuel or salvage it as a vehicle. I only prayed that Bule would pay the fee we had agreed upon, or the Trog would be understandably upset at the loss of his cart.

The woods around us were deep and thick with trees and bramble. In the falling sun the forest looked preternatural and eerie.

I shook off a chill and tried to comfort my heart.

The afternoon wore on. No carts passed.

Eventually, the road entered an even darker knot of trees. Even the Oracle's brilliance could be concealed in that wooded place.

Erdo sniffed at the air. "I had a grandfather who lived in a knoll like this."

"The same one that was crushed beneath the boulder?" I asked.

"No, the other one. He had horrible red eyes, and lots of warts."

I did not vocalize my suspicion that *all* Trogs were plagued with warts.

Once again, my simple comments prompted Erdo to tell tales of his relations. I would have told him to be quiet if my leg hadn't hurt; I was hoping that listening to his prattle would take my mind off the pain.

"...You can imagine the stink that my great-grandma's run-in with the Soda People caused. And I mean *stink!* They say that the stench was so terrible, that my grandfather deserted her but minutes later, and that the stink even permeates her very grave." Erdo shuddered at his own imagery. "Can you imagine? Everyone told Grams not to chase that darned pig into the mineral flats, but she just *had* to have that extra bacon..."

Erdo ceased speaking; his oversized ears pricked up to a

sound in the distance. "Hello, hello! I smell people."

"What?" I asked, curious.

"I can smell a fresh beet from a mile away, " Erdo explained, "and I can smell humans from about half the distance."

He leaned over to allow one of his ears to take in the sounds. "Voices, Lord Seer—and they're coming this way. And they sound quite merry, too."

As the voices neared, I began to become suspicious. "Merry" was not the proper word to describe the tone. "Drunken" and perhaps even "belligerent" was better suited.

Erdo saw them first; his eyes were better suited to the forest environment where the light was scattered by the canopy of foliage overhead. The four men that were shambling down the road toward us were dressed in leather armor. Their generally unkempt appearance spoke of their generally uncharitable actions.

"Robbers, your Seership!" Erdo exclaimed, coming to the same conclusion that I had. Such bands of scalawags had long been expelled beyond the boundaries of the Thirteen Kingdoms by the joint efforts of the kings.

I grabbed Erdo's arm and began to drag him into the forest where we could hide, but we had already been spotted. The rogues stepped up their pace, closing in on us quickly.

"Robbers!" Erdo repeated. "Why haven't King Clayton's men dealt with them?"

"Shh!" I urged, clinging to the thin hope that we still might be able to hide. It was obvious to me that if Clayton were indeed preparing for war, attentions would be turned from the domestic situation, allowing such lawlessness to filter across the border.

And then the band was at the side of the road, laughing at our pitiful attempts to escape.

"What have we here?" one of them said. He was very rough looking and sported an eye patch that surely was not for effect, as mine had been.

"A nobleman and his Trog!" the man exclaimed, and then turned to his companions.

Nobleman? *What* nobleman? I realized that they were referring to me. Damn those fine clothes that Priory had given me!

Attempting escape being futile, I turned to face our antagonists. Erdo continued to plow into the underbrush; if I had not kept hold of his arm, he would have blended into the woods that Trogs called their home.

One of the men's eyes fell to the golden knob on my cane. "A *rich* nobleman!" he said to Eyepatch. "See his fine cane! I wonder what other valuables they might have…"

Erdo ceased making for the woods and tugged at the hem of my blouse. "Give them the gold you promised me," he pleaded. "Give them the gold and maybe we'll escape with our lives!"

Eyepatch nodded. "Aye, good sir," he said. "Give us your gold and maybe we won't kill you—*maybe*." He stepped off the road and onto the grass, brandishing a knife in one hand. The other hand was empty and extended, asking for the gold I supposedly had.

It is odd how in such dire situations one can behave as one wouldn't normally; the outrage of the situation filled me with foolish bravado.

"I suppose you will be wanting my cane as well," I said.

Eyepatch grinned with greed. The scar on his forehead twisted menacingly in response to the change in expression.

"Here it is," I said, and then I hit him with it as hard as I could. Blood splashed from his temple as Eyepatch fell to the ground, stunned.

At the side of the road, the other robbers burst into laughter. "Downed by a cripple!" one jeered. "Downed by a cripple!"

Eyepatch was not amused. He stood, wiping his brow with the back of a grungy hand. He examined the blood. "You wretch!" he growled. His grip on the dagger grew tighter, and he stalked toward me, eliminating the last bit of space between us.

Sheer hatred smoldered in his good eye.

Suddenly the air was filled with a howl like that of a ravenous Demon. Startled, Eyepatch made the mistake of taking pause. In a blur of motion, a brawny figure leaped from the bush and disarmed Eyepatch with a powerful blow. He then delivered a punishing blow to the jaw of my would-be assailant. Eyepatch fell backwards to the ground. Blood from his wounded lip arced through the air, spattering one of his companions. Rather than see his own blood spilled, the second vagabond took flight into the forest with his friend following but a heartbeat later.

I righted myself with my cane and turned to face our hero. He was obviously a scoundrel, from the way he was dressed in leather pants and a brocade shirt, which was open just enough to expose his powerful chest. This was no robber, but a despoiler of women and honest folk. He was obviously a mercenary.

"Well!" I said, trying to sound grateful. "You saved our lives."

"Nothing to it," the man said with a grin. His curled back lips revealed that one of his front teeth was made of gold. "A Trog and a dandy have no business in these woods these days."

"Trog, yes, dandy, no." I said. "I am a member of King Phyllaman the Second's court and am on my way to the Third Kingdom."

"He's the Lord Seer, Claimed of the Golden Oracle!" Erdo blurted before I could stop him.

The man threw his head back and laughed heartily. "Well, you can't see much if you're foolish enough to pass this way," he said between chortles.

I grit my teeth. "Well, it's obvious, isn't it? I knew you would be here to save us."

The man stopped laughing. He scratched his head, picking a leaf out of his long hair. I had obviously caused him to think thoughts that stumped him. "Did you really foresee that?" he asked in awe.

"Naturally. Furthermore, it is in your destiny to

accompany us to King Clayton's court in order to assure our safety. There will be a rich reward waiting for you if you do."

Now I was talking his language. He bowed to me and introduced himself. "I am Derek, son of Elrack. I am at your service."

"And I am Kyle, Claimed of the Golden Oracle. My friend here is Erdo."

Erdo waved.

What a mess I had made. I was forced to admit to something that was a falsehood once again. I wasn't claimed of anything, for there was nothing to be claimed of. I was weaving a dangerous web from which there may be no escape. Sooner or later, someone would realize that I was a fraud.

There were more pressing matters at hand. Erdo and I returned to the road while Derek went into the forest to retrieve his steed. It was a magnificent animal. I had been around horses all my life, but I had never seen one so sleek and muscular. It was taller than I was at the back (well, most horses were) and Derek set astride it like a master. They loped onto the road, and we were once again on the way. He pulled me up to ride behind him. We would make better time that way. However, being close to his body caused me pain. This was the kind of body that Sariah would be attracted to, not mine.

As we rode, Derek spun tales of his bravery that were completely ludicrous. He had been at the battle of Ch'ga-zam, he had personally beheaded over a hundred robbers who burst into villages and tried to rape the women. (I'm sure he bed the grateful wenches too since everyone was so obliging of him.) He spoke of great wealth he had stashed in the caverns of the mountains, and that he had even seen one of the Nevermen.

Erdo's eyes bulged at the lie. "You saw one of the Nevermen and lived to tell?" he asked, the tone of his voice bordering on worshipful.

"Sure did," he said, brushing a wisp of that awful long, brown hair from the bridge of his nose. "They're a terrible sight to see. All white and crusty, with their genitalia hanging between their legs. Yes, a terrible sight."

Oh, he sounded so masterful, so heroic, and Erdo was hanging on his every word. I had never been so disgusted in my entire life. Derek was as big a liar as I was.

I tried to ignore him as the forest became darker and closer to the side of the road.

Many questions had been raised by the events of that day. What were robbers, who had been expelled into the Great Desert, doing in the area? Was there a significance that they were between Clayton and Phyllaman's territory?

There was much to be said about King Clayton. If robbers were in his lands, then someone had used the banned magicks to bring them back. It followed then, that perhaps King Clayton himself had someone cast a spell, either to gather robbers and mercenaries like Derek together into an invading horde, or someone else had loosed the Desert Bonds and was sending them to attack Clayton.

The former seemed more reasonable. There was a great deal of hatred for King Clayton in the land; he was depicted as an evil and cruel king who subjected his people to terrible taxes and brutal laws. I never saw firm proof of these allegations, but they were common.

I could not be sure that my deductions were correct. Further investigation was required before I could bring the matter before the Council, which I intended to do should it be warranted. If the robbers and Derek's presence was but an accident and Clayton was not planning a war, to accuse him of such could sacrifice the peace that I was trying to protect. Derek, therefore, was possibly evidence of evil magick.

I found Erdo tugging once again at my blouse. The tugging was an irritating habit, but then being a dwarf he could not exactly tap me on the shoulder to gain my attention. "I've got a sensitive nose—if you're looking for a magick laboratory, I could sniff out the powders and such!"

"Where did you get such an idea?"

"You said, "magick," like that, under your breath."

"So?"

Erdo blinked. "I'm not a simpleton," he said, "and I can assemble the evidence and come to a conclusion, just as you can. Robbers in the forest? Must be magick. I can help you! You know that we Trogs have excellent sense of smell. I can sniff out potions over a huge distance."

I brushed his grimy hand off my clothing. "So you can smell something specific from a long distance?"

"Yes, yes!"

"Did you smell anything back there, at the scene of our altercation?"

Erdo rolled his eyes. "Oh Gods yes! Those men smelled awful!"

I could have told him that. Erdo was fishing for gold pieces, to be sure.

"I can do it, Lord Seer!"

"We'll see."

But—"

"I said we'd see.

*** *** ***

We rode the bumpy trail for what seemed like an eternity. Conversation was minimal until shortly after the sun slinked below the horizon.

"We're coming up on the castle," Erdo abruptly said.

"Good," I replied, for my seat was aching. Derek sat in the saddle merrily, whistling a tune he didn't know.

I strained my eyes in the failing light to glimpse the signs of the castle that Erdo had. I could see nothing but countryside before us. "How do you know we're near the castle?" I queried.

"Because I can *smell* it, and believe me, it's terrible," Erdo replied.

Shortly thereafter we rode over a knoll that had hidden the castle and city from our view.

Clayton's city, Caz Bar G'Zan, was very unlike Rind. Here, the streets were littered with garbage and the stench of decay was everywhere, just as Erdo suggested. The windows of most of the houses were dimmed; most of the activity in town was centered on crowded pubs where citizens had chosen to celebrate the council meeting with drunkenness.

Clayton's castle loomed ominously on the horizon. Thick vines snaked up the walls and turrets, but could not hide the state of general disrepair the structure had fallen into. It was merely a cube of a building that had been ugly to begin with and was now uglier in its disrepair. Clayton was a distracted man indeed to allow the centerpiece of his kingdom to become so shoddy.

We crossed the stagnant moat and entered the courtyard without challenge. What guards we did see were listless with liquor. Here there was none of the pomp or pride that colored the Second Kingdom. Even the silliness of Phyllaman's court was palatable when compared to the gloom that hung about this foreboding place.

Derek tied up the horse at the entrance to the castle. There was no sign of the horses or the throngs that had come to see the Council save the massive amounts of dung on the stones that paved the street.

Derek and Erdo followed as I entered the castle proper, looking for someone to point me toward the banquet that the Kings were undoubtedly treating themselves to. There were no servants about; I assumed they were quite busy attending to the Kings and their knights.

We were just entering the main hall when I saw a drunken Priory stumble out of a smoky chamber. Who else but Phyllaman would bring his costumer along?

"Priory!" I called.

The old man dropped the goblet he was holding and came to attention. "Yes, your g-g-g-grace?"

"These two gentlemen are my escorts," I said, indicating Erdo and Derek. "Please find them something suitable to wear."

Priory stumbled toward us and looked my companions over. "Oooo, he's a short one," he said of Erdo, and then "Oooo, he's a big one," he said of Derek. "Come with me, kind sirs, and I shall have you outfitted in no time."

As Priory started off down the hall, I pulled Derek and Erdo aside. "Meet me in this very spot as soon as you're dressed," I said. "Don't go wandering about the castle, for I don't want to raise any suspicions. Understand?"

"Right," they said in unison, and followed Priory. I would be much relieved once Derek was in proper clothing and not as obviously foreign. If Clayton had indeed commuted Derek from far away, he had not managed to land him in the castle and therefore would not recognize him—but anything was possible.

Alone, I realized that the floor plan of Clayton's castle was very similar to Phyllaman's and that the throne room was probably behind the huge doors at the far end. I slowly walked along the dirty floor, coursing through the web of torn and singed tapestries that hung from the wall.

I reached the entrance to the main hall. Here too were inebriated guards, and so I casually made my way into the chamber, opening a rotted door and slipping inside.

The banquet scene was one of unbridled hedonism. The thirteen kings, knights, lords, and ladies were seated around a huge round table that was piled with viands of every kind imaginable. An orchestra warbled in the far corner of the room; the music was all but muted by the laughter and bellowing of the revelers. Tapestries that had once hung on the throne room walls had been torn from their hooks and trampled into the floor, along with discarded food. There was going to be quite a mess to clean up before the Council could meet on the morrow.

I scanned the room for someone I recognized, having never seen any kings other than Phyllaman the First before. At the far side of the table sat an unamused Bule, whose expression went taught when he saw me in the doorway. Bule immediately jumped to his feet and scurried my way.

"Oh Lord Seer, I am so pleased to see that your illness has passed," he cried. "I was most disappointed when I was told that you would not be accompanying us."

"I am not ill, nor was I this morning," I informed him.

Bule's expression slackened, becoming a frown of worry. "But I was told this morning that you were ill."

"Who told you I was ill?"

"Well, one of the servants came to me as I was coming up the stairs toward your chamber and-"

"*Who*, Chamberlin Bule? Who told you that I was ill?"

"I don't know the old man's name; there are so many people working in the castle and—you—you don't think-"

"Someone tried to keep me from coming here," I said, completing his sentence. I looked about the hall warily. "Something must be afoot after all."

Bule took me by the arm and began to lead me from the room. "You can't speak with the Kings now; they far too full of themselves to listen now. Come, I want you to meet the cook I was telling you about."

We stopped short of the doorway, for we had come face to face with a king and a lady who were returning from elsewhere in the castle. Bule stiffened visibly before bowing the presence of this nobles; I knew who the man was even before he was introduced.

"King Clayton of the Third Kingdom, may I present Lord Kyle, Claimed of the Golden Oracle."

"Your highness," I said. I bowed up and down slowly, taking in full stock of his countenance. He was thin and pale, with a strangely knotted beard that sprouted from beneath his chin. A character indeed.

King Clayton smiled quite unexpectedly, his brown eyes twinkling. "I am ever so pleased to make your acquaintance," he said with a nod. His voice was high and thin but did not suggest the flippancy that Phyllaman's did. "It has been a long time since we have had a Seer in our midst."

"Oh, a very long time," Bule added. "Ten generations or more."

"Quite. May I present my sister, the Princess Elwynna?" Clayton motioned to the lady beside him. She was a very stern woman with a turned-up nose and blotchy skin. I pitied the man who would marry her—not just because of her ugliness, but the unsavory chance of inheriting a degenerate kingdom.

"Your Highness," Bule and I said, and bowed.

Elwynna remained silent.

"I trust you have a message from your mentor to deliver to the Council tomorrow?" Clayton asked.

Bule cut me off. "He surely has. I was just about to show him to his quarters for the evening."

"Excellent. Now if you will excuse me…"

Bule and I bowed again as Clayton and Elwynna slid past us and into the banquet. I watched him closely as he passed; in his regal attire and with his presence he seemed nobler than any of those in the hall, albeit in a strange way.

Bule sighed with relief as the door closed on the hall. "Now, to the kitchen," he said, and led me away.

Confused, I could not help but mention the impression I had received. "King Clayton hardly seems the monster of his reputation."

"Ha!" Bule snorted. "He's an awful person; there's all sorts of tales of his nefarious doings. Why, just ask any of the servants here. They'll tell you. And just look at the place, Lord Seer. This castle is a disgusting dung heap that would fall easily to another King."

"Yes, I see now," I said. "Perhaps he is building an army in peace to keep the peace."

"Phsssh! He's a cretin. Clayton is guilty. Anyone can tell you that."

I stopped arguing with Bule for there was no point. His mind had been made up. I had come to the castle sure of Clayton's guilt, and something was telling me otherwise. As for the servants, well, one cannot listen to and believe in rumors when it comes to matters of war and peace. If Clayton was up to no good, I wanted to see it with my own eyes.

*** *** ***

The cavernous kitchen was isolated from the rest of the castle, as is the custom. As soon as we entered, I spied Erdo and

Derek leaning against the wall, stuffing their mouths with food taken from trays that servants bore as they passed. "Excuse me for a moment," I said to Chamberlin Bule.

"Oh, hello Lord Kyle!" Erdo said, seeing me approach. "Do you want some chicken?"

"No," I said sternly. "I thought I told you to wait in the hall."

"I got hungry," Derek said.

I chose not to scold them further; hunger was surely a powerful drive with someone whose stature was as large as Derek's. "Fine," I said, "but wait here until I get back. Don't go anywhere, understand? And whatever you do, don't drink the wine."

"Right," Erdo said through a mouthful of chicken.

I returned to Bule's side. He was watching the exchange with disgust. "Such uncouth people! Who are they?"

"Friends of the Oracle," I said. "Now where's that cousin of yours?"

Bule led me through the maze of counters and servants. There were many worktables where cooks were rapidly creating delicacies that a drunken tongue cannot taste.

The air was heady with the aroma of roasted meats and fine sugar candies. It was a mixture that produced a sweetness tinged by smoke. I heard my own stomach growl at the stimulus.

We came to a fireplace on the far wall, where a thin rail of a man was stirring a huge cauldron. "Thaddeus?" Bule asked.

The man jumped visibly, clutching his chest. "Oh, it's only you!" he replied in relief. "I thought it was—never mind."

Bule motioned toward me. "This is Kyle, the Seer," he said. "Is there someplace we can talk?"

Thaddeus thought for a moment and then pressed a finger to his lips, pleading with us to be quieter. He then led us into a dark pantry and closed the door. The space was redolent of preserves of every kind.

"We must be very careful," Thaddeus whispered. "Something is going to happen. His majesty came to me earlier with a vial of liquid and bade me to put it into this evening's wine."

Bule cast me a concerned glance.

"And did you do so?" I asked.

"Well…yes, I had to. He wanted to watch me do it. The Gods only know what sort of horrible bewitching he would have brought down on me if I hadn't. And there was no other wine to take its place, or I would have substituted another barrel. Here."

Thaddeus produced a small bottle from the pocket of his apron and handed it to me. I opened it and smelled the dregs at the bottom; they were fetid, rancid.

In the kitchen, Erdo's nose began to audibly whistle.

"And there have been other miserable deeds afoot," he continued. "Almost a season ago his Majesty threw many of the knights into the dungeon. I've been trying to feed them as well as possible, but not much more than slop gets past the dungeon guards." He nervously pressed his eye against a crack between planks in the larder door, looking for suspicious ears.

"Do you know why Clayton threw these men into the dungeon?" I asked.

"No."

"Oh, but it's obvious," Bule offered. "If Clayton is planning on war, most sensible men would refuse, hence their imprisonment. Look at the guards who now man the palace! Absolute rabble! You must warn the Council, Lord Seer. You must tell them of Clayton's plot!"

Now was one of those times when I had a difficult decision to make. Bule was right in being suspicious and fearful of Clayton's challenge to the peace in the Land, but to run to the Council and cry foul was a dangerous plan of action. War would almost certainly be waged against Clayton to dethrone him and put a more peaceable king on the throne. In that regard, strife was inevitable. Nevertheless, I owed responsibility first and foremost to my office as Seer, whether my being Claimed was a true thing or not.

Why couldn't Bule do the job himself? At the time I

reasoned that he did not want to be accountable should his accusations prove false and the strife they cause be for naught. It was better to find someone else to do the dirty work for him, and my being of young years led him to believe that I could be coerced into the task. Very well. However, I was going to be sure that Clayton was guilty as charged before I said anything.

"There are things I want to see first," I told the two men in the larder. "I must visit the dungeon."

Bule protested. "Lord Seer, surely you see the plot that is-"

"I see a plot, but I'm not sure where the threads lead," I explained. "Some unknown person tried to keep me from coming to the Council meeting. Am I to believe that, too, is Clayton's doing? I have a feeling that you and Thaddeus have only scratched the surface."

The Chamberlin was dismayed, but agreeable. "Very well," he said.

*** *** ***

With the vial that contained the mysterious substance, I returned to Erdo and Derek's company.

"Ugh! What is that awful smell about you?" the Trog complained.

"Didn't you smell it when you came in?" I asked, challenging him.

"Well…no. There are so many smells in here that it's hard to separate them. But that bottle smells *vile*."

I held it under his nose, and he recoiled. "It's a terrible concoction," he exclaimed. "I smell wort, and moss and, oh please, take it away."

I capped the bottle. "Magick?" I asked.

"Definitely."

Derek spat the gristle he was chewing onto the floor. "What went on in there?" he said, indicating the pantry.

"I'll tell you about that later," I said. And then to Erdo: "If there was more of this concoction about, do you think you could track it down?"

"There's no more of that in the castle, believe me. I could

smell it through stone if it were. Now if it were in a bottle like that, then maybe I'd have to be close. That bottle is made from Harga stone, a very fine stone indeed. It's almost impervious."

I bit my lip. Could Clayton have managed to hide his magick laboratory so well that we might not be able to locate it and find an antidote for the poison's effect, whatever that might be?

"Let's go down to the dungeon," I said.

*** *** ***

A castle's dungeon is never difficult to find; all one must do is seek the lowest point in the structure and follow the stairs down into the dank bowels of the Earth. Erdo put his nose to work, and soon thereafter we were negotiating narrow stairs when we came upon a closed door.

"Locked," I said dismayed, after trying the handle.

Derek sniffed the air and pushed me aside. He took the handle in one large hand and yanked the door off, leaving a ragged hole. "Rotten wood," he explained.

I was stunned. "Look what you've done! We're supposed to be careful and not let anyone in on our investigation." I pointed to the hole in the door. "Clayton will surely know that someone has been down here nosing around."

"Yeah, but he won't know who it did," Derek reasoned, and opened the door.

The frightful moans of the imprisoned assailed us. Erdo clamped his warty hands over his ears. "Do they have to carry on so?" he wailed.

"Shh!" I urged, but it was too late. Advancing up the dim steps the led further down into the castle were guards, one armed with a sword the other with a mace.

"Who goes there?" one of them called.

"Oh, just the Lord Seer of the Golden Oracle and his men," I responded.

The guards looked at each other, and even in the dim light of their torches I could see they were shaken by my presence. What luck!

"Er, what can we do for you, my lord?"

I rolled my eyes up into their sockets (a gruesome trick that had always annoyed Sissy) and slapped a hand to my forehead. In the spookiest voice I could muster, I said, "I'm following a vision, and it's leading me this way..."

I headed down the stairs and past the guards; Erdo and Derek did the same without challenge. The superstitious beliefs held by everyone but myself made many tasks easy.

The walls of the dungeon were black with the soot of the torches that were their only source of light and heat. Deep inside, filthy hands reached out for us through barred cells, pleading for release. I stopped at the nearest cell and peered through the bars. I checked over my shoulder to see that we were out of the guard's audible range.

"Are you the knights Clayton has imprisoned?" I whispered.

The nearest prisoner nodded his head. He was so underfed that his skin was pulled taught about his gaunt frame.

"Aye," he replied. A bug crawled from his filthy, gray beard; he brushed it away casually. "I am Sir Slakely. Until a few months ago I was the captain of the King's Guard."

"Why has Clayton imprisoned you?"

"Because I would not take up arms," he replied flatly. Who are you to be concerned with us?"

I did not want to reveal my identity, lest Clayton hear of my speaking with the prisoners and use it as fodder for further aggression. It was bad enough that the dungeon guards knew who I was.

"I am a friend sympathetic to your plight," I replied, "For me to be able to help you, you must help me. Tell me: Against whom did King Clayton wish you to take arms?"

"He said the kingdom needed an army; that there was a war brewing. And when I suggested that peace was strong in the Land and any war in the making was of his own design, he imprisoned me and those knights who agreed. Here we will die, for none of us will wage war unless the cause is just."

Here Thaddeus' whisperings were confirmed. What other evidence was needed to convince the remaining twelve kings that evil was abroad? Hopefully they could unite against Clayton, and he would bow to their pressure and release the good knights rather than face strength of twelve combined armies.

There was still the matter of the potion that Clayton had distributed. We had but one night to uncover the laboratory.

"Be patient," I said to Sir Slakely. "If all goes well, you will be free in a matter of days."

I turned to Erdo and Derek, but they weren't beside me. Now where in the hells had they gone? One moment they were standing behind me, and the next they had disappeared.

"Excuse me," I said to the knight, and continued further into the dungeon.

From the lower dungeons came the sound of cheers. I ambled my way back down the stairs to see that Derek was ripping the cells open with his bare hands. The cheering came from the poor souls who we set free. They congregated at my feet, all gaunt and thin and dirty, and began to sing my praises. "Blessed Seer!" they cried. "Oh Gods, glory be! You are our savior!"

Behind them, Derek was smiling and rubbing his hands together. He loved it.

I took the vial from my pocket and handed it to Erdo, who shied away from it before taking it from me. "Follow that smell," I said. "Take Derek and search the dungeon as best you can, and then come find me—I'll be at the banquet. We must find Clayton's laboratory."

"What about them?" Derek asked, indicating the freed knights. It was a quite a predicament.

I raised my voice. "Listen to me, all you. It is my intent to set you free. However, er, this is not the proper time."

The men looked at each other, and then back at me.

Once again my hand was forced, and I had to invoke the supernatural. "I have a vision, a vision of glory and freedom for you all."

"Hooray!" came the cheers and hoots.

"Shh!" I urged as the sound reverberated in the stone corridors. "Tomorrow will be a grand day of liberation. But for now, you must go back to your cells and feign confinement. You know that the locks are broken, and that freedom is near. Heed the words of the Oracle!"

Everyone in earshot cheered. I wanted to scream out of annoyance. I had made another prophecy, and I had to make it come true.

And do you know what happened? All the men went back to their cells, and they propped up their cell doors. Theirs was the sweet promise of freedom. Mine was a premonition of doom.

Just then, the two dungeon guards came down the stairs. "'Ere," one of them said. "What's all this?"

"Nothing!" I said nonchalantly and pushed Erdo and Derek between the guards and me.

One of the guards narrowed his eyes suspiciously. "I thought I heard cheering."

"Oh, you just heard the men groaning," I said. As if on cue, everyone in the dungeon began to moan.

The guards looked at each other. Apparently, they were stupid enough to fall for the trick.

"Now if you don't mind," I said, "I am going to leave my two men behind for a while. So beautiful is this dungeon, that we would like to know how it was constructed in order to model the new one being built in our kingdom."

Both guards took pause.

"It is the will of the Oracle," I added.

The guards shrugged. "Well, I suppose that would be alright," one guard said to the other. :You two, make it quick."

"Yessir!" Erdo replied and saluted. I didn't know who was overdoing it more: him or me.

*** *** ***

Erdo and Derek continued their search of the dungeon as I returned upstairs. The previously absent guards at the entrance to the dungeon backed away warily as I passed; both appeared inebriated. I greeted them with a smile and continued toward the throne room and banquet hall.

I poked my head into the banquet hall. Around the great table conversation had become that of drunkards. Everyone was slack in the chair, many with a "wench" (for lack of a better word) in their laps. The air was ripe with the smell of mingled wines and heady herbal liquors. Even the guards around the perimeter of the room were slack with drink. It was a most undignified sight, and one that was ripe for invasion. But that wouldn't happen, of course. All the powerful were together in their revelry. It was the next morning I feared when the poison—if it really had been poison—would take effect.

The kings and their lords took no notice of me as I hastily made my way to Chamberlin Bule's side. Next to him was seated King Phyllaman, who was chatting with the Lord to his right.

"Did you discover anything useful?" Bule whispered to me. He motioned for me to sit in the chair that was presumably reserved for myself.

"Your cousin was right about the knights in the dungeon," I replied. "We haven't had much luck in locating Clayton's potions and spell books. The search continues; I decided that it would be less suspicious if I was present here."

Across the great table, one of the kings threw his jewel-encrusted goblet at another. The second king laughed heartily and returned the jest by throwing a leg of roast fowl.

"Do they always behave like this?" I asked noting the less than regal behavior.

Bule nodded. "I'm afraid so. As I told you, all the kings are very full of themselves—and the suspect wine as well."

I looked past Bule at Phyllaman, who did not seem as boisterous as the rest of the crowd. He clutched his stomach momentarily. "I feel a bit ill," I heard him say to his lord.

"Aye," Sir Mackret said. "Clayton's food hasn't settled well with me, either. Soon I will be off to bed."

Bule (who had also heard the comments) and I looked

at each other. Were Phyllaman and his men simply too full of drink, or were they suffering from the effects of the poison? What would happen if everyone at the table suddenly dropped dead?

"Surely Clayton wouldn't kill all twelve kings at once," I thought aloud. "Their twelve respective princes would wage a war he couldn't win!"

"*Ten* princes," Bule whispered. "Neither Phyllaman or Clayton have an heir."

How could I have forgotten such a dreadful complication so easily?

"What does your mentor have to say about all this? Surely you must see something."

"I see the same as you: trouble," I told him. "There is nothing that either of us can do right now. We'll have to wait until the kings sober up, and then we can bring our case before them as the Council."

As Bule sighed with resignation, I directed my eyes toward King Clayton. He and Elwynna were watching the revelry with keen eyes, though Clayton's lords seemed as drunk as the rest, which puzzled me. Would he poison his own men? And who was to sit in the unoccupied chair to the right of His Majesty?

"Have you seen Clayton's Chamberlin this evening?" I asked Bule.

"You mean Lord Cummings? Why no, I haven't. Why?"

"Just a thought. Chamberlin, we must tread softly tomorrow. The more I consider the evidence surrounding Clayton, the more dubious I find some of the allegations."

"What?" Bule exclaimed. "The potion! The knights in the dungeon! What further evidence do you need?"

"An army," I replied. "Where are the men to fight this war Clayton is planning? He suggested to his Captain that a war was brewing, but what if he was planning strictly *defensive* tactics rather than offensive ones?"

"That does not explain the poisoning," Bule snapped.

"No, it doesn't. However, if someone is proficient in magick enough to summon men from distant lands, could they not disguise themselves as a king in order to issue commands?"

Bule's expression was one of shock. "What do you mean, summon men from distant lands?" he asked.

Had I not mentioned Derek and the robbers? Something told me the less spread about, the better such things would be. "Another rumor," I replied.

Bule sat back in his chair, rubbing his square chin.

The banquet and the orchestra droned on for some time.

Lords and kings eventually got up from the table, bid their fellow nobles goodnight, and headed for their respective chambers. I too grew weary and was anxious to see if Erdo and Derek had come up with anything. I bid Phyllaman and Bule good night and left the throne room. As I walked I said a prayer to the dead gods, a wish that the kings would still be alive the next morning. The potion—the magick—was an evil thing, a rotten fruit on the vine. I had to stamp the evil out before the entire Land was in ruin.

Now exactly where were Erdo and Derek? I wandered about for a few minutes hoping to run into them, but such was not the case. I quickly became lost, for the tapestries and banners all looked the same to my tired eyes. I yawned; after such an arduous day it was difficult to think of anything other than sleeping.

Just as it occurred to me that I had no idea as to where *my* chamber was, a prissy little man came rushing down the hall.

"Ah, you must be the Seer!" he exclaimed.

"Yes, I am."

"I am Lord Cummings, King Clayton's Chamberlin," he said with a nod. I noticed that his manner was as fussy as Bule's and wondered if all Chamberlains behaved as such. "Have you been shown to your quarters for the evening?"

"Actually, no. I was just wondering where they were."

"Splendid! Right this way."

Lord Cummings motioned for me to follow, and I did so.

He led me down several halls and then up a great staircase. My chamber was just to the left of the landing.

"I hope this will do—it's difficult to put so many guests up for the night, even in a castle of this size."

I poked my head into my room. It was not as elegant as the one I had stayed in back in the Second Kingdom, but still far better than anything I had previously known.

"This will do very well, thank you."

"Excellent! Now if you will excuse me, my lord." Chamberlain Cummings vanished as quickly as he had appeared, pudgy little legs carrying him off deceptively swiftly. The remarkable gleam in his eyes was so much like Bule's, I thought. Here were two men who obviously relished the power they held, even if it was only jurisdiction over the mundane day-to-day chores of running a castle.

I was still quite anxious to find Erdo and Derek, but the sight of the bed made me think of nothing but rest. Surely there was nothing wrong with stretching out for a few minutes before continuing the search for my companions...

There was still much to figure out. Who had told Bule that I was ill, and would not be accompanying the king to the Council meeting? Was someone in the Second Kingdom's castle involved in Clayton's plot?

The bed was soft and my mind and body tired. Before I could stop myself, I drifted off to sleep.

Later, at some point during the night, I sat bolt upright in bed. I looked nervously around me and heard a tapping noise at the sole window. The light of the moon was streaming through its stained glass, sending rivulets of multi-colored light into the chamber.

Tap, tap, tap.

Surely it was the wind outside.

Tap, tap, tap.

Curiosity got the best of me. I slid out of bed and taking my cane to lean on, walked across the cold stone floor to the window. There appeared to be nothing outside, and yet the tapping persisted.

I opened the window and was greeted by a rush of air. A large bird—an eagle—had been perched on my windowsill. The air came from the beating of its great wings as it flew away into the night.

Suddenly my heart was as cold as my feet. Was it an omen, or a coincidence?

I quickly returned to bed and pulled the covers over my head. As I drifted off to sleep, I wondered where Derek and Erdo were.

*** *** ***

CHAPTER FIVE: THE COUNCIL BREAKS

But men greedy and always lack
The jewels and gold of another
And so it was that a magick act
Turned one against his brother
-The History of the Second Banderwallian War, verse 1535

I woke with a start to the sound of someone knocking at the door to my chamber. I saw in horror that the morning sun was creeping higher into the sky—Erdo and Derek had been left unsupervised for most of the night!

"Lord Seer! Lord Seer, are you alright?"

It was Bule who was pounding at the door. I jumped to my feet and attempted to open it when I realized that in my fatigue, I had locked it. I undid the latch and opened the door.

"Oh, thank the Gods you're all right," Bule said, relieved upon seeing me. "Something terrible happened last night, and we were worried that you had become a victim."

"What happened?" I asked in dread.

Bule shuddered. "A nasty affair. All the prisoners in Clayton's dungeon escaped. Not only those knights Thaddeus referred to; I mean, they're all good men to be sure, but Clayton has spread word that quite a few notorious criminals were locked up in there too, and now they're free!"

My stomach churned with grief for the conditions that had befallen me. Erdo and Derek freed the knights.

"The dungeon guards—were they injured?"

"Well, that's the strange thing," Bule said. "They must have been in on the break, for they've completely disappeared. So much for evidence of Clayton's wrongdoings! But no more of this talk; the Council is to convene shortly."

I hastily dressed, grabbed my cane, and followed Bule down the stairs. I reasoned that I had slept through breakfast, but it was of no consequence, for I was too ill to eat.

"How are the King and his men?" I asked. "Are they showing any ill effects from the banquet?"

"That's another strange thing. They're all a bit grumpy, but given the quantity of wine they consumed, they have warrant to be so. Other than that, I'd say they were fine. Lord Seer, whatever do you think is going on?"

I did not answer him, for I had no answer. At this point I was totally confused by the events that had transpired and would have done anything for a beacon to point my thoughts in the right direction. Without hard evidence against Clayton, it was all I could do to warn the Council of impending strife and leave it to the collective wisdom of the kings to act.

The throne room appeared quite different in the morning light, and so did the kings. Without wine to fuel conversation and an orchestra to add to the din, the chamber was as quiet as a mineral flat. The various nobles spoke among their lords in hushed tones, either out of reverence or after-effects of strong drink.

Phyllaman perked up noticeably when he saw the Chamberlin and I nearing him. "I am pleased to see that you came after all," he said quietly to me, with sagging eyes. "Do you feel better?"

"Worse, in a way," I confessed.

The King frowned. "May I introduce to your Sirs Mackret and Dowry, captain of the King's guard and advisor to the throne, respectively? Phyllaman motioned to the men seated on the other side of him. Sir Mackret was a relatively young, burly redhead with a full beard, while Sir Dowry was older, taller, and clean-shaven (and obviously the more dignified of the two). Both men nodded at me indifferently; there was no room for awe or fear of the Oracle in their aching heads.

Across the table, King Clayton held me heavy in his sight. I puzzled at his stare. Had he heard of my snooping about the castle? Was he alarmed by my presence? At that moment I wished that I really could read minds, as Bule had suggested.

As was the custom, the Council meeting was presided over by the eldest king. The honor fell upon gaunt King Delwyn of the Sixth Kingdom.

King Delwyn was the oldest man I had ever laid eyes upon. Of course, no one knew exactly how old he was (kings are so very vain) but it was rumored that he was well past ninety —and every year of life had been etched into his gray, wrinkled features.

Delwyn coughed a wad of phlegm from his throat. "This meeting of the Council of the Thirteen shall now come to order," he said, hardly above a whisper. "Before we commence the general diplomatic discussions, I ask if there are any important, immediate issues that need be brought to the council's attention."

Beside me, Chamberlin Bule rose to his feet unexpectedly, without prompting from King Phyllaman. "As most know, by the grace of the Gods the Land has been provided with a Seer Claimed of the Golden Oracle. It has come to the attention of the Second Kingdom that there are foul deeds brewing in the Land, and that there is a traitor amongst us."

Angry mutterings rippled across the table as my jaw dropped in abject horror. What in the hells was Bule thinking? The man was putting words into my mouth!

Bule took his seat. "Speak, speak!" he urged me in a whisper. "Now's the time, while the morning is fresh, and we have their attention."

I stood nervously. "Good kings of the Land," I began, nodding in their general direction. How was I to get out of this mess? "Er, as Chamberlin Bule suggests, there is some evidence that the practice of magick has resurfaced in our midst."

More angry growls, this time the Lords and Kings scoped the room, each seeking to pin the traitor with their eyes.

Quite suddenly, a knight bearing a lion's device seated at the far side of the table jumped to his feet. "It's him!" he shouted, pointing to a shocked monarch to the left. "It's the foul creature Edwin of the Eighth Kingdom!"

King Edwin pounded a meaty fist on the table and rose in response. "Liar!" he shouted. "How dare you accuse me of sorcery! Where is your proof?"

The knight (whose king had buried his face in his hands out of embarrassment) spat his accusations: "You put a hex on robber bands and they invaded—and that caused them to shun your kingdom for ours! I lost twenty good men last season alone because of your devilry!"

Edwin shook with anger, his eyes narrowing to black slits. "So what if I did?" he conceded. "Conrad did the same thing to me! How was I to ensure the safety of my people?"

King Conrad was obviously shocked by the allegations against him. "I only did so because Horace did the same to us! It's only fitting that his cursed kingdom be pillaged,"

The king that was lord to the knight who started the row groaned audibly. "I told you the spell would backfire on us, you oaf!" he shouted to the knight, who sat down, red in the face.

"Gentlemen, gentlemen!" Delwyn cried, trying to regain control of the meeting. "This Council was formed in order to deal with such situations as the proliferation of robbing curs in the Land! Where is our unity, our allegiance to one another? Why was there not a combined effort to rid ourselves of the nuisance, as we have done in the past?"

"The past?" Conrad asked. "I never had a problem until we drove the robber tribes into the Great Desert. From there my kingdom was an easy target. Dozens of men were lost in the Purge and *then* the piracy began! See what the Council has brought on my people?"

Not knowing what else to do, I sheepishly took my seat. All my good intentions had turned upon me and the men at the table, just as the magicks had backfired on King Conrad.

"Such behavior," I heard Phyllaman whisper to Sir Dowry. "Where indeed is the unity? You'd think the kings were suffering from sour stomachs, as I do."

A chill ran down my spine. Could it be that the effect of the potion Clayton allegedly tainted the food with had finally made is effect manifest? If Clayton suspected that other kings were breaking the conventions of the Council, what better way to start a war than force confessions and create disharmony?

I looked back across the table at Clayton. What a fine actor he was. He looked as surprised as the other kings at the words of the others.

After a moment of strained silence, Delwyn spoke once more. "The use of magick is intolerable," he proclaimed. "For over a hundred years we have been free of its blight. Magick breeds nothing but suffering, as we now hear. I motion that once again that such practices be abolished. If such a motion is not honored, I see no other choice than to motion for the expulsion of those guilty parties from the alliance."

A new wrinkle developed, confirming my theory. Sir Mackret, who had seen fit to be silent during the initial stage of the meeting, suddenly turned to Phyllaman. "Why don't you do something?" the knight hissed. "Ours is the richest kingdom in the Land. Why don't you use your influence to end this nonsense? Threaten to end free trade."

"Be silent, Sir Mackret," Phyllaman commanded, in a manner most unlike his genial self. "This is no time to be taking sides. We would not want to bring the wrath of a fool sorcerer down on our kingdom. We will remain neutral and wait for further developments."

"Further developments? You spineless fool!" Mackret stood and bowed to King Delwyn. "The Second Kingdom joins the Sixth in the motion against the use of magick-"

With swiftness I never suspected him of, King Phyllaman was on his feet. "No, the Second Kingdom does *not* support the motion on the grounds that we have not been party to the skullduggery, nor a victim of it. We remain neutral."

Mackret's ruddy features reddened deeper still as angry blood rose to his head. "Fool, if your father was still alive, he would not be so afraid to make a stand."

"Sit down, Sir Mackret."

"You're not fit to rule a kingdom—why, *I* could do a better job than you, you fop!"

"Sit down, Sir Mackret!" Phyllaman bellowed. He was too late; the entire table was aghast at the scene before them. Never in written history had a knight questioned the divine rule and wisdom of a king in the Land—such an event suggested that Phyllaman was not as divine as the rest of the men in the room who wore crowns

Mackret opened his mouth, and at first, I thought he was about to speak again, when he expelled a stream of black, wormy, stinking vomit that splashed on the table. Several lords and one king at the table did the same consequently. Mackret clutched at his stomach and tore from the chamber, presumably to find a better place to expel last night's repast.

"Devils!" King Delwyn said, wiping his mouth with the back of his hand. "I recognize the stink of evildoing—we've been poisoned!" He leveled his gaze at Clayton, who put a hand to his chest, stunned at the implications of Delwyn's gape. "Never in my ninety-eight years would I have suspected so many good men would fall prey to the temptations of magick and its promises of easy gain. Fools! I have a prophecy of my own: all you will rue the day you turned to conjuring!"

With that, Delwyn spun on his heels and left the room, followed by his disgusted lords and knights. The final lining in the armor that girded the Land from strife had been broken.

One by one the kings silently stood from their places and filed out of the room. Soon there was naught but Phyllaman, his men and Clayton's and his entourage.

Phyllaman sighed heavily and turned to face me. "Your prophecy of foolishness running rampant in the Land was all too correct, Lord Seer," he said. His face was pale, presumably from the same ills that afflicted the other former members of the council.

"That was a prophecy that I had hoped would not find truth," I said honestly.

As Phyllaman stood and we began to march for our carriage and horses, darkness fell over my heart. Nothing was as it seemed in the Land; kings and their men held nothing in esteem but their own good fortune and were wont to destroy that of others. I could not find it in myself to place the blame for the events of the Council on Bule or myself; Bule had asked me for guidance, believing that I was given knowledge beyond that of other men and that his decision to reveal Clayton's wrongdoings was for the good of the Land. How was either of us to know that other kings were doing the same as Clayton? Never in ninety-eight years, as Delwyn had said.

*** *** ***

Interlude: The Queen

The light in the room grew dim.

Edwin, son of Kyle, hastily replaced the wick in his lamp and returned to his father's writings. What a scandalous tome they comprised!

"King Phyllaman, I, Bule and the rest of the representatives from the Second Kingdom made our way to the horses and carriages and quickly loaded ourselves and our things aboard-"

Lost in the prose, the young prince did not hear the key in the lock to his chamber door, or the rattle of the latch. It was not until light streamed into the room and his mother entered that he quickly shut the book and sought to hide it behind his back.

"What have you got there?" the Queen demanded.

Edwin swallowed, trying to force down the lump that had entered his throat.

"Give me that book."

The prince remained motionless.

"Did you hear me, Edwin? *Give me that book!*"

"But it's not yours, it's-"

The Queen reached around the boy and snatched his birthday present from his hands. She opened to the first page and scanned the handwriting with her gray eyes.

Darius has a way of twisting things, as all historians do...

I swear on the Golden Oracle that the words contained herein are true...

The secrets were too hard to resist. Without further debate, the queen closed the book and left the chamber, locking the door behind her.

On the bed, Edwin sighed.

*** *** ***

CHAPTER SIX: TRAGEDIES ABOUND

And so the battlements did crumble
Shaken by magick's thunder rumble.
-The History of the Second Banderwallian War, verse 2098

King Phyllaman, Bule, the rest of the representatives from the Second Kingdom and myself made our way to the horses and carriages and quickly loaded ourselves and our things aboard. Erdo and Derek and the knights, wherever they were, would just have to make do.

Personally, I was sick with dread, for my prediction of strife had come all too true, and the reality of it was worse than I had ever contemplated. Were *all* the kings in the Land using magick? All thirteen of them had gone mad if that was the case. Any student of history could see that magick paid in suffering and strife—how could so many men forget the flesh-eating demons that had infested the Land when a king last attempted to use magick for gain?

With the horses harnessed to the carriages, I moved to enter that which was reserved for the lesser lords.

"No no, Lord Seer," Phyllaman called to me. "You must ride in the royal coach. There is much for us to discuss."

I bowed graciously. Being confined in a small space with both Chamberlin Bule and King Phyllaman did not appeal to me, but I gave in to the king's wishes and climbed aboard his carriage. Phyllaman motioned for me to sit across from him and Bule.

"Well!" Phyllaman sighed. "I suppose the first thing I should ask you, Lord Seer, is if you see anything regarding the future of the Second Kingdom."

At this point I was inclined to keep my mouth shut, but if King Phyllaman was so blind that he did not see the trouble on the horizon, then it was my duty to draw it to his attention.

"I see war in the Land. Surely you must see the same with your own faculties."

Phyllaman frowned. "Yes, as a matter of fact I do. I just thought…"

His voice trailed off as he gazed wistfully out of the carriage.

"I just thought that perhaps I was wrong, and that the Oracle had shown you that peace would remain intact. That's something of a vain, foolish wish, isn't it?"

"The desire for peace is never foolish," I said. "To remain peaceful as others around you gird themselves for war? Now *that's* foolish. I understand and respect your desire for neutrality and hope the Second Kingdom can remain so. Yet with all due respect, Your Highness, I must say that sooner or later you will have to take a stand on the issues at hand and seek to ally yourself with other kings. Never in the history of the Land has a sole king been able to defend his kingdom from invasion."

Phyllaman's eyes shifted to me. "You have been well taught," he said, "but an alliance with any of the twelve former council members implies that I agree with the use of magick. Bule has just alerted me that even Clayton has had his nose in a spell book."

I looked at Bule, who shrugged. The Chamberlin's assertion that Phyllaman would not listen was apparently unfounded—or was it that the grave nature of the morning's events had purged him of his giddiness and let good sense take the forefront?

"As you wish," I replied. "May I remind you that you have no heir, and your untimely death would throw the Second Kingdom into chaos?"

"Lord Seer!" Bule exclaimed.

Phyllaman raised a hand to silence Bule as the carriage began to roll from the courtyard. "Go on, Lord Seer."

I nodded.

"As I was saying, your death would throw the kingdom into chaos, for without an alliance there will be no one with the authority to step in and run the kingdom, leaving it ripe for conquest. I would say that the situation makes you something of a target for assassination, given the desire of the other kings to expand their boundaries."

King Phyllaman remained silent, contemplating my words. I was surprised at myself for being so blunt with him, but I saw no other way to prevent damage to the lands that I called home. Still, I was in the presence of my king, and yet the words had rolled from my tongue as if I had no control over them, as if they were not my own.

Phyllaman stuck his head out of the window. "We must make haste," he called to his driver. "I must be back in Rind as soon as possible."

The driver's whip cracked, and the horses increased the speed of their gait. I sat back in my seat, relieved that my words had found their way into Phyllaman's ears.

The three of us inside the carriage remained silent for quite some time after that. My mind wandered, focusing on the clatter of the carriage's wheels on the stones in the roadway. And then something terrible came to mind; they were Erdo's words.

I spoke up presently. "Your Highness, we will be reaching Gallman's Bridge soon and-"

The clatter intensified as the wheels hit the pave stones of the bridge. Before I knew it my stomach was wrenched from its comfortable position low in my body as the carriage lurched and the world toppled on end. Suddenly I was sixteen again, and hurrying home from the market to fetch medicine for my mother's dyspepsia, but the cart had flipped and I was heading for the rough ground of the ditch, this time with the knowledge of what was going to happen to my leg-

The cold water of the Great River against my skin brought me back to my senses. The sound of horses thrashing madly in the drink reached my ears and then the water covered my head, and I was torn from the upset carriage by the rushing current. The fine clothes Priory had given me grew heavy with water; I sank deeper, deeper into the river, heading for the bottom and a death by drowning.

My head broke the surface of the water long enough to hear the voices of panicked men: *"The King, the King! Where is-"*

And then the light was gone again, blotted out by the dark green waters of the river. My nostrils filled with fluid, stinging my sinuses, and choking the breath from my lungs. Pressure closed in around my throat; even if there had been air down there it would not pass the blockage created by-

-and then the light was back again. It was not the grip of death that had seized my throat; rather I had drifted close enough to the shore for a knight to wrap his arm around my neck and drag me from the river. I coughed and sputtered, my body seeking the air it had been deprived of.

"There he is!" someone shouted. *"There he is! I see the King!"*

The knight immediately dropped me and dashed off in the direction of the commotion. My eyes stung from the green water, but there was no doubt as to what my sight revealed: an anonymous lord that had dived into the water and was sloshing his way toward the bank of the river with King Phyllaman's limp body under his arm.

Men crowded around the lord as he laid Phyllaman on the ground and tried to revive him. However, I knew that the king was dead, and that I had warned him of the possibility of an untimely death only moments before.

"The king is dead!" I heard someone whisper, and then repeat his words, shouting: *"The king is dead!"*

Shivering through the wet clothes that clung to my skin, I watched as several knights tied their horses to the coach and dragged it from the stream. The coach's horses had surely drowned or had at least been swept downstream, but there was no sign of Chamberlin Bule.

As the carriage wept muddy water from every seam, I found myself at Lord Dowry's, side, examining the wreck. The left rear wheel had slipped cleanly from the axel, hence the accident that claimed the King's life. Phyllaman's crown sat in a pool of mud on the upholstery, but still there was no sign of Bule.

"Gods!" Dowry exclaimed, shaking his head in woe. "This is truly a dark day for the court."

"And for the rest of the Second Kingdom as well," I added.

Dowry turned his head toward me. "What do you mean?" he asked.

"King Phyllaman left no heir behind. I surmise that the situation would put you in command, Sir Dowry—but do not expect your control of the kingdom to go unchallenged."

Dowry's serious facial features hardened with anger as he leveled an accusing finger at me. "Is that an official prediction from the Gods or is that a threat from a boy charlatan?" he snapped. "If you're truly a Seer as Phyllaman and some of the less wise men in the court believed, why didn't you warn us of this tragedy?"

A voice: "He did."

Dowry and I turned to see Chamberlin Bule, arms draped around the shoulders of two knights, being led toward us. Bule's pale skin was still blue from his time in the frigid water. "The Lord Seer warned the king that he should prepare for his sudden death, but alas, the warning came too late."

Dowry was humbled by Bule's assertion that I had correctly made the prophecy. They did not understand that I had simply followed the lines of logic to reason out that the king was subject to being assassinated, given the current political situation. There was nothing mystical about my method. Had I come to the point where so many true prophecies had piled up behind me that I could no longer run away from them?

Spurred on by my thoughts, I took a closer look at the axel from which the wheel of the carriage had slipped. Surely a servant at the castle checked on a regular basis the wooden pin that held the wheel in place, looking for signs of wear.

"What is it?" Bule asked as I kneeled on the wet ground. "What do you see?"

I reached out with a finger and poked it into the hole in which the retaining pin was normally placed. Inside I did not find the expected fragments of wood that would indicate the pin had broken. Instead, my finger met with a slightly sticky brown substance.

"Wax."

Lord Dowry and Bule quickly kneeled beside me, eager to see the new evidence I had uncovered.

"Someone replaced the wooden pin with a fake made of wax," I explained. "The wax was firm enough to hold the wheel in place as long as the road was smooth."

Bule and Dowry remained silent in contemplation of the wax, as did the other knights and lords who had congregated behind us.

Bule's hands made their way to his hips. "I don't understand," he said. "The wheel could have fallen off at any place along the road and no one would have been injured."

Dowry interrupted. "Rubbish," he said. "The road is as flat as the Great Desert until..." His words trailed off, the situation piecing itself together in his head. "...flat as the Great Desert until we reach Gallman's Bridge! Good Gods! The king has been *murdered!*"

A murmur of horror swept through those that crowded around the carriage that had been Phyllaman's death trap. But who would seek to kill the king? If expansion of another king's territory figured in the plot, then the deed had surely been planned well in advance, for no king who attended the Council meeting had time to rig the pin after the brief meeting. There was one other possibility: someone inside the Second Kingdom's hierarchy had been hired to fix the axel or had done it on their own volition.

"Mackret!" I heard Dowry say under his breath. *"Mackret!"* He jumped to his feet and turned to the other knights. "Where is

Sir Mackret? Has anyone seen Sir Mackret?"

Bule stroked the wet brocade of his blouse, thinking. "Didn't Mackret rush out of the council meeting before we left? Has anyone seen him since?"

"Villain!" Dowry exclaimed. "Yes, he did! And did he not also say Phyllaman was not fit to wear the crown, and he himself had aspirations of ruling?"

Dowry was set in motion his own conjecture; he broke from the crowd, shouting to those who still milled about the banks of the river, lamenting their king's death: *"Knights! Squires! Mount your horses! The criminal Sir Mackret must be hunted down and brought to justice for the murder of King Phyllaman the Second!"*

Beside me, Chancellor Bule sighed with relief as the men scrambled to obey the call their new leader. "There is nothing to fear," Bule thought aloud. "Dowry will see that Mackret is punished."

"Yes, they'll surely chop his head off," I said. "What if Mackret didn't do it? Suspects abound."

Bule's eyes shifted this way and that. "Oh. I never thought of that. Whatever are we going to do?"

*** *** ***

A hastily made pin to replaced the wax in the dripping carriage. (I had learned something from my father after all!) had bad feelings for riding in the carriage that was the instrument of the king's death, and even more reservations about the makeshift pin that held the wheel on the axel. However, I was unable to walk the distance back to Rind, and the horses were already laden with the armor-clad men. I had no choice.

I cannot describe to you the mournful feeling that gripped my consciousness as we made our way back to the city of Rind. Sir Dowry and his men had the scent of Phyllaman's blood in their nostrils and it caused them to thirst for Mackret's own. As for Derek and Erdo, I assumed that they were still making their way to Rind in search of a prize for performing so well.

The thought that Mackret may not be the killer distressed me, but such a mistake was trivial compared to the situation that faced the Second Kingdom. Magsur, the God of War, was waiting just outside our very door, seeking his way past the fortifications that the end of the Council had left shattered in its wake. The most cursed knowledge I had was that I was powerless to prevent the coming strife; all that was left for me to do was to watch peace crumble around me.

The heart of Rind was as quiet as if the Nevermen had come down from the mountains and abducted the citizens as food for the coming winter. The shutters and doors of the houses and businesses had been tightly closed to shut out what the people of the city surely saw as a great evil that was lurking in their midst. Even the marketplace was quiet, but in a curious way. The stalls and carts were all in place, and it appeared that the merchant folk had fled in haste from a fright. I almost mentioned to Bule and Dowry how strange the inactivity seemed. Then I realized that it was not so out of place. The city was in mourning for their King, who had passed on to the Underealms—and then I realized that the denizens of the city couldn't have any knowledge of Phyllaman's demise. The people of the Second Kingdom had fled/barricaded themselves for some other reason.

Soon the caravan was crossing the bridge that led into the castle's main courtyard.

"Chamberlin," I said, shifting in my seat, finding the carriage cramped (lesser lords were forced to make room for those of the royal entourage that survived), "Something is wrong. The city is too quiet."

It was dreadful sitting there, with the wet clothes adhering to my skin in the death vehicle of the lord my king.. Bule was inattentive; he had done nothing but stare blankly out the hastily repaired and completely soaked carriage since we left Gallman's Bridge. "What?" he asked.

"I said that something-"

My words were cut short by a tremendous mechanical

thud that caused everyone in the cabin to jump in alarm. I thrust my head through the window to see what the matter was.

The drawbridge had been abruptly raised as soon as the last horses of the caravan cleared the archway. Knights in full battle armor poured from their hiding places inside the horse stalls, dribbled down from the battlements, rushed from every door. Horses reared in terror at the catcalls and hollers of battle, throwing the startled and unprepared knights of the caravan to the cobblestones. The scrape of metal against metal rang about the courtyard as dozens of swords were simultaneously drawn from their sheaths.

"Devils!" I heard Dowry scream. "We'll execute you all for treason to the crown!"

Hot breath bore down on my neck; Bule was leaning over my shoulder, aghast.

The knights who had been thrown from their mounts were the first to enter the fray. Swords clashed, throwing sparks that splashed like tears on parched ground. Without a battle plan each knight found himself on his own, being driven back toward the wall. Steel was no match for linen; combatants not clad in armor bled quickly. A terrified part of me sought to avert my eyes from the impending slaughter but couldn't.

A rebellious knight and a lean lord whose blouse bore the device of the royal family dueled but a stride away from the carriage. The knight thrusted, the lord parried, the knight thrusted again. Stunned, the king's second cousin looked down in disbelief at his wound, as if he could not fathom that his assailant's sword had met with flesh. He crumpled to the ground in a pool of his own blood.

Across the courtyard, Sir Dowry valiantly defended himself against the best efforts of two opponents. Even so, the swings and thrusts of the adversary swords forced Dowry to the wall with the rest of his men. "Fiends!" he shouted. "I'll kill you all myself!"

Alas, in Dowry's rage his grip on the hilt of his sword grew lax. One of the knights slashed venomously at his target; Dowry blocked the blow, but his sword was jolted from his hand. The blade clattered to the ground ominously.

Dowry's back stiffened; he inhaled deeply, expanding his chest in pride. It was a noble thing to be struck down in defense of one's cause, and Sir Dowry was ready to accept his defeat at the hands of the traitors. Both of his foes raised their swords. I covered my eyes with my hands; Dowry's demise was going to be an ugly sight indeed.

"Stop!"

At the sound of another voice, I peeked through my fingers. Flanked by guards, Sir Mackret stepped from the main doorway and into the courtyard. He was hastily bedecked in the raiment of the King, an ill-fitting costume at best.

Action in the courtyard ceased, sword-points halted but inches from Dowry and his defeated men.

Mackret strode brazenly through the courtyard, winding around the frozen combatants and those who had already fallen. A mad gleam poured from his eyes; this was not the after effect of the potion he had been given the night before, no, this was true madness that was streaming through the holes in his countenance torn open by the poison.

"How *dare* you raise arms against the King and his men," Dowry snarled as Mackret neared. "The Gods will strike you down for your impertinence!"

"The Gods are dead," Mackret snapped. "Now where is his former majesty?"

"He lays dead in the rear coach—dead by your foul hand, demon!"

"Dead?" Mackret shouted. *"DEAD? Villains! I* wanted to kill the sniveling fool myself! I'll have the murderer's head—no, I'll have *all* your heads for not ensuring the King's safe passage so I could kill him!"

"Sever your own head, oaf," Dowry said. "I've seen through your plot. I know of the wax pin you put on the rear axle."

Mackret raised an eyebrow. "Oh? I know nothing of what

you speak." He turned to his guards. "Take Sir Dowry and his men to the dungeon. They are to be tried and found guilty of the murder of King Phyllaman the Second."

The guards motioned in turn to the knights, who began to force Dowry's men from the courtyard at sword point. Dowry said nothing further; the muscles in his jaw bulged as he clenched his teeth in anger.

I could not hear what Mackret said next, but his message became clear as the guards headed for the nobility's carriages. None of the vassal princes or their wives had set foot into the courtyard; battle was not their calling, nor was it the Chamberlin's or mine.

"Out!" a ruffian demanded, tearing the door to the carriage from my grip. I nervously stumbled down, followed by Bule, who was virtually in tears. We were past offering resistance; only one knight was needed per ten nobles.

And so we marched across the courtyard, toward the dank bowels of the castle from which we would never exit to see the sun.

"Wait," Mackret said. "You—the gimpy boy in the funny costume, the prophet. Come here."

I looked at Bule, who looked back at me, eyes trembling. I swallowed my fear and did as I was told.

The smell of wine still hung about Mackret, as if he had not ceased drinking since the night before.

"You're a charlatan, a fraud, but a very perceptive one," he said to me. "Your speech at the council meeting betrayed your intelligence. Serve me well and you will live to grow old. Come."

What was I to do other than follow? Perhaps I could use my influence to somehow insure that Dowry and company would live to grow old.

"King Mackret" led me into the castle and toward the throne room. Gone were the tapestries and gilded torch-holders; I surmised that Mackret had pilfered these and other valuables and used them to pay off the knights he had in his service.

"You must think I'm a terrible man," Mackret said as we

walked, "I only want what's best for the kingdom."

"Oh?" I replied brashly. "And what might that be?"

Mackret laughed unexpectedly at my sarcasm. "Phyllaman is—er, *was* a fool. As a governing body, the Council of Thirteen hasn't been effective for years. Over that same span of time I tried to convince Phyllaman that a parting of ways was inevitable, that kings were eyeing each other's holdings greedily. And did he listen to me? No. And so when you "prophesied" that war was brewing—not a particularly astute observation, considering the fact that it had been staring us in the face for so long—and Phyllaman still would not prepare for battle, I realized that drastic measures would have to be taken to ensure that the Second Kingdom remained safe. Conquest. "Remember that, young lord. Conquest is sweet"

I stifled a groan. Mackret was saying that I was responsible for his usurping the rightful rulers of the kingdom.

We paused briefly outside the doors to the throne room. Mackret turned to me, speaking in grave tones. "I didn't kill Phyllaman," he asserted. "I could never have killed him in the face of his nobility. At the most I was planning on permanent exile to the Great Desert. That's beside the point now. I had no trouble finding knights who would be loyal to me, for most of them had seen the trouble brewing in the Land as well but hadn't the nerve to do something about it. Still, I need legitimacy to rally the people to my cause. That's where you come in." His eyes twinkled with intrigue; he was obviously pleased with himself for being so clever. "The peasants believe you to be the mouthpiece of the Gods, and so do most of the gentry. I want you to calm the fears that my ascension to the throne will stir." Mackret pointed to the doors. "I want you to go in there and announce that the Oracle, who serves the Gods, has instructed you to bestow the crown upon me."

This time I groaned audibly. Yes, I had made up prophecies on my own, but never anything as outlandish as this. And that Mackret wanted *me* to coronate him! Ridiculous.

The fact that Mackret did not believe in the Gods made

the situation all the more difficult. A more superstitious person I could have put off by telling him not to tempt the Gods. And the look in Mackret's eyes told me that I had only to obey or to die by the executioner's blade.

Steeling myself for the ordeal, I took a deep breath. Mackret responded by opening the doors and ushering me inside.

The scene in the throne room was more ludicrous than that Phyllaman and his men had played out for me but two days before. Gaiety was too light a word for the happening; the vagabond knights and lords who had sided with Mackret were participating in a clamorous drunken revelry. Unseemly ladies congregated about the hall, lighting on laps here and there, tittering and giggling. Clearly these men were inebriated with the most intoxicating of liquors: their own ambition. And such behavior was to make the kingdom safe for its people?

Once aware of Mackret's presence, the chatter ceased long enough for goblets to be raised in salute. "All hail King Mackret!" someone cried, and the crowd cheered.

Mackret stepped up to the dais, waving a hand in recognition. "I salute you, my brave friends," he bellowed. "We seized the kingdom's destiny and have shaped it anew. Long shall we prosper!"

The crowd cheered again.

Amidst the throng, I stood bewildered. How long would it be before these men woke up to their senses, if ever?

"We need no longer fear the wrath of those who oppose us," Mackret continued. "The Gods are in our favor. I present to you Lord Kyle, claimed of the Golden Oracle."

No cheer greeted me. Instead, hushed, reverent eyes fell upon me. The last thing I wanted to do was concoct a prophecy in favor of Mackret and see it come to fruition as my other predictions had. There was no use in resisting.

"Er, good lords and ladies of the Second Kingdom," I began. My eyes nervously shifted to the left; I briefly spied Mackret, who was sitting on the throne, beaming. "As the agent of the Gods, I stand before you today...stand before you...st-"

My words failed to flow, choked by the indescribable chill that had crept into my bones. The hair on the back of my neck stood on end. Never before and never again had I been racked with such portentous feelings; I knew it was only a matter of seconds before-

"Go on, go on!" I hear Mackret urge.

The immense masonry of the castle shuddered under some unseen stress. I was no longer the center of attention; the lords and ladies scrambled in terror as the quaking of the floor and walls intensified.

Jostled from his seat, Mackret fell to the dais on his behind. "Stop this!" he shouted to the castle. "Stop this nonsense at once! I'll not have this in my kingdom!"

At the conclusion of Mackret's vain commands a great pulse swept through the room, wrenching at the very fabric of space. The far wall the room split from floor to ceiling, and from that black tear came a hot blast of the foulest air imaginable. It was then that the Demons began to pour through the rift. They were a terrible sight, creatures tall and knobby and girded with scales. Their twisted faces with framed by bony extrusions were horrendous. On their hands their bore claws that would rip through armor and flesh as easily as the parchment this book is written on.

Someone screamed (it might have been me) and then *everyone* was screaming and running in various directions except for Mackret, and myself who both stood frozen in bewilderment.

Eyes wide in curious terror, I watched as a creature larger in stature than the others strode through the rift into our kingdom. The Commander Demon wore no armor (there was no need of it, considering the thick scales that covered his body) and at his signal the lesser, but equally terrifying demons poured into the crowd and found their first victims, setting them aflame with their foul breath. They chortled as their victims burned, and then began to devour them, clothes, ornaments, and all. The Commander himself seized Mackret by the throat and dragged him close. The monster threw its head back and laughed in glee, its gills bulging obscenely with air. "Hardly a conquest!" it cried to the king in a most articulate manner. "If such tasty morsels as these seek to defend this world, then our victory will be quick and delicious indeed!"

All the beasts joined in the laughter then, air sacs flopping madly, singed flesh and gore dribbling from their fanged mouths.

As I closed my eyes against the horror, I felt a tug at my garment and cried out in terror, sure that it was the touch of a demon at my hem. I whirled to see a previously unnoticed, gnarled little man standing behind me, finger pressed to his lips in a gesture begging for silence. "Quickly!" he whispered and dashed toward the dais. I came to my senses and followed as the man ducked behind the sole tapestry that remained hanging. I followed behind the throne and into a small hole in the wall: a secret passage.

Once inside, the man activated some unseen mechanism that closed the secret door, shrouding us in darkness. "This tunnel will lead us to the stables," he said, crouching over and ducking into a passageway that branched to the left.

Without a word I followed my savior on my knees, hoping that there weren't any rats dwelling in the tunnel.

"Damn!"

The old man stopped crawling long enough to sweep his white beard from beneath his knees. "I just washed my beard, and now look what I've done: I've ground it into this dirty floor! Oh well."

The tunnel eventually came to a dead end. I was amazed that the old man could activate the switch that opened the door; I couldn't see my hand in front of my face in that black passageway. Something told me that years of negotiating these tunnels made my guide an expert.

The small door opened into a stall in the royal stables. A horse, which was chomping on a wad of hay, gave us an annoyed glance as we climbed to our feet. I watched as the man took a leather rig from the wall and began to outfit the horse to pull a cart.

"Don't just stand there!" the man snapped. "Help me!"

"What do you want me to do?"

The man cast his eyes to the roof. "Oh, what is wrong with the young people of today?" he cried. And then to me: "Go into another stall and hitch up another horse. We'll need as much speed as possible if we're to get out of the city alive."

Remembering the horror I had left behind in the throne room, I sprang into action and trotted from the stall to another. As I hitched the horse across the way the acrid smell of burnt flesh reached my nostrils—the diabolic creatures that had invaded the Land were having a barbecue—spurring me to haste.

By the time I had the second horse hitched, my mentor had his hooked to a flat cart at the rear of the stables.

"Come on!" he urged. "What are you stalling for? Do you want to be the next course on the Banderwallian menu?"

The mere mention of that cursed name made my blood run colder from fear than it already did, nearly freezing in my veins. *"Demons?"* I asked as I led the horse to the cart. "Were those creatures *Banderwallian* Demons?"

"Naturally," the man replied, and jumped onto the cart with surprising agility for his advanced years. I did the same, but much less gracefully.

"Here. You drive," he said, and thrust the reins into my hands. I gave them a tug and we were rolling.

Once in the courtyard I saw that smoke was pouring from the main door and windows of the castle, rising from the turrets, wisping from the seams in the masonry. Soot was beginning to force itself upon the gilded stones. I shook my head, thinking of poor Dowry and his men, still trapped in the dungeon. Everyone knew that Banderwallian Demons had an insatiable hunger for human flesh. It was only a matter of time before the dungeon was depleted of vittles and the demons moved into the city and countryside to satisfy their hunger.

Lucky for us, the drawbridge was mysteriously down, allowing for a quick escape. Beyond the archway Rind lay quiet.

"We should spread some sort of alarm," I said. "These poor people will be easy prey for the demons."

"Why bother?" my companion asked. "The city is full of nothing but insignificants as well as the castle these days. History won't miss them."

"That's a terrible thing to say!" I argued, guiding the cart quickly through the streets.

"Terrible but true," he responded. "I should know; I write history. I am Darius, the Second Kingdom's scribe."

I thought for a moment, wondering where I had heard that name before. Of course! Here was the man whose tomes my tutor had forced me to practically memorize. And what wretched books they were.

"I've read some of your work," I said.

Pleased, Darius smiled. "Oh grand, grand! Chamberlin Bule said you were educated—very much so. We should work well together."

As the cart entered the deceptively calm countryside, Darius produced a tiny brown packet from a fold in his robe. He fingered it for a moment, and then it suddenly grew twenty times in size, revealing itself as a large parchment book.

"Magick!" I cried, nearly steering the cart off the road. "Gods!"

"Calm down, boy," Darius chuckled. "Magick in and of itself isn't bad. The value depends on the person working it. Look here."

I watched from the corner of my eye as Darius produced a feather quill from inside the book. "A magick pen," he said, licking the tip, which left a black mark on his pale tongue. "It never runs out of ink."

"I don't care," I said. "Magick is still dangerous."

"Oh, but you're a stubborn one! Let me tell you something, boy Seer, I wouldn't be alive today if it wasn't for the magick arts." He reached into his robe again and produced a small vial.

"Extract of Goren root," he said, holding it up into the light. "In a magick bottle, too—it never goes empty. A dose of this every morning and you'll live to see more than a hundred harvests, just like me."

"Goren root?" I asked. "Isn't Goren root juice supposed to be an aphrodisiac?"

"What better tonic is there than intercourse?" Darius asked. "But enough of this chatter. We have work to do." Darius turned to a blank page in his book and set his quill to paper. "Now then, let's hear your prophecies."

It seemed to me that this was no time to trifle with such banalities (given that the demons had invaded) but since there was surely nothing to do about the latter, I resorted to satisfying the former. Besides, it kept me from wondering if Darius had saved my life only so he could record my mysterious utterings.

"Well, I told old Jezzidiah where to dig a well, and then I told King Phyllaman that there was trouble brewing-"

"Come on! Can't you remember exactly what you said?"

I thought for a moment. "When I came into the throne room I was disgusted by the court's behavior, and so I said something like "I see nothing but woe in the future if such foolishness continues.""

"Ye Gods, but that's terrible!" Darius exclaimed. "It's a wonder anyone listens to you at all. You've got to develop a style, my boy. Now, what specific information caused you to believe there was woe on the horizon?"

"Um—well, King Phyllaman didn't seem very regal and-"

Darius cut me off. "You need to come up with something more colorful and make sure it rhymes. For instance, you could have said:
> "Lo, as the King is wont to merry be,
> In the heavens plots Queen Destiny.
> And if the King does not grow stern,
> His land with demon-fire will burn."

I suppressed my urge to label the scribe's poetry as horrendous. "I didn't know anything about the coming of the demons," I pointed out.

"I wasn't suggesting that you did. Always end your prophecies with a threat. That way you ensure that your audience will pay heed."

"In other words, you want me to lie."

"Correct," Darius said. "What's a fib here and there? Sometimes there can be good reason for not telling the truth."

"Such as?"

"Since you have been tutored, I assumed that you read my history of King Phyllaman the First's reign?"

"Yes, I did," I replied.

"Excellent. It's one of my better works. I'll let you in on a little secret: that book is chock full of lies. Take the incident with the Banderwallian Demons. You remember that, don't you?"

I thought as hard as I could, not wanting to embarrass my tutors. "Yes, I think so. Someone—I don't remember who—was tinkering with magick and let down the barrier between their dimension and ours, causing them to come across the rift and attack the Land."

"Ha!" Darius exclaimed. "Nothing but fiction. What would everyone think if they knew the truth: someone in Phyllaman's court *created* the demons intentionally, but couldn't control them?"

"What?" I asked, stuptified. "Who would do a foolish thing like that?"

"Why Lord Banderwall, naturally. You see, Phyllaman wanted to find some way to ensure that if attacked, he would come out on top. And so he summoned Lord Banderwall, who was known for his propensity for conjuring, and asked him to cook something up, purely for defensive use, understand. Banderwall did as told. He created the perfect army. The demons are ruthless, intelligent, and almost impossible to kill. And I tell you, it was a good thing that Banderwall came up with a spell to banish his offspring to the empty dimension as quickly as he did: in just three days the Demons had devoured nearly a hundred people and over three hundred cattle!"

"Anyhow, The task fell on me to clean the mess up so future generations would still smile upon Good King Phyllaman the First. Politics, my boy. It doesn't matter what you do on the throne if you look good doing it. It's all a matter of perception. Come, what are your other prophecies?"

Outrage filled my body. Phyllaman had toyed with the life and death of every man, woman, and child in the Land. All this historian wanted from me was my prophecy. If I did not tell him something, he would likely make something up if he didn't like it.

"There's no time for that," I said, jerking on the reins and speeding the horses' gait toward the farm. "If we can't kill the demons, then we'll have to find some way to banish them back to the empty dimension."

"That has nothing to do with me," Darius insisted with a smile that exposed empty gums. "That's strictly *your* problem."

"*My* problem?" I asked, stunned. "It's everyone in the kingdom's problem and that includes you, too."

Darius laughed. "Ha!" A new twinkle had appeared in his eye; it was the flash of secret knowledge that I didn't have lurking in his head. "I'm not the one Claimed of the Golden Oracle. The Gods speak to men only through the Oracle; She is their agent, their link to our world. And if you've been claimed to work the will of the kind and goodly gods, then there must be others claimed of the bad and evil ones, no? Your opponent is not the Demons themselves, rather, their master. He or she is surely Claimed of the Black Oracle."

A line from the Litany of old ran through my head: *All that is just and good is countered by an opposite that is not. It is thus that the balance in the cosmos is maintained.*

I had studied the oral traditions of the Land but since I hadn't believed them to be true, I had never subjected them to any degree of scrutiny. What Darius had told me while we sped toward the farm should have been obvious, but still I resisted the belief that there was anything more powerful than men in this world and the next.

"Don't take it so hard," Darius said, mistaking my disbelieving silence for melancholy. "By the same logic, the demons must have opponents, too. Somewhere there is an army waiting for you to take command and ride on the back of the Oracle to victory."

"I hope so," I muttered, not considering the implications of the scribe's choice of words.

*** *** ***

I decided that we should head for the farm as a haven. Even Darius knew of it, bearing what was almost a legend.

As our haste drew us closer to the farm, Darius continued to babble about history and the lessons it held for humanity. However, after hearing him confess to altering the details of Phyllaman the First's reign, I wondered how much of his talk he expected me to believe.

The village on whose outskirts I had grown up was completely deserted, just as Rind had been. I looked over my shoulder to see the city in the distance; thin wisps of black smoke drifted high into the air, the smoke's source concealed by the myriad buildings of town. Where was everybody?

Once the farm was in sight, the terror of flight was replaced by curiosity at the goings on ahead of the cart. My father's land was bustling with activity; scores of people dotted the fields, hastily harvesting and replanting. I recognized old Jezzidiah as we crossed the property boundary that was marked by the edge of the cornfield. Why had father enlisted the villagers to assist with the harvest? And who were those haggard men I didn't recognize?

"Say, this is quite an operation," Darius noted. "You really *are* a farm boy, aren't you? And I thought Priory had cooked up a humble lineage for you along with your costume. Oh, this is grand, grand! Students forever more will *love* to hear about this."

The only words I wanted to hear were those that explained the sudden surge in activity. I guided the cart to the stables and stopped the horses. My ears were immediately assaulted by Erdo's coarse holler: "There he is, next to the stables!

The Seer is here, the Seer is here!"

I turned to see activity in my proximity come to an abrupt halt as men threw down their hoes and scythes and bags of seed to come rushing toward me.

For a moment I thought I was about to be lynched, and then much to my surprise the men threw themselves on the moist ground and genuflected before me, weeping in gratitude for some unknown favor.

"Bless you Lord Seer!" they cried. "That the Gods would grace this world with a heart so noble is a miracle! Bless you, bless you!"

Confused, I dared not set foot off the cart lest the throng I had attracted suffocate me. Darius sat quietly beside me, madly scribbling in his book, and muttering to himself something about my popularity and how it would be preserved for future generations.

Proud as a peacock, Erdo strode through the wailing admirers of mine. "Isn't this incredible?" he said, patting the horses as he passed.

"What is going on here?" I demanded. "Who are these people?"

Erdo rolled his eyes skyward in the gesture of a guilty child forced to confess. "Well, it's a long story, but when Derek and I freed these men, we just couldn't bear to see these poor wretches boiled in oil or stripped of their skin and-"

Clarity filled my head as I realized what Erdo, and Derek had done: Chancellor Bule had mentioned that prisoners had escaped from Clayton's dungeon, and I had failed to see the connection. Derek and Erdo had freed Clayton's imprisoned knights and brought them back to the farm, which Erdo knew since it was on the edge of the Great Forest.

"-and since there was all this talk of war, I figured that we could use all the help we could get." Erdo continued. "The funny thing is that the guards *gave* us the keys and begged to come with us!" The Trog shook his head out of pity at the prostrate throng, which by now numbered almost one hundred.

My first reaction was to scold Erdo for being so rash, for when Clayton discovered the true nature of the escape, he would certainly use it as an excuse to fall upon our kingdom with his mercenary horde. Then again that was the least of our problems. Besides, Clayton's men could possibly help in the battle against the Demons. Who would wage better war against Clayton than those he had wronged?

"That was a smart move, freeing those men," Darius said behind me.

"But I had no knowledge of it, " I said.

"Yes, but there's no need to record that little detail. You're going to be a legend, my boy! That is, if you manage to banish the Demons before they have you for supper."

Darius chuckled then, a dry, throaty sound that was completely unpleasant.

I turned my attention back to Erdo and the crowd. So soaked with tears of joy was the ground that the emaciated knights were wallowing in a mud puddle, still lauding me for their rescue. Apparently Erdo hadn't seen fit to tell them it wasn't my idea.

"Where is Sir Slakely, the captain of Clayton's guard?" I asked.

Erdo shrugged. "He was out in the fields somewhere."

"And Derek?"

"In the barn."

"Find Slakely and tell him to meet me in the kitchen of the main house."

"Right," Erdo said, and was on his way.

Now came the uncomfortable task of getting off the cart and making my way into the barn. Darius saw me begin to move; he leaned toward me and whispered in my ear. "Be magnanimous," he suggested. "Remember, you're their savior."

I groaned at the thought of gaining the distinction as such and stepped down off the cart. Immediately did the knights clutch at my trousers and douse my shoes with their tears. Such excessive laud made me nervous and a bit angry, for I had done nothing to deserve it. This would not be the only time I felt that way; indeed, there are many days that I feel that Darius and Erdo and all did too thorough a job in seeing that I was firmly entrenched as a hero.

"I'll die for you," one knight muttered to my foot. "I'll fight 'till the last drop of my very blood is spilt for your cause, O noble Seer, Chosen of the Gods!"

This was too much. I callously forced my way through my army's ranks and slipped into the barn, barring the door behind me. I could hardly fathom what was next. Surely, they wouldn't make me a general.

I thought I would find solace in the barn, but instead I found Sariah and Derek. They did not see me at first, and so I made no sound.

"Then there was the time I was faced by five robbers and the women who had fallen into peril," Derek said. He had an arm raised and leaning against I post, his shirt fallen open to reveal his muscles.

"Oh my!" Sariah exclaimed, her hair shining in the light like the straw—golden and perfect.

"Ahem," I said, stepping into the light. Sariah reacted to my sight.

"Oh, Kyle!" she said, stepping toward me but staying short. "You're safe!"

"I'm Claimed of the Golden Oracle—of course I'm safe." I said, playing my card. I was so jealous that I didn't know what to say. I found words. "I'm ever so glad the two of you have come to be so close in such a short interval of time," I said dryly, "but there are more important things to be done: the kingdom has been invaded by Banderwallian Demons, and if we don't act soon, we might be burnt and devoured by the same. Would you mind joining me in the kitchen, Derek?"

"Uh, sure," he said. He looked at Sariah and took her hand, stroking it lovingly. "You're safe," he said to her. I felt nauseous.

Outside, my followers had dispersed into the fields and the harvest was on again. Hoping that the adoration would not begin anew, I hurried past them to the main house.

Clear of the house I saw my Father walking toward me, heading from the kitchen. "Kyle!" he said, joy and relief highlighting his ruddy, handsome face. And then he grew serious, mannered; I was no longer his child, but a Seer who was to be treated with reverence and caution. "It's good to see you, son," he said stiffly.

"It's good to see you too, Father," I replied.

An uncomfortable moment passed between us, making me long for the days in which I was but his son. That time seemed so distant now.

My father shifted his feet in the brown soil. "I take it from the army you've raised that something terrible has happened." he said.

"Yes. King Phyllaman is dead."

Father's already stoic expression grew saddened, grim.

"He was murdered," I continued. "That's beside the point now. The Banderwallian Demons have come through the barrier."

Sadness grew into the visage of absolute horror. "Demons?" Father exclaimed. "How?"

"I don't know. Our kingdom is surely lost; it will be all we can do to keep them from spreading across the Land and devouring it completely. In the meantime, I think it wise for you and the farmhands to pack up the families and head for the Great Sea. Maybe the Demons can be stopped before they get that far."

My father was resolute; I knew he would not question me and my position. He sighed and looked past me to the fields, many of which he had cleared with his own hands. A new sadness welled up in his eyes; both he and I knew that the Demons would not leave much in their wake.

"Yes, I guess that would be the best thing to do." And then his eyes shifted towards me. "But what about you?"

What about me? I could think of nothing but Darius' words: *I'm not the one Claimed of the Golden Oracle. Your opponents are not the Demons themselves, rather, their master. He or she is surely Claimed of the Black Oracle.*

Your opponent, Kyle. You're "it." The Demons are your problem.

"They'll need my help," I said, referring to the "army" Derek and Erdo had procured for me. The Gods only knew what that help consisted of.

Father looked at me then, and it was the despair behind his eyes that forced a terrible, hope-filled prophecy to my reticent lips. "Everything will be all right," I said. "*I'll* be all right. Trust me; I'm a Seer, remember?"

As my father sighed, I silently prayed that this one prediction would come true.

*** *** ***

CHAPTER SEVEN: THE RAID

And the Demons poured through the rift
Looking for flesh and skin to devour
Through the Gods the people did sift
And the Golden Oracle would have her hour.
-The History of the Second Banderwallian War, verse 4820

Through the open kitchen door poured the aroma of Sissy's cooking along with the rhythmic rise and fall Darius' voice; he was babbling to the beleaguered Sissy, who was frantically stirring the contents of two huge pots that boiled over the fire.

"Count Cedric was an idiot," Darius said. "I tell you, he—ah! The Seer is here!"

Sissy stopped cooking and turned to me in disgust. "So!" she sighed. "The wandering prophet has come home. I hope you appreciate what I'm doing for you. Those cretins you dug up from Gods know where are running me crazy with the way they eat. I can hardly keep up with the cooking!" She jerked a thumb in Darius' direction. "And as for this old fool, he talks too much! I thought scribes were supposed to be silent."

Darius laughed heartily; he was obviously used to such derision. "What a tongue she has in her head," he said of Sissy between guffaws.

"I have a good mind to yank yours out and throw it into the stew," she snapped.

Darius stopped chuckling immediately, as any sane man

would. Sissy rarely made idle threats.

"I'm sorry to trouble you so," I said. "Those men were held prisoner in Clayton's dungeon for treason. They refused to wage war against the other kingdoms."

"Oh," Sissy said, returning to her fire. Her concise comment led me to believe that she was not as annoyed as she was trying to seem; something told me she enjoyed being put to such full use.

I cleared my throat, preparing to deliver bad news once again. "There's trouble, Sissy. Serious trouble. The Banderwallian Demons have broken through again."

"Oh."

"Mother and Father and the field hands are talking of going to pack up and head toward the Great Sea. Perhaps we will find a way to send the Demons back where they came from before they spread that far."

"Perhaps we will," she said, not diverting but the slightest sliver of attention from her cooking.

I was puzzled by her lack of concern. Didn't she understand the gravity of the situation?

"I-"

Sissy cut me off. "Don't even say it," she said, wiping her hands on her apron. "I'm too old to go anywhere. Besides, you need me here to feed your army."

"Absolutely not," I insisted. "It's too dangerous. Besides, we'll manage on our own."

"Rubbish. Who's going to do the cooking? You? Men don't fight very well on an empty stomach. And what would hungry Demons want with something as gnarled and tough as me? I'm staying."

"Don't argue with her, boy," Darius said. "Her mind's made up."

Sissy cast an annoyed glance at the scribe, as if to say that his comments had not been solicited. "I take it you're staying as well?" she asked.

"I wouldn't miss it for the world," Darius said. "Besides,

who would record the glorious events for future generations?"

"Stay if you want. Maybe the demons will get hungry and rid us of you, you nuisance."

What was I to do? I couldn't make Sissy go with the others; she was free to choose her fate. If that fate included death at the hands of the Demons, I would never be able to forgive myself. I couldn't help but wonder why I had been singled out above all other men to bear witness to the tragedy that I was undoubtedly facing.

Just then, Derek, Erdo, Sir Slakely and a man I had not been introduced to crowded into the kitchen. The knight I did not know immediately threw himself at my feet

"Please get up," I begged him before he had a chance to start drowning me in thanks. Sir Slakely gently prodded his fellow with his foot as Darius and Sissy watched the proceedings with interest.

"This is Sir Colin, my second in command," Sir Slakely said.

Sir Colin jumped to his feet and snapped his scrawny body to attention. "At your service, O noble Seer!" he exclaimed.

Embarrassed, I motioned to the table. "Please sit down. We have much to discuss."

Everyone joined Darius around the table, including Sissy, who was wide-eyed with interest.

Sir Slakely folded his hands on the table and cleared his throat. "I suppose the first order of business is to determine what the first order of business is," he said.

"Indeed," Darius agreed.

For several moments everyone was silent. Derek tapped his foot on the oiled dirt floor, Erdo picked at his fingernails and the others were likewise distracted. It was painfully clear that there was a lack of ideas about, and so I threw a suggestion out onto the table: "Perhaps if we lured the Demons out into the countryside and distracted them long enough to find a way to send them back to where they came…"

Slakely snapped to attention. "An excellent idea! We'll lure them into the woods. In the forest there are less lives to lose. Why would the Demons give up a safe and comfortable home in the castle?"

"Safe?" Darius chuckled. "*Safe?* The Demons are safe wherever they go, my friend. They're totally impervious to our weapons; I should know. Sooner or later their larder will be depleted, and they will seek victims outside of the castle to satisfy their hunger. We needn't lure them out; they'll come on their own."

"Yes, but at the expense of the lives of Lord Dowry and his men and the others trapped in Rind."

Darius rolled his eyes. "People are going to die regardless of what we do. Why bother with those already in the Demon's clutches and risk falling into the same?"

Sir Colin pounded a fist on the table angrily. "Have you no pity?" he demanded of Darius. "Would you let the Demons feast as they will without a fight?"

"What is twenty or thirty lives?" Darius retorted. "In the face of thousands of years of history, Dowry and his men don't count for much."

Now the situation around the table began to grow tense. Sissy, Slakely, Derek and even Erdo moved to debate the significance of the individual and his place in history—an admirable point to debate, but this was hardly the time for academic dialogue. I opted to take control of the situation and steer the informal meeting away from becoming an ethical brawl.

"However, Darius, you would not argue that the Demons need to be dealt with and that the feat will take time?"

"Oh absolutely," he replied.

"And by your own philosophy would you not reason that those who should give up their lives in this affair should be those who have pledged their lives to defend the Land?"

The Scribe's eyes narrowed as he looked at me; I was backing him into a philosophical corner. "Well, yes," he said warily.

"Then in order to provide the time we need to learn how to banish the Demons, we must free Dowry's men. Dowry and Slakely can then lure the fiends out into the Northern Forest and away from the populous of the Land."

The participants looked at one another and nodded in agreement with my logic. Darius did so reluctantly.

"Good," I said. "Now Darius, is there a secret passage that leads to the dungeon?"

"Of course."

"Perhaps you could draw us a map..." Sir Colin suggested.

"Absolutely not. I'll lead you to it. You aren't going to keep me from witnessing history in the making."

Rubbing the red stubble on his chin, Sir Colin leaned back in his chair and frowned. I initially thought that the prospect of Darius accompanying us on the raid was troubling him, but other aspects of the current situation were weighing heavy on his mind. "Exactly how do we get rid of the Demons?" he asked.

Darius shrugged. "I'm not exactly sure, but it probably goes something like this: First you take the shells of two eggs, and you put them in a pot along with a goblet of newt bile or some other odious substance-"

Slakely and Colin offered their protest in unison: *"What?"*

"Don't interrupt," Darius said. "Now where was I? Oh yes: a few drops of tincture of bowling-beetle dung-"

"Are you saying we have to cast a *spell*?" Sir Slakely asked in disbelief.

"Well of course you must cast a spell to get rid of the Demons. They were summoned by a spell, and so only a spell can dispel them."

A new pall tinted the knight's already sullen features. "What a fiendish lot we've drawn!" he howled. "To rid our land of one evil we must invoke another."

"Rubbish," Darius said. "Oh, if you only knew." He turned to me, shaking his head. "Lord Seer, are you sure you want to let the fate of the Land hinge on the actions of these idealistic dolts —no wait, I forgot. None of us have a choice."

"Enough of this," Slakely said. "Let me rouse our best men and we'll be off."

"Nonsense," Darius repeated. "You can't go now."

"Oh? And why not?"

Once again Darius attempted to start a brawl by offering me an aside. "Couldn't you have found a better band of vagabonds than these?" And then to Slakely: "Use your head, man! Banderwallian Demons crave human flesh, which they have been denied for years. I say let them gorge themselves. And then when they are languid from feasting, we can slip in to and out of the castle while the mere sight of such delicacies as us will make their gorges rise."

I found the knights looking to me for guidance. I had absolutely no idea what to tell them. To wait would mean that there was less of a chance of finding survivors in the dungeon.; to rush in while the Demons' lust for food was at a fever pitch would undoubtedly prove just as fatal.

"Perhaps Darius is right," I said impotently.

*** *** ***

As I lay on my cot in the dark, I prayed to whatever gods there were that I was doing the right thing in delaying the raid. Through the window I could see the glow of the fires still burning in Rind. Soon I would be heading straight for them and toward whatever burned in them.

*** *** ***

The next morning, Darius, Derek, Erdo (who complained sorely of his inclusion in the affair) Sirs Slakely and Colin and ten of their best men piled into three carts and started out for Rind.

"Shouldn't we wait until after nightfall?" Erdo said, undoubtedly hoping that the dark would aid our quest.

"Absolutely not," I responded. "Darius says that the Demons are more active at night. They will hopefully be tired from yesterday's revelry." It was a feeble line of reasoning to be sure, but the best that I could manage. Today, tonight, yesterday, tomorrow—to me it did not matter when we acted so long as we did. There was no better time than the here and now.

As we began on our way, I caught a glimpse of Sissy coming out of the front of the farmhouse. She wasn't exactly smiling, but she seemed assured that everything was going to work out for the best.

Sariah appeared beside her. Curiously dressed in a deep blue dress, I smiled at her and waved. Two words formed on her lips: *Goodbye, Derek.* I looked over my shoulder, and Derek blew a kiss at Sariah. My heart sank in my chest. How could I, the cripple, have thought that I would win the maid? I was even more foolish than I thought.

We could smell the city long before we entered it, and its aroma was a distinctly cooked one. Outside of the gates we abandoned our carts and made cautious, quiet way into the city.

The houses and fortifications of the periphery were in pristine condition but abandoned; clutter in the streets implied sudden flight. As we drew nearer to the marketplace the clay streets and shops were scorched and blackened with soot; timbers and straw roofs still smoldered and smoked.

I felt a tug at my sleeve. "Where is everybody?" Erdo whispered up to me. "I haven't seen a single living thing since we entered the city."

"Neither have I," I said out of the corner of my mouth. I nervously looked to either side of the narrow street, thinking that our words might suddenly draw attention to us.

Up ahead, Slakely and three of his men were skulking about with swords drawn, peeking around corners, and peering through smashed shutters for signs of a demon ambush. Behind me strode Darius, who seemed so at ease that he might as well have been whistling a cheery tune.

There was still no sign of the Demons. Slakely stopped briefly to confer with his men and then we were pushing onward toward the castle and whatever lay ahead.

I lamented as we continued our way through the ruins of the market. The wooden stalls and carts had been overturned, smashed, and burned. Fanciful merchandise lay shattered and scattered. Here and there, scorched bones picked clean of meat and gristle jutted from the debris. Those who had stayed behind had been routed from their hiding places and had obviously not been able to escape before the Demons poured over the drawbridge, hungry mouths open wide. I found myself wondering if anyone at all in the city had managed to escape—and why the demons had apparently returned to the castle.

Sure of their own immortality (and blinded by their own glory) the Demons had not seen fit to raise the drawbridge. Looking back, I see it would have been perfectly safe just to step across the planks that spanned the moat and enter the castle as any man would, but instead Darius lead Slakely, his scouts and the rest of the party down the slope of the moat channel and to the edge of the murky waters that butted against the more defensible stables.

Slakely watched in disbelief as Darius began to wade into the fetid water. "The water-serpents, man!" he said. "What about the water-serpents? There's no cure for their venomous bite."

"All rubbish," the scribe said. His going was slow; the bottom of the moat was sucking mire that impeded his progress. "Just look at this water. Do you think any of natural creatures could live in such pollution and filth? Now come along before a Demon spot you and curbs your tongue permanently."

The party began to do as told. I hesitated for a moment, hoping that Darius was right. Derek, who had kept rear guard in our approach, appeared beside me; he plowed through the mud with considerably more ease than I did. "When are we going to get to kill something?" he asked.

"Sorry, but I don't think there'll be much of that," I said. "This is more of a covert mission."

"Damn," Derek muttered, and plowed ahead. If ever a Demon had a formidable enemy, it was Derek. His brash attitude alone served as a shield of which many a knight's sword would glance.

Darius had reached the far side of the moat and was feeling along the joints of the great masonry stones for some unseen mechanism. I had not seen him complete the traverse of the moat and was surprised to see that his garments were thick with mud only as high as his low waist. What was the point of having a moat if it could be easily negotiated? I assumed that the trench was for effect rather than true defense; it was a trick, just like the tales of poisonous snakes and goodly kings banishing marauding demons.

In the daylight I had a better view of the door that led into the maze of passages that Darius knew so well. When the scribe's gnarled finger finally found its mark, a large block in the castle wall melted from sight, dissolved by a magickal contrivance. "I'll go first," Darius beamed, and then he crawled on his hands and knees into the dark maw before him. Slakely and his men followed, then Erdo, Derek, who yawned with boredom. He was probably thinking about Sariah and her breasts—I certainly was. That is, I was trying to distract myself from the menacing situation at hand.

A thought struck me: crawling through tunnels bored in the dank earth while hideous, supernatural beasts lurked above ground was not the best situation for a cripple to be in. Why hadn't Slakely or even Sissy tried to stop me from tagging along? Would I not slow them down if the need to flee arose? Could it be that my cohorts were somehow unaware of my handicap's implications?

I was not aware that the hidden door had closed behind us until I found myself in utter darkness. Perhaps it would have behooved us to carry torches, but since we were reduced to crawling on our hands and knees, I realized torches would be of little use.

Eventually my eyes adjusted, eking as much light from the surroundings as possible. The walls of the tunnel were of the same dark stone that constructed the rest of the castle; the ground below was damp and aromatic of mold and fungus.

We had not been moving long before Erdo started coughing and sputtering without warning. "Gods!" he exclaimed, knobby fingers pinching his nose shut.

"Shh!" Slakely hissed, as if the Demons could hear through

stone.

"What's wrong?" I whispered, urging Erdo to continue forward. The Trog resisted, turning his plump, squat body to face me.

"Can't you *smell* that?" he asked.

"Smell what?"

"Gods, it's that awful stuff that was in that vial Clayton's cook had. This part of the tunnel *reeks* of it."

"Are you sure?"

"Look at this nose," Erdo said, tapping the bulging bridge of his proboscis. "My nose never lies. I tell you I smell that junk that Clayton poisoned the food with."

Realizing that Erdo, Derek and I had fallen behind, Slakely ignored his own admonition to keep quiet. "Keep up!" he yelled from several crawl-paces deeper into the tunnels.

"Hold up!' I insisted. "Erdo may have made a discovery."

Before I knew it, Darius was pushing his way past the scouts; if there were any new developments, he wanted to witness them so he could record a perverted version of the event for posterity's sake. The scribe had swept his long beard back on both sides of his head and had tied a neat knot in back to keep it from dragging in the dirt. "What's the matter?"

"It *smells!*" Erdo whined.

"Rubbish. You're smelling your upper lip," Darius insisted.

"I don't think so," I asserted. "Erdo claims he smells the making of a potion that Clayton used to cause unrest at the Council meeting. Are there any old laboratories down here?"

"Absolutely not. If there were, I'd know about them."

"Are you finished chatting back there?" Slakely called.

"Just a moment," I responded and returned my attention to Darius. "Are you *sure* there are no secret chambers down here?"

In the darkness I envisioned Darius' features becoming indignant. "Why would someone put secret doors *within* a secret tunnel? I tell you there's nothing behind these walls but foundation stones!"

Darius must have pounded a fist against the masonry to punctuate his pronouncement, for light suddenly flooded through the door activated by his actions.

In the queer light that bathed the tunnel I saw Erdo's eyes roll up into his head. "Phew!" he exclaimed, before swooning into a heap. I understood his displeasure; the stench that emanated from the secret chamber was noxious.

Darius ducked into the new passage before Slakely could tell him not to, and though the strange, dancing illumination made me nervous, I did the same.

Within the space of a few paces the tunnel opened into a full-sized room. Shelves fragile with age completely lined the walls; upon them were stacked moldering books of odious composition and a myriad of jars and jugs. Many of the vessels had burst with rot and age, oozing decayed herbs and offal onto the dust-covered shelves. The stench would have driven me back into the tunnel if Slakely and his men had not been blocking the entrance.

"Mother of Goodness and Fortitude!" I heard one of the scouts exclaim. He made a holy sign over his head and averted his eyes from the countless atrocities of a forgotten magick laboratory.

Sir Slakely followed up with curses of his own, his red beard inflamed in color by the light whose source was still unidentified: "Devilment! Evil in the Third Kingdom! Gods! We best not disturbed this cursed place—it was sealed and should remain so lest evil befall us."

Darius was not as horrified. He poked about the worktable. "This must have been Lord Ban-" and then he caught himself almost revealing the Demon's true source. "I mean I wonder who this laboratory belonged to?"

"Who cares?" Slakely said. "By the looks of it the sorcerer is long gone. Why disturb his evil accouterments? Out, men! The dank tunnel is preferable to this den of iniquity."

Darius snickered as Slakely and his men retreated.

Derek stuck his head in—"Hey, what's-" and then the

smell registered with his apparently sluggish olfactory sense. "Holy holy! What stinks?"

"Wormwort, and a lot of it," Darius said.

As the scribe continued to examine the magician's trappings, I was drawn to the bench in the far corner of the room. Upon it I found a flickering, bluish globe, the source of illumination of the room, concealed behind a box of small bones. Next to the orb was a glass bottle half-full of a red powder that looked suspiciously like that Clayton's cook gave me. Something struck me as strange about that bottle and globe, but I could not pinpoint what it was-

Fingerprints.

While a uniform coating of dust covered the rest of the equipment on the table, the bottle and orb were clean in places where someone had recently handled them. I snatched the bottle from the table and dashed as quick as one can on all fours to the still unconscious Erdo. I shook the Trog gently, trying to roust him. "Erdo, Erdo, wake up! I need you to smell this for me."

Erdo's eyelids fluttered for a brief second, then slowly opened. He moaned softly, clutching his stomach in nausea.

"Can you hear me?"

"Mmmmmmmuh-huh."

"I need you to sniff this powder and tell me if it's the same as that Clayton's cook gave us."

I removed the cork from the bottle and held it under his nose. Suddenly the Trog's oversized eyes sprang open— "Yes. Oh *Gods* I'm going to be *sick*!" He passed out again.

I rocked back on my heels, contemplating the situation. Darius crept up behind me, torn from his keen discovery by curiosity. "What's going on?" he asked.

"I'll explain it to you later," I said, handing him the bottle. "Is there anything in the lab that might help us banish the Demons?"

"Possibly."

"Good," I said. "I think it's time we moved to free Dowry from the dungeon."

*** *** ***

Sir Slakely was thankful that we had finally decided to move on, for his back was aching from stooping over in order to negotiate the tunnels. However, he was not elated at the sight of the globe that Darius bore in one free hand. "What are you doing, you fool?" Slakely spat. "Haven't we enough trouble with magick already?"

"Yes," Darius admitted, "How could using this little device to light our way possibly make the situation any worse? It was already aglow when we found it."

The knight did not offer any further argument.

The tunnel ended in a circular chamber high enough for a man to stand in. With light provided by the globe, the room was revealed as a juncture between still more tunnels. Several of them branched off from various points around the walls' circumference. Darius paused, puzzled. "Now let's see... the dungeon is through the third tunnel to the left—no, the second—oh bother."

I took the opportunity to check on Erdo, whom Derek was ushering through the tunnel in front of him.

"Oooog," the Trog groaned, hand to his forehead.

"How are you doing?" I asked.

"Aw, he's okay," Derek said as he stood up, straightening out his strapping frame.

"Oh, it must be the fourth tunnel to the left," Darius said, and crawled into the dark, pushing the globe before him.

"I hope the old man's right," one of the scouts bemoaned as he watched a rat run across the stone floor. "These tunnels are scary."

Not half as scary as what's upstairs, I thought. None of these men had ever beheld a Banderwallian Demon in all its terrible glory.

The secret door at the end of the tunnel opened into a hall in the deepest bowel of the castle. Here the floor was decorated with some queer mosaic and as I stood in full presence of Darius' glowing orb, I saw that it was not art but rather the work of an unknown number of rats. In places guano completely obscured the pavement beneath. It was hardly imaginable that these cells could still hold prisoners; most of the wooden doors were rotted beyond functioning, revealing manacles and torture devices in the rooms beyond. The castle's dungeon had been empty for as long as anyone in the party could remember; King Phyllaman the First had built a more humane prison out near the southern boundary of the city.

"I hear voices further up," a scout whispered to us as he returned to the group. "Human voices."

Sir Slakely looked at me and then at Darius, as if we were supposed to give him some sort of sign or suggestion. I had the impression that he was not as experienced a commander as he led us to believe.

Slakely cleared his throat and then started up the hall, followed by his scouts. Darius shrugged and started after them; Erdo, Derek and I did the same.

"Not even the rats live down here anymore," Erdo said to no one in particular. "These are old droppings; they hardly smell at all, and it's a good thing, too."

The upper levels of the dungeon were in a lesser state of disrepair than those below. At the very top were those cells reserved the less heinous of criminals. Cells consisting of three solid walls and wrought iron bars replaced dark, dank rooms.

No sooner did we enter his sight did Lord Dowry run to the forefront of one of the cells and peer through the bars. Though his eyes were reddened by the smoke that still hung thick in the air, they were lit with hope. "Lord Seer!" he exclaimed. "Thank the Gods! Release us so we may behead the demon Mackret and his fiends and set the kingdom right again!"

The men in Dowry's and the surrounding cells roared and grumbled similar sentiments.

"Mackret is dead—I think," I said, not knowing if the Demons had eaten him or not, although they had no reason not to. "But there are other demons to worry about: Banderwallian Demons."

There was no need to describe what would happen if the demons heard the cries for justice and the calling for Mackret's death ceased. The only sound in the room was the clanking of a scout unlocking the cells (he had found the keys on a peg at the guard's station).

Dowry and his men were undoubtedly glad to be free but did not rush from the cells with any great haste. For all they knew there was nowhere to escape to. Roughly thirty men stood in the cramped upper dungeon, looking for direction.

"They'll need swords," someone whispered in my ear. I looked to my left to see Darius next to me. "If we tell them they can't kill the Demons they'll never go along with the plans. Give a knight a sword and he will be driven to use it."

"Where will we find thirty swords?"

"In the armory."

"Good," I said. "Can you lead us there?"

"Yes, but..."

"But what?"

"There isn't a secret passage that leads to the armory. It was added to the castle later, whereas the secret tunnels were laid down with the foundation. We will have to risk exposure to the Demons."

I looked at Dowry, Slakely, and what was to be my army. All their eyes were on me. This was the cruelest of all Destiny's tricks so far: not only did I find myself in command of an army, but I was about to ask them to fight an unbeatable foe.

"Er, we will have to raid the armory if we are to offer a defense against the Demons."

"Then let's get to work," Dowry shouted. His men cheered, driven into frenzy first by Mackret's plotting, second by the invasion of the Demons. Darius knew the soldier's psyche too well; his picture of the knights as single-minded killers was not far off.

"Let's go *quietly*," I begged, hoping that the Demons would remain (presumably) asleep, as Darius insisted they were.

The men filed from the room led by Sir Slakely, oddly

enough. Dowry either loved life too much to take the lead or hadn't taken notice of Slakely's attempts to take control.

I scanned the former prisoners, and when I did not see who I was looking for I stopped Lord Dowry as he passed. "Where is Chamberlin Bule?" I asked.

"Bule?" he asked. The knight turned slowly in place, scanning the dungeon as I did. "The Chamberlin was in the cell with us to begin with—no—to be honest Lord Seer, I don't remember seeing that fop since those heinous crimes were perpetrated in the courtyard."

It did not seem unlike Bule to save his own skin by sneaking off when his captors weren't looking; I only hoped he had not fallen prey to the voracious Demons. I needed his confidence.

With no desire to lead the raid on the armory, I joined Darius, Derek and Erdo at the rear of the group as it quietly began to file out of the dungeon.

"Is it time to go yet?" Erdo whined.

"Not yet. We have to secure weapons for the men."

Darius reveled in the prospect of battling Demons with steel, but truly, his eyes lit up in macabre anticipation of bloodshed.

He rocked back on his heels, smiled maliciously, and repeated himself: "Let's do it."

With all those men sneaking out of the dungeon ahead of me it made no sense to skulk about as the knights did, peering this way and that and hugging the walls with their bodies. After all, if the demons hadn't noticed the first thirty men who crept out into the stairwell, why should they suddenly take notice of me? I walked with head held high, and, not knowing any better, my three curious companions did the same.

The lower halls of the dungeon were cloyed with a preternatural silence underlined by the acrid smoke the feast had produced. I cannot describe the anxiety and dread that gripped my heart then, for all we knew we could be walking straight into the very clutches of the fiends we sought to expel.

That was when I heard the voice in my head, as clear as if its owner was standing beside me, speaking into my very ear: *No. The Demons are asleep, just as Darius said. And yet...*

I shook my head to physically rattle the internal monologue loose.

"What's wrong?" Darius whispered over my shoulder.

"I'm hearing voices."

I must have sounded quite worried, for the scribe patted me on the back with a bony hand. "Good man," he whispered. "Seers *should* hear voices. I knew you'd catch on sooner or later."

Just down a broad stone hall but steps from the staircase that led to the dungeon was the armory.

"An idiot built this castle, to be sure."

For an instant I was sure that the phantom voice was back again and that I had gone completely mad, but it was only Darius whispering to me again.

"Why would an architect put the armory so close to the dungeon? What if there was a prison break? It would be far too easy for the criminals to gain entry and arm themselves...say, that's a good story! I'll have to remember that. Someday I might be able to use that in one of my books."

That part of me that was not pre-occupied with the matters at hand took note of Darius' confession that he would substitute outright lies for history should he deem it to boring. His works deserved a second, enlightened reading.

Slakely, his scouts and I kept watch at the door as Dowry quickly distributed arms. Derek chose a huge, gleaming battle-axe for his own, but Erdo refused to take even as much as a dagger. "I hate violence," he said self-righteously, though I surmise he did not care to enter the fray.

It was exactly that fray that bothered me. Where *were* the Demons? We had seen neither hide nor hair of a single living creature since we left the dungeon, not even a rat. Something was dreadfully amiss. Asleep or not, surely the clatter of armor and weapons would roust the hungry monsters from their slumbers and set them drooling for flesh.

The Demons serve no threat at the present time; they will not stir until you are long gone. Another threat is near, however, and growing closer even as I speak.

"What?"

I found Darius gazing at me intently. Was he speaking to me? "I beg your pardon?" I asked.

"What are you babbling about?"

"I didn't say anything at all," I insisted.

The scribe squinted one eye at me suspiciously. "Yes, you *did* say something—something about the Demons not stirring and another threat growing closer."

Given the ugliness of the current situation, the last thing I wanted to encounter was fear of losing my sanity. I opened my mouth to offer Darius further rebuttal, but none came forth. Either I could not compose any or my disbelieving tongue refused to utter them.

Darius was quick to draw his own conclusions. He skittered from my side and headed straight to Dowry. After a hushed exchange Dowry cleared his throat: "The Seer has proclaimed that the Demons will not wake to battle us on this day," he announced loudly. "This is a boon to us, for the Scribe has just pointed out that the tunnels would be a death-trap in the instance that the Demons woke and moved upon us. We must busy ourselves tallying the invaders so we may better prepare ourselves for battle."

My numbed ears could hardly believe what they were hearing. Dowry wanted to take a census of the Banderwallian Demons! What difference did it make how many of them there were when one of them could gnaw the flesh from a man's bones between beats of their evil hearts?

I watched in horror as the men drew lots pertaining to wings of the silent castle. Damn Darius for putting the knights up to this!

My yanking at the sleeve of his robe startled Darius. "What in the hells did you say to Lord Dowry?" I demanded angrily. "He could be sending these men to their deaths!"

"What are you worried about?" Darius said calmly. "You were the one who told me the Demons wouldn't wake up while we were here."

"I said nothing of the sort."

He shook his head and smiled the knowing smile of someone who had dealt with angry pupils for more years than there were Demons in the castle. "Yes, you did tell me the Demons wouldn't wake. What's the matter? Don't you have faith in your own powers of prognostication? Now if you will excuse me, there are things I would rather not abandon to the Demons."

With that, Darius turned and headed toward the stairs that led higher into the castle.

"Wait!"

Darius stopped. Shadows thrown by the orb's light elongated as he turned toward me.

"Didn't I say something about another threat in the castle?"

"Don't you remember?"

I confessed that I didn't.

A free hand flew to a waiting hip. "Good Gods boy, it's a good thing I have a fertile imagination and memory or there'd be no words of yours to record! I quote: "Another threat is near, however, and growing closer even as I speak." A crude line, but an effective one. It will have to be re-worked so it rhymes."

"Did you warn Dowry?"

"Of course not. Where's your sense of suspense? If we're not going to battle the Demons just yet, there has to be some sort of surprise to keep the historical river running."

I've had enough of surprises, I thought, watching Darius vanish up the stairs, and I hadn't even considered the implications of finding the source stomach-souring poison in Phyllaman's castle.

"Lord Dowry, you must-"

Erdo was leaning against the far wall; as for the others they had vanished on their missions, including Derek.

"Lord Dowry left," the Trog said.

Panicking, I flew across the hall and grabbed Erdo by the shoulders. "Which way did he go?"

Eyes bulging in alarm, Erdo turned his head ever so slightly and sniffed air through his misshapen nose. "Uh, that way!" he said, pointing up the stairs opposite those Darius had mounted.

I ran up the stairs as quickly as my bad leg would allow me to. At this depth there was considerable moisture in the air; green moss clung to the stone walls and occasionally to the stairs and so I had to be careful not to slip and take a tumble. I had no idea where I was going. I raced up to what I was sure was the main level of the castle. The smoke was noticeably thicker but there seemed to be a breeze, indicating the floor was above ground.

A strange grating sound reached my ears; in my haste I mistook it to be that of gruff, hushed voices and started off toward it. Though the tapestries were nothing but charred ashes on the ground and an occasional rope or swath of material on the wall, I reasoned I was in the great hall that led to throne room. Its doors were partially closed but clearly that was the location where the voices originated. I hit the doors with the full weight of my body, slamming them open.

"Be on your guard! There might be—"

The Demons were flat on their backs on the sooty tile floor. Their number was terrific; hardly any of the intricate mosaic was exposed between their slumbering bodies. Their breathing was a terrible clamor as air rushed in their gill slits, bloating their air sacs momentarily before expelling the exhaust over their thick, barbed tongues. Bones lay strewn about the room, as did shreds of discarded clothing, armor, and jewelry. Here and there a Demon slept with a skull or leg still in its clutches. Beyond them lay the gap in the throne room wall through which they had invaded: the nothingness beyond still writhed and boiled menacingly.

The Demons and the gap I had seen before, however, there was a new element in the room the puzzled me as

I squinted against the fading torch-glow. The Demons were bloated presumably from their devilish feast; their great bellies had swollen to protrude well over their belts and weapon-slings (which, dare I say, looked as if they had been fashioned from human remains). Scales had parted from the swelling to reveal new, finer scales beneath,

When my terror-induced paralysis began to loosen its grip, I slowly turned and began to tiptoe out of the predicament my haste had gotten me into. To my astonishment I had stepped *over* three slumbering Demons coming into the room. There was no other way I could possibly have made it so far into the room because little tile was exposed between myself and the main door.

My body trembled with fear of becoming a meal for the Demons. Yes, they slept, but clumsy me, I could surely waken one if I fell on top of its tender, bloated stomach.

What's the matter? Don't you have faith in your own powers of prognostication?

No, no, no! This was not the proper time and place for my troubled mind to begin to believe that I truly was the font of the Golden Oracle's endless wisdom.

Nervous sweat rolled from my cold forehead and into my eyes. The sooty, singed walls bulged and warped obscenely in my blurred vision; every Demon talon, every movement of their thick gills, every raspy breath was intensified by my fear.   I cannot recall how I got out of that room; perhaps an instinctive part of my mind took over for the numbed, rational self, perhaps I *floated* over the Demons by sheer force of will. Regardless, when I wiped my eyes clear with the back of my hand, I found myself in the hall, just outside that cursed lair.

Though the Demons were now out of sight, the anxiety they brought on remained heavy on my being. I felt so encumbered by my fear that I could hardly move nor utter a sound.

Mingled with the rasping of the demonic respiration was the distant clank of armor and weapons. Accompanied by this percussion was the sense of a presence moving in on me, its dread eyes fixing on me as a target, moving ever nearer-

A hand/claw/tentacle touched my shoulder. Out of reflex and duty to fulfill the call the unholy dread that assailed me, I whirled about to face my tormentor.

It was only Darius. Derek and several of the men accompanied him.

"My, you *are* jumpy!" Darius chimed, and then jerked a thumb in the knights' direction. "These dolts haven't seen as much as a Demon-spoor—and neither have I, for that matter. Where, do you suppose, they went?"

"In—in—there," I stuttered, indicating the throne room.

Derek bravely/foolishly pushed past me and kicked the door open with a booted foot. All at once that rasping sound filled the air, and the odor the Demons and their work exuded wafted into our collective nostrils. Someone drew in a startled breath.

Derek strode into the room, staying within the patch of light the torches in the hall provided. At the end of this wedge of illumination lay a Demon. Derek prodded it with his boot, and then with the tip of his sword. "Interesting," he said. "If these foul things weren't breathing, I'd say they were dead."

"Yes, it certainly is interesting," Darius said. He joined Derek, kneeling at his side to examine the thing more closely. He ran two fingers over the scales that girded the creature's chest, moving down toward the stomach. "Fascinating. I wonder why they would the sleep so deeply?"

"And why are they so bloated?" That was my own voice I heard; I must have been the one who gasped, too.

"A good question."

Darius leaned over, placing his right ear on the demon's swollen belly. His eyes rounded and widened in surprise.

"Uh-oh."

"What is it?" Derek asked.

"Well, it—it sounds like a heartbeat! Good Gods, I think the Demons are hibernating because they're *pregnant!*"

Derek's jaw dropped in disbelief, as did the jaws of everyone else in earshot. "Pregnant?" he said incredulously. How can they—I mean, they all look the same!"

Darius stood and shrugged. "I'm sure that each and every one is quite the same in a rudimentary way." He approached me, eyes wild with the thrill of intrigue. "Just think of it: not only are they the perfect army, but they can duplicate themselves in just a few hours! Oh, what brilliance! *Brilliance!*"

I was not as impressed with Lord Banderwall's creation. Who knew what else the Demons could do? "And so it's all the better that we find the spell that sends the damned things back to where they came from," I said.

Darius waved an unconcerned hand in my face. "Oh that—it's no problem; the spell is surely downstairs in the laboratory."

"Then what are we doing up here?"

Derek waved his sword. "Let's kill them."

"What, and wake the lot?" Darius asked. "There are too many of them. Divide and conquer, that's the thing."

The afflicted wail of someone in some unknown distress came screeching through the castle. This was the punctuation of the distant clattering I had ignored while entranced by the sight of the Demons; apparently my friends had not come from that direction and had not taken notice of it either.

There was no need for a call to action. Derek and the other men drew their swords and ran for the source of the sound. I was left with Darius, but I could hear his explanation for his next actions; his eyes spoke to me as he shrugged: *"As a historian, I just can't afford to miss anything, no matter how dangerous."*

Not knowing what else to do, I too followed, albeit at a slower pace.

We didn't have to walk far, for the clamor was headed in our direction. Backing up the stairs were Derek and his men, forced back to the main hall by unidentified soldiers in full armor and bearing swords, maces, and axes.

Who were these men that offered us battle in the very

castle? Apparently, no one bothered to stop and ask who or why. Derek swung his axe mightily; I had to avert my eyes and finally sought refuge from the spouting blood by heading back toward the throne room and points beyond.

And still the knights fought, giving and taking ground on the blood-soaked staircase. I passed the throne room quickly, but as the doors that led to the kitchen and servant's stations came into sight I slowed, for the din that emanated from behind them was certainly that of further conflagration. I heard Dowry's unmistakable voice ("Die, villains!") and then the kitchen doors splintered and burst under the force of axes swung behind them. Pinned to the door by Dowry's sword was one of the "villains". Blood poured from the seams of his armor. At once I was reminded of the blood-soaked scene that had taken place but a short time ago in the courtyard when Mackret's men assailed those of the deceased king. Philosophers and poets may write of the sophistication, honor, and wisdom of the race of men, but do not let such romantic notions as these delude you my son, or you and your kingdom will be lost. Man's natural state is that of conflict, and if he cannot find it, he is well prepared to produce it.

The tide of violence began to close in on me. In such affairs it is very unclear who is winning and who is losing; there was so much blood spattered about that those who were injured were indistinguishable from those who were merely soiled by the ichor.

"That one!" Darius roared above the noise. "You—the big one! Get the one who's going for the stairs!"

Taking Darius' direction to heart, Derek dove for the opponent who sought escape by pushing his way back toward the staircase from whence he had come. I couldn't bear to look; I had earlier speculated that Derek had come from a warlike people (his sheer size suggested that such men would undoubtedly seek dominance) but the glee with which he wielded the battle-axe was terrible to behold.

Severed limbs flew here and about but soon the supply of meat for the butchering was depleted and a retreat was in the works.

"*After them!*" Derek bellowed, and dare I say no one disputed his authority. The chase was on.

"Just like the old days!" Darius beamed as he ran past me, face splattered with blood.

Out of duty (or perhaps sickened fascination) I followed.

Exactly where the marauders were withdrawing to became more and more clear as Derek, Dowry and men continued pursuit. Whoever they were they sought to exit the castle and flee for their very lives; obviously they hadn't expected the Second Kingdom to be prepared for battle—which left me to contemplate who in the Land would have an army ready to strike.

I followed the combatants at a safe distance, though I never once considered myself to be in danger. By now a part of me had decided that I had been chosen by the Gods (for whatever reason they might have) to observe the events unfolding around me. I now realize how wrong I was. I was not an observer of events, but the very catalyst that produced them. It was naive of me to think that such hatred and violence could erupt so quickly without having roots deep in the past; indeed, if I had truly listened to the accusations that the kings had slung at each other during the final meeting of the Council of Thirteen I would have understood that there *never* was true peace in the Land.

Suspicious activity thrived. I was flint, and my ascension to Seership and subsequent prophecies ignited the flames of war as casually as my father's fields had burned by my own hand years ago. And no matter how hard I tried to fight my fate and role by falsifying prophecies and trying to reason with the rulers of the Land, the outcome would be the same. Not only was I a prophet, but the very means by which many of my prophecies came true.

What was the ultimate end the Gods were trying to achieve?

I hope, dear son, that you do not expect to find the answer to that question within these pages. No, the answers that men seek are written elsewhere; they are recorded in that marvelous and terrible book in which Destiny scratches her prose in invisible ink.

My lofty musing had caused me to fall behind the pursuers and the pursued, and so I hastened my pace toward the courtyard. If the Gods wanted me to be a witness, I couldn't disappoint them by being tardy.

The carnage in the courtyard made my head light with nausea. The gilded stone walls were awash in crimson blood. Severed limbs, along with the former owners lay strewn about the pavement and ornamental garden. And yet the bloodbath had not ended, for standing proud in front of the raised drawbridge was Derek, Dowry, and Slakely. Before them kneeled four figures whose faces were obscured by the crowd of knights who surrounded them, holding them in supplication with the points of their many swords.

Dowry's booming voice echoed ominously in the courtyard. "We hereby sentence you to death for your deeds, villain!"

With both hands Dowry raised his sword above his head; the blade paused in the air briefly before it reversed direction, ready to deliver the decapitating blow.

"Stop!"

My plea for mercy startled the onlookers; they glared at me as I pushed through their bloodthirsty midst. I slipped in a thick puddle of blood, nearly losing my balance.

Dowry's arms bulged with effort as he halted the sword's weighty descent but inches from the condemend's exposed neck.

"Sheath your swords!" I commanded. "Have you all gone mad with bloodlust? The Demons breed around us and all we see fit to do is slaughter each other!"

This time the virtue of my office was not enough to hold impetuous Dowry in check. "This criminal must die!" he exclaimed, prodding his intended victim with his sword. "He has brought the curse of the Banderwallian Demons upon us seeking to weaken our kingdom so he could plunder it. *He must be executed for his crimes!"*

"I didn't call the Demons! And I came bearing arms only to *expel* the creatures from our beloved Land!"

Dowry grabbed a knot of Clayton's long locks, yanking his face from the pavement. *"Liar!* You raised the fiends only to have an excuse to march on us. I'll feed you alive to your murderous brood! I'll-"

I am not one for being valiant, but some unseen force threw my body between Dowry and King Clayton (who was, from this point on, *ex*-King Clayton). "He says he didn't do it," I heard myself say.

"And you *believe* him?"

"I'm not sure what I believe," I said, "but to slaughter him without considering his side of the story is utterly unjust."

Dowry sought support from the men with his eyes; no one would meet his gaze.

"Uh, the Lord Seer is right, you know," Slakely said. "Maybe we should hear Clayton's plea."

Dowry sighed and cast his eyes skyward, as if looking for a lightning bolt to strike Clayton dead and prove him guilty. The Gods, however, did not oblige him.

*** *** ***

CHAPTER EIGHT: DESTINY'S AGENT

From the bowels of perdition the Demons did rise,
Of men to make a feast,
Only in the Seer, He was so wise
Was the fortitude to dispel the beasts.
-The History of the Second Banderwallian War, verse 5680

    I managed to convince the men to withdraw with the prisoners to the relative safety of the farm. I made it clear that we were not ready to battle the Demons, and that their slumber would be long. I bade Erdo to stay behind with a cart. He did so only after I assured him that the Golden Oracle did not reveal his death by Demons. No one was happy with the arrangement, but it bought me some time to try to sort things out.

    I watched the men pull away, hoping that my ruse would work. Darius was not among them, and I knew where he was.

    I left Erdo out in the bloody courtyard with the cart and returned to the tunnels.

    I crawled through the secret tunnels on my hands and knees guided by sheer instinct, for my mind was caught up in the whirlwind of events that had befallen me. Ahead I could see the gentle glow that the orb provided; I was right in my assumption as to where Darius would be.

    Grateful to be able to stand, I entered the lab. The scribe was busy perusing a selection from the laboratory's shelves; he looked up when he heard me enter.

    "Don't tell me the Demons are awake already," Darius

asked.

"No, they aren't."

"Good."

He returned to the book propped up with jars on the table in front of him; his ancient hands were not strong enough to support the tome themselves. I remember thinking that Darius looked almost fragile in that blue-gray light, as if he had not discovered his magickal tonics until he was well into his later years. And still, perhaps the Gods had a hand in that too; he was enjoying an extension of his agency here only so that he may facilitate the fulfillment of Destiny's whims.

I wrung my hands. Darius was quite an amiable man, and yet he seemed so wizened that it made me uneasy.

"Darius?"

Brittle with age, the page he held between his thumb and forefinger cracked free of its binding. "Hmm?" he said, paying more attention to the damage he had done to the parchment than to me.

"I need your counsel on certain matters."

That got his attention. His already wrinkled brow creased with marvelment. "You *want* my opinion? I cannot remember the last time someone actually asked me what I thought."

This much I knew to be true; Darius had a habit of letting his thoughts be known long before anyone had a chance to ask for them.

As Darius closed the book I did likewise with the secret door.

I found a seat on a curiously designed chair that sat next to the bookshelves. Darius remained leaning against the table of apparatus that undoubtedly delighted him.

"I am a peasant, the son of humble farmers," I began. "A few days ago I fell ill and stumbled off into the forest in a fever dream, only to fall at the base of our village's shrine to the Golden Oracle. Since then I've been dubbed a Seer and everyone is saying that the Gods have awakened and this and that and now, I'm stuck in the middle of this mess, I-" I exhaled loudly, running out of words.

"You say that you have been 'dubbed' a Seer. Do you deny this to be true?"

Irritated, I rose from my seat and thrust my hand into the orb's bright light. "Look at this scar on my hand! Does that look like an eagle to you?"

Darius closed one eye and squinted like the other. "If you say it does..."

"I don't," I snapped.

"Then it doesn't."

Confused, I stared at him for a moment.

"Look son, does it matter whether the scar on your hand looks like an eagle or a chicken? I'd wager not. If you aren't a Seer, it's too late to convince the world of that. You're in this muck up to your neck. The fact of the matter is that the rest of the world is convinced that you are indeed Claimed of the Golden Oracle, and from what I've heard, you've given them every reason to believe it."

My hand found its way to my head, fingers raking through my hair in frustration. " I never made any *real* prophecies; all I did was use that common sense that all of us have and made several good guesses."

"Who said being a Seer was anything more?" Darius retorted. "All men may possess this 'common sense', but how many of them ever use it? To the dullard your perceptions would seem miraculous, and believe me, there are a lot of dullards about. Your gift is more than that Kyle. If you'd only stop fighting it and allow it to become a part of you."

I sighed, seeking support against the table as Darius did. "Why has all this befallen me?"

Darius shook his head. "Why, why, why! Why is why all that youth ever asks? Ask yourself how many times you've asked yourself "why?" and how many times you've arrived at the same answer: if there are indeed any "whys" they are beyond our grasp, and perhaps even that of the Gods themselves. Now what did you want to ask me about?"

My thoughts were jumbled by Darius' deft manipulation of the conversation. "Well, word spread quickly of my Claiming—so quickly that it was uncanny—and before I knew it, I was on my way to the Rind to see the King. It was in his court that Chamberlin Bule approached me; he had heard from a relation that Clayton was dabbling in magick and planning hostilities against the other kings in the Land. At the Council meeting this relation—a cook—produced a vial of poison that he claims Clayton commanded that he taint the food with, causing the kings to be irritable. Darius, *all* the kings are playing with hexes and curses and who knows what else. I had instructed Erdo—the Trog, you know—to see if he could sniff out the poison but he couldn't locate it. And then! Then someone rigged the wheel on the King's carriage with a wax pin and the King drowned. So Dowry goes running off after Mackret—oh, you know about that part.

"The important thing is that Erdo sniffed out the poison here, in this lab." I produced the bottle

Darius jumped, startled by the silence of my pause (he had been dozing with his eyes open as I spoke, to be sure). He held the bottle up to the light. "Yes, I was wondering about that. I thought perhaps the Golden Oracle had blessed you with the location of this lab."

He gripped the cork of the bottle with a few gnarled fingers and tried to unplug it. "Here," he said, shoving the bottle back toward me in frustration. "You open it."

I did so, averting my face in order to minimize my nose's exposure to the substance's noxious fumes

Darius hardly had to bring the bottle under his own beak before the smell hit him. "Phew!" he exclaimed. "I'll bet that got their stomachs churning. It has no real flavor of its own, and it causes great fires in the belly. So, what does this suggest?"

"It suggests that Clayton *didn't* poison the food, and that someone in this castle is responsible for the dyspepsia that caused the Council break. But..."

"What?" Darius asked, waiting for an answer.

"But the cook said that Clayton asked him to put the poison in the food."

Darius eyes lit up. "Aha! So the cook lied—or something else is afoot. Did you not say that all the kings were dabbling in magick? If one of them knew enough about the Old Arts to use tincture of firewort, could they not devise a spell to disguise himself as Clayton and do the deed?"

"Yes," I conceded, "If it wasn't one of the kings, it was someone in this castle."

"And why not King Phyllaman?"

"Because he said he wasn't dabbling in magick—unless he was lying, too. Yet by the same reckoning it could have been Mackret, or Dowry. Or you for that matter."

The scribe chuckled deeply. "Oh, thank the Gods that I'm not too old to be above suspicion of mischief!" he said to the ceiling. And then to me: "Anything else?"

"And then there's the problem of the Banderwallian Demons. Who broke the barrier and let them across? After we split up to count the demons, Clayton and his men invaded the castle."

Darius' expression opened in surprise.

"Clayton claims he came to fight the Demons—I don't know how he found out about them yet—but Dowry maintains that Clayton called the Demons in order to have an excuse to march on us. I'm not even going to debate how Clayton knows what he knows."

"Now does that make sense to you?"

"No," I replied. "Who in their right mind would summon such monsters unless he knew how to repel them? And that answer is presumably here, in this laboratory. I just can't figure out which one of them is behind it all."

"One or *ones?*" Darius asked. "You've listed a curious amalgamation of crimes, my boy." He smacked the worktable with a flat palm to punctuate his announcement. "Perhaps two criminals, say—for the sake of the argument, Mackret and Clayton—conspired to usurp Phyllaman without knowledge of the other's plot? Mackret kills Phyllaman, marches in and takes control. Clayton summons the Demons and expects to find that paunchy Phyllaman has become the new item on the repast, banishes the Demons, double crosses Mackret and takes over the throne out of the goodness of his black heart."

"But what about the Council?"

"What about it? With conquest on all the King's minds no one is going to cry foul if another king spreads his armies thinly over two kingdoms, or even if an upstart knight murders his lord. Mackret may have poisoned the food to insure disunity."

I sighed once more. "I just don't know. It's all so confusing."

"And it's all in your hands," Darius added.

Suddenly I felt my blood turn to vapor in my veins. "No, it's *not* in my hands. I'm not the King or even a knight. I'm supposed to be the wandering Seer who spooks the peasants and mutters vague prophecies."

Darius grinned and shook his head; a strand of hair fell out of the knot in back. "It's too late for you to go back to a life of such in distinction and historical unimportance," he said. "You've already been accepted as an authority figure. Now all we need to do is give you that last push and you'll be set."

"Set?" I barked. "Set for what?"

Now it was Darius who grew exasperated, his eyes ignited with a fire I did not care to witness. "Good Gods, boy, you can't be that blind. Phyllaman the First was the mortar that held the Council of Thirteen together—not by virtue, but by wit. He was not an imbecile, like the others who sat around that stupid Council table twice a year, belching and patting their fat bellies. Phyllaman the First wasn't perfect either, mind you—the Demon episode was a grave mistake—but he *cared* for the people of all the kingdoms. He was a dear, dear friend to me, and on his deathbed, he extracted a favor from me as payment for forgiving my impropriety with his youngest daughter."

Darius snickered a bit, and then continued.

"I promised that I would watch over the Council and the

Land and do my best to preserve all that Phyllaman had done. Alas, the Gods had not seen fit to bestow me with a royal lineage, and so my hands were tied. I watched as Phyllaman's weak-kneed son took over the throne, and though he may have preserved the quality of life in this Kingdom, he was not one for being involved with the Council. The old kings, who remembered Phyllaman the First and his noble efforts began to wither and die out, replaced by greedy, distrustful sons who have brought our Land to the brink of ruin. That's a historical development that I would rather not record as the final work of my prolific career. And so I've spent all these years chomping on Goren root and performing a few other rituals too embarrassing to describe in order to keep myself alive, not just in order to fulfill the bargain I made so many years ago to protect the people, but to devise a work as the capstone of my career. In my own mind I care nothing for the commoners, as you may have surmised, but a deal is a deal. And all this time I have searched high and low for an amiable, educated, caring someone and it's *you*, O noble Seer! I'm passing the care taking of the Land over to *you*. But first I will provide you with the tools with which you will be able to fulfill this wonderful destiny outlined for you: I will make you a legend in your own time. I, Darius, will author your destiny and it will be spoken of for generations to come. Your story will be my greatest historical work—the greatest work of all time!"

The room spun about me; my own head felt as if it was spinning on my neck like a mad sort of top. I summoned all the strength left in me to force the tiny word from my lips: *"No."*

And still the scribe beamed. "Too late! I won't live much longer, and then there won't be anybody to watch over these fools except for you. If you don't step in, I guarantee that the Land will be barren with man and Demon war within a season. These people need to be led, Kyle. Can you conscience the destruction of the Land you love?"

"But I'm not royalty!"

"Royalty? Bah! You're better than royalty: you're the

chosen of the Gods."

Darius jumped up and grabbed my hand, gawking at it in mock reverence. "Oh look! The mark of the Golden Oracle! O blessed be, the Gods live! *The Gods live!*"

I closed my eyes to try to shut out the sight of the future that stretched out before me. Darius was as mad as his scheme. To think that I could be propelled to as lofty a position as he described was ridiculous. And surely the recipe for greatness involved rectifying the troubles that now plagued that Land.

"And now for the bad news."

I opened my eyes to see Darius holding a dust caked jar in one hand and a lid in the other. "We're fresh out of dragon's blood."

*** *** ***

CHAPTER NINE: MORE TRAGEDIES

In time of war there is no time
To contemplate the outcome but to win
Read further on in this rhyme
And learn of the Seer's ken.
-The History of the Second Banderwallian War, verse 9320

Not much later, Darius loaded herbs and books and unspeakables into a black bag he produced from inside the sleeve of his robe. I wondered how he expected the two of us to carry the sack, for completely full it was almost as large as my own person and surely weighed as much.

No sooner did he tie the bag close did it shrink to palm-size, becoming that much more manageable. "Remind me to show you that trick," Darius said, and then we returned to the tunnels.

Erdo was waiting just inside the courtyard with a cart to take us back to the farm, as I instructed him. I had half expected him to run away, but I was glad he didn't. It was on to the farm, where Dowry, Slakely and crew were surely waiting impatiently to begin the trial of King Clayton.

Once or twice I looked over my shoulder at Darius, who was sitting quietly in the rear of the cart. It is a wonder that he did not expect difficulties along the road that led to my greatness. If I had told him how fraught with mishaps my childhood was, he might have thought twice about his choice for keeper of the peace.

"Where are we going to find dragons in this day and age," he muttered to himself. "And if we should find a dragon, how will we talk him into giving blood? What a predicament."

I turned my eyes on the road ahead. I knew this would be the last calm moment I would have for quite some time. That knowledge immediately fell under scrutiny. Was I using my own common sense or that of the Golden Oracle? Could She be responsible for that voice I was only now hearing in my head?

If you'd only stop fighting your gift and allow it to become a part of you...

If I was going to accept the existence of dragons, then I had to accept the rest of the trappings that went along with them. There was plenty of evidence for the reality of magick, and magick meant gods who created it. All the wild stories the farm hands told were true. The Litany was true. But *dragons?* The thought of their existence was as idiotic as the belief in the Nevermen and the Soda People.

"Are you feeling okay?"

Erdo's voice trounced me from the state of shock I had fallen into. "I feel...I don't know how I feel," I confessed. "Erdo, we're in trouble. We don't have one of the ingredients needed to work the spell that banishes the Demons. We need dragon's blood."

Erdo's eyes bulged so in his head that I was fearful that if the cart should hit a bump his eyes would plop out onto the road where they could be squashed by a passing cart. "Dragon's blood? Are you serious? Who ever heard of such a thing?"

"My thoughts exactly," I said. "Perhaps if someone else in the Land has a magickal larder..."

Darius interrupted. "Don't count on anyone being able to lend us any dragon's blood. Toad gonads or bee's venom perhaps, but *not* dragon's blood. There hasn't been a dragon in these parts since long before either of you two children were born. If any sorcerer stocks such exotica, it has surely dried up or clotted since then."

The dismay that tinged Darius' words was of a grim

hue indeed. I reasoned that he had not allowed for unexpected occurrences such as the dragon's blood shortage, and for the first time I saw him grow somber. If I had been inclined to be insolent (which I am not) I might have suggested that such a turn of events could only heighten the suspense future readers of His Greatest Work would undoubtedly encounter.

"I gather that you don't have any dragon's blood in your lab, do you, Darius?" I asked, hoping for the best.

"*My* lab?" he said, craning his neck to look at me. "Boy, I don't have a laboratory of my own. Phyllaman the First ordered all the magick implements burned. Banderwall must have sequestered his away in that secret chamber for his own reasons. What items I have I hid under my bed." His eyes grew narrow, indignant. "And besides, I only cast *clean* spells. Some of the potions Banderwall cooked up required ingredients that no self-respecting sorcerer would admit to having."

I almost asked what those items might be but didn't.

*** *** ***

The cart traveled as fast as my or Erdo's conscience would let it, considering the accidents that seem to befall those whose haste proved too much. I could not help but dread returning to the farm and perhaps finding that Slakely and Dowry had already executed Clayton; the prisoner king was our only link to the identities of those who had plotted what was surely to be the downfall the entire Land.

The perimeter of the farm was as quiet as the slumbering Demons' lair. I suddenly became aware that I was biting my fingernails. The thin drops of blood accumulating on my fingertips told me I had been gnawing in anxiety for some time.

Derek was leaning against the great oak that grew next to the house. Garments still spattered with blood, he was paring a green apple with a wicked knife. At least he had the decency to wash his face.

"'Bout time you showed up," he said, mouth full.

I did not wait for Erdo to stop the cart, jumping out as best I could.

"Where are the others? Where are they holding Clayton?"

"Out back by the silo. The knights seem pretty bloodthirsty."

And he was one to talk! I bit my tongue and rushed for the silo.

"Wait for me!" I heard Darius exclaim, but I did not tarry.

Even if Derek had not been present to guide me, it would not have taken long to locate the captive and his captors. No sooner did I pass between the barn and the house did the clamor reach me. My pace quickened.

The silo was surrounded by a crowd composed of the sum of Slakely and Dowry's knights, all which pushed and shoved to get a glimpse of the proceedings inside the silo. These men had not taken the time to wash as Derek did (they weren't concerned with impressing a certain lady) and it was a disgusting sight. The brotherhood of knightship had become a fraternity of would-be lynchers.

Dowry's angry, booming bass echoed through the silo as I began to push through the crowd. So intent on seeing the spectacle were the knights that I was afraid that I would not make it to Clayton in time, but one annoyed knight turned to bark at one of his brethren and saw it was myself who sought to squeeze past. "Lord Seer!" he gasped and stepped aside. Soon my way began to clear as others took notice of my presence.

Between the bodies of the horde, I caught a glimpse of King Clayton. Stripped of his armor, he was bound with rough hemp to a kitchen chair. My glimpse was but fleeting, but I could have sworn that his cheeks were stained with tears.

"*Enough!*" Dowry bellowed, looming over Clayton like Death itself. "We'll have no more of your lies and denials! The Land has bled by your hand, fiend! You will be put to death!"

"Wait!" I shouted, finally breaking through into the open —and then the smell and sight hit me. Piled waist high behind the captive king was the remainder of his men and suddenly I realized that it was not the blood of battle that soiled the knights, but that of wanton anger and merciless disregard for human life. The confined air of the silo was foul with the odor of fresh blood. It was a smell that I will never forget nor want to; to forget the carnage, my soul would first have to shrivel and disintegrate inside me.

I finally found words to express my outrage. "Gods! What have you done?" I cried. "Didn't we agree to hear Clayton's plea?"

"We've already heard his plea and find him guilty!" Dowry shouted, and then looked about the crowd as if he expected cries of support from the rest of the men who had taken part in the bloodbath. Instead, the knights stood about looking each other like children caught cheating at a game. I was beginning to think that Darius was right: perhaps the rest of the men in the Land *were* fools. And if I was the best-fit man to rule over them, then Gods help us all.

"This is an outrage," I continued. "If we all went about putting those we distrust to the sword, there wouldn't be a soul left alive in the Land. You all come to me for counsel and direction, but do you listen?"

The words were flowing hot from my tongue; there was no shunting of the current this time. A part of me that still cringed in the cage of my skull was dimly aware that I was letting someone else put words in my mouth, that I *was* the mouthpiece of the Gods, for better or for worse.

"Listen to me, one and all, and mark well my words: if we continue to shed blood while faced with the Demons shedding *our* blood, then *all* blood will be shed, and all will be lost."

At the conclusion at my words, I swear that I could hear Darius chortling with delight at my new prophecy; it was so cryptic and overwrought that it had to suit his taste. Now if I could just make them rhyme...

Regardless of how well they were thought out, my words had a solemn effect. Dowry's flushed expression paled considerably at the prospect of bringing doom upon the Land. Still, to admit that he had given in to his passions and acted in haste was beneath his dignity; he pushed his way through the ashamed, thinning crowd into the open air.

I heard a voice at my side. "I tried to tell him to wait, but he just wouldn't listen. You know how soldiers are."

Slakely, clean of blood, stepped out of the shadowy corner of the silo. "There was nothing I could do," he insisted. "His men outnumber mine."

The knight's words were cut short by a sudden increase in the volume of Clayton's wailing and moaning. "Please, please Lord Seer!" he sobbed. "You must believe me! Surely you can see that I'm telling the truth!"

"Perhaps," I said with a sigh. For a moment I contemplated untying the poor wretch, but I did not want to seem too sympathetic, lest the men grow wary of me. Instead, I tried to be as comforting and warm as possible, given the situation.

"The knights are leveling severe charges against you, Your Highness," I said. "They insist that you summoned the Banderwallian Demons."

"No, *no!*" he wailed, and most un-kingly like. "I didn't! I'm a peaceful man! Why would I bring something so horrible down upon our Land?"

Beside me Slakely inhaled as if to offer rebuttal, but he stopped short, remembering my presence. How interesting.

"Did you know the food at the Council banquet was tainted with a potion?"

"*What?*"

I frowned. "One of your kitchen staff insists that you provided him with a potion to put in the Council's wine; I have reason to believe that potion caused tempers to run short and disunity to settle in."

"Who told you I gave them poison?" Clayton wailed, writhing in his bonds. "Who told you that? He's a liar, whoever he is! *A liar!*"

Perhaps, I thought, because we found the poison in Phyllaman's castle. Then again, firewort was common.

Slakely whispered into my ear: "*Ask him why he came to your kingdom bearing arms.*"

"When you were taken prisoner, you insisted that you came to our kingdom to help rid the Land of the Demons. My question is, how did you know that the Demons had come across the barrier?"

"Chamberlin Cummings told me!"

"How did *he* know?" I pressed.

"I don't know. He just told me that the Demons had invaded and that the Second Kingdom was crying for help!" He shook his head to free his face of the tears that clung to his pale skin. "Honestly, Lord Seer, you must believe me! Why does everyone think such foul thoughts of me? Have I done nothing but stood by and guard the peace of the Land? Why? *Why?*"

Clayton burst into great heaving sobs then, so great that I could hardly bear to watch or listen. I turned in pity and disgust and exited the silo. Slakely followed.

Derek and Dowry were standing not far outside; their voices fell hush as I neared.

"You must send a party to the Third Kingdom and inform those knights still there that their Lord has been taken captive. And then you must fetch Chamberlin Cummings and bring him back here at once." I said.

"Who?" Dowry asked.

"Chamberlin Cummings. King Clayton insists that Cummings instructed him to march into our kingdom."

"What good will questioning the fool do?" Dowry asked. "Surely Clayton instructed him to authenticate his story on pain of death."

"Then we will offer him our protection," I insisted. "Please, Sir Dowry. There isn't much time. Who knows when the Demons will wake?"

Dowry frowned, growled deep in his throat, and then turned to do my bidding. Suddenly he stopped short and turned to me once more.

"Say, what does Chamberlin Cummings look like?"

"He's short and prissy," I said. "You know the type; just keep Chamberlin Bule in mind and you'll have no trouble in locating his counterpart."

Derek's attention seemed to peak at the mention of Phyllaman's Chamberlin. "Say, that Bule was looking for you," he said.

"Bule?" I asked. "You've seen him here, at the farm?"

"Yeah, sure. He was talking to Erdo out by the kitchen."

"Very well."

I started in the direction of the kitchen but stopped momentarily to instruct Derek further. "Stand guard over King Clayton. Make sure that no harm comes to him."

"Right," and then the mercenary trotted off to the silo.

"And Derek, do as I say this time—*please!*"

*** *** ***

Bule was indeed chatting with Erdo, who was greedily devouring a bowl of stew that Sissy had begrudgingly provided.

"Oh, Lord Seer!" Bule exclaimed, jumping from his seat on a tree stump at the sight of me. "It is ever so good to see that you are all right!"

"Only partially right," I corrected, but by the look on Bule's face the intent of my words escaped him. "Where have you been?" I asked. "When we rescued Dowry, we couldn't find you and feared that you had fallen victim to the Demons."

Bule shuddered visibly at the mention of the Banderwallian menace. "As you can see, the Gods were with me," he said. And then he looked about for prying ears and tiptoed to my side. "Vile Mackret came to the cell offering to let me live if I served him loyally," he said quietly. "Now I ask you Lord Seer, what was I supposed to do? I couldn't save the others in the dungeon, but at least I could save myself."

"How lucky you happened by our farm," I said. "The Gods truly *do* smile on you, don't they?"

Bule shrugged in modesty. "Well, one never knows how long one's luck is going to hold."

"Quite."

"And now if you will excuse me…" and Chamberlin Bule trotted off past the kitchen, on some fussy errand.

I stood beneath the oak tree, mulling over the Chamberlin's story. Erdo muttered something I couldn't tell what, for my mind was too occupied.

"What?"

"I said that you looked worried," Erdo replied.

"Only because I *am* worried," I said, and took Bule's seat on the stump. My bad knee creaked ominously; the joint had seen too much excitement in too short a time. "Dowry doesn't seem to recall seeing Bule in the dungeon at all."

The Trog shrugged. "It *was* dark down there, and Bule is kinda short."

"Short of stature yes, but he makes his presence known all the same. Perhaps…perhaps he was in on Mackret's scheme."

Erdo laughed heartily, clutching his round stomach with his hands. "Bule? *Chamberlin* Bule? He's completely harmless!"

"At least he appears to be harmless," I corrected. "Things are often not what they seem. For instance-"

My explanation was disrupted by the shrill, panicked cry of an anxious knight: *"The traitor has escaped! KING CLAYTON HAS ESCAPED!"*

"Gods!" I exclaimed.

Erdo and I bounded to our feet and quickly made our way to the silo. The Gods were obviously too busy keeping Chamberlin Bule alive to see that things went smoothly for me.

A steady stream of men with swords drawn had already begun to scour the area about Clayton's former prison. Into the fields they poured, out toward the mineral flats or forest, depending upon which direction they went.

Inside the dusty silo Dowry was cursing the bonds that had held his quarry. The hemp was not broken; Clayton had managed to work the knots free, apparently with ease.

I looked about the chamber. "Where's Derek?" I asked.

"Derek!" Dowry exclaimed, dropping the bonds. His face took on its frequent shade of red. "I'll throttle that lout. I swear I'll kill him with my own two hands!" He stormed out of the silo, bellowing at the top of his lungs: *"Bring that boor Derek to me at once!"*

At that moment I needed not to ask what Dowry was thinking; he had verbalized his thoughts, and his demeanor and avoidance of our eyes meeting spoke clearly: *This is your fault. If you'd let me kill that monster earlier, he wouldn't have escaped.*

I figured that the chances of Dowry throttling *me* were low; surely the old superstitions forbade slaughter of the Oracle's own.

Erdo was leaning against the door; he sighed heavily. "Now what?" he asked.

"I wish I knew," I replied. "Without the dragon's blood, all we can do is try to sort out the mess that caused the Demons to be summoned in the first place. For now, I think it would suffice to find Derek and make sure Dowry doesn't kill him. As for Clayton..."

Erdo gave me an odd look and then quickly looked away, as if trying to downplay the manifestation of his thoughts.

"What is it?" I asked.

"He went that way." he said and pointed out the door toward the farmhouse.

"Who? Clayton?"

"No, Derek. That leather he wears *smells*."

Once again, Erdo's sense of smell proved to be remarkable. In this case I felt a bit sorry for the poor Trog; his nose had betrayed his friend.

"Where to?" I asked as we neared the house.

"Around back—toward the kitchen."

The kitchen indeed!

Voices reached my ears; Erdo had picked them up several paces before I did, and his demeanor darkened accordingly. His loyalty to Derek was very interesting to me.

The door of the kitchen was open again; in order ventilate that smoke which did not find its way up the skewed brick chimney. I took a deep breath, totally prepared to tell Sissy to cover her ears lest I offend her with my language when I confronted Derek. Perhaps I would have fared better to cover my own eyes: Derek was lounging at the kitchen table, chatting with Sariah as Sissy prepared the next meal.

"*What in the hells are you doing in here?*" I shouted. "Why aren't you out at the silo?"

Derek cocked the crooked smile of his that I always found so annoying. "Relax," he said with a smooth gesture of his hand. "Clayton's not going anywhere."

"No, he's already *gone,* you imbecile."

Derek jumped up so quickly that his chair toppled over beneath him. He dashed for the door, face red as Dowry's, but from embarrassment rather than anger. As he rushed outside, I gave Sariah (whose face was also red) a stern look, and then turned to exit before I said something in anger that I would later regret. Sariah said something that I regret hearing: "Don't let them hurt poor Derek!" she called, running to the open door.

I could have vomited.

The scene that I was faced with as I came to a startled stop in the doorway was the realization of the worst turn of events possible: Derek had stopped not three paces out of the door, coming face to face with Sirs Dowry and Slakely. Next to the latter was Clayton's crumpled body. A bloodstain had blossomed on the bosom of his blouse, stemming from a clearly fatal wound. A semi-circle of knights flanked the tableau, barring flight to either side.

The impasse caused by the severity of the situation ended. Dowry leveled an accusing finger at Derek. "Tie him up," the knight commanded, his voice icy but rattled. "He stands accused of conspiracy with King Clayton."

Three of the lesser knights moved toward Derek, who stood as motionless as a stone martyr. Much to my surprise, Derek did not offer a fight nor offer a word of protest. He allowed himself to be led to the silo, the scene of Clayton's fatal attempted escape.

Coupled with the troubled gazes of Slakely and Dowry, the silence that settled in upon the remaining company was dreadful indeed. I floundered for words to ease the tension.

"How did it happen?" I asked.

"Clayton was in the barn," Slakely explained. "Sir Colin interrupted his attempt to saddle a horse. Clayton armed himself with a pitchfork and..." He completed his sentence with a troubled shrug of his shoulders.

I buried my face in my hands to conceal my desperation. "This is a terrible time for such a terrible thing to happen," I moaned. My hands unwillingly fell away from my face, bringing me to investigate Slakely's eyes. "If Clayton really did march into our kingdom with benign intentions, then we have waged an act of outright war."

My logic misconnected with Slakely's; his eyes lit up and his voice quickened. "A war which we've already won!" he shouted. Several of the onlooker knights cheered in reply.

"At what cost?" I demanded. "Our army is too small to spread into the Third Kingdom in order to hold it as our own. Doing so would only thin our defenses here, and if the outer kings truly are planning conquest, it leaves us weakened. And the Demons? Remember them? We still have *them* to contend with."

Slakely thought for a moment, his conviviality temporarily shunted by my concerns. "On the other hand..." he muttered but did not finish his thought.

"What?"

He pursed his lips, disgusted that he had discovered yet another barrier to the simple solutions he sought. "Those knights that remained in Clayton's service are cutthroats. If we can't take control, there will be anarchy as they vie for the throne. I fear that no king will succeed unless all other competitors are eliminated."

My heart was wrenched with pity for the poor souls who called Clayton's kingdom home. Clayton had left no heir, just as Phyllaman had not. It was only a matter of time before the bloodshed that occurred in Rind swept over our neighbor land.

"The situation is beyond us," I said to the clouds above. "First and foremost, we must rid ourselves of the Demons."

"And then?" Slakely asked. His eyes shifted left and right a bit, as if the brain behind them was contemplating saying something he oughtn't. "Perhaps," he whispered, "Perhaps if you plead with your mentor to divulge our route to success..."

Gods, but Slakely was convinced that by divine grace we would prevail over the tumult we were witness to. The last thing I needed right now was the intellectual insult of superstition.

"Perhaps," I said, and turned toward the kitchen to end the conversation. Unfortunately, Sariah was barring entrance to the same. I looked into her pale eyes briefly and, not liking the storm brewing in them, looked away.

"Excuse me," I mumbled.

Sariah remained frozen on the steps. Over her shoulder I could see Sissy, who looked at me and shook her head in a telltale, knowing manner.

"Why didn't you protect him?" Sariah demanded crossly.

"It's Clayton's own fault that he got killed," I blurted in a feeble attempt to play the fool.

Sariah saw right through my ruse. "Not Clayton you dolt. *Derek.*"

"Oh, him. Given the opportunity, I'd explain to you that because of Derek's inability to follow orders we could very well be at war with the deceased's minions in a matter of hours—but then again, such an explanation probably wouldn't do much good."

Sariah's jaw dropped in response to my flippant words. "What's *that* supposed to mean?"

"It means that you're obviously too smitten with the man to find fault in his actions."

"I'm *what?*" she exclaimed. Her pale hands moved to her hips in the universal gesture of displeasure. "You're jealous!" And then she called out over my shoulder: "Everyone! The Lord Seer is human after all!"

It was a miserable taunt that no one except Sissy heard, but the words struck an already tender nerve. Sariah was right, of course, but I wouldn't admit it.

"Stop shouting," I growled, face turning red with a mixture of embarrassment and anger. "Why would I be jealous of Derek?" I demanded. "Because he has two good legs? Because people don't gawk at him and throw themselves at his feet, moaning and babbling about long-dead gods? Because people don't forget that he's a human being and not some cold creature from the stars? No, I'm not jealous. I'm envious, perhaps, but we demigods are *never* jealous."

Sariah's hands fell to her side, fists clenching so tightly that I heard her knuckles pop. She shuddered with frustration for a split-second and then stomped past me, off the porch and on toward the barn.

The departure of my beloved cleared a visual path to Sissy, who was still at the fireplace.

I cut Sissy off before she had a chance to offer me the advice of her advanced years. "Not a word from you," I spat.

"From me?" she asked innocently. "I wasn't going to say anything at all."

"Oh yes you were," I corrected and, without further contemplation, left to seek Darius' counsel. After all, it was his fault I was in the predicament that I was.

My reign over Slakely and Dowry was tenuous at best, and though many of the men had sworn their lives to me (a meaningless gesture, to be sure). I had the feeling that I would be deserted if I did not play up to my hallowed, divine station. The authority of that lofty position was still in the making and Darius apparently held the keys to success.

From overhead there came thin, high squawk. I looked upward to see the eagle gracefully circling the sky above the fields. *The bird is obviously a heavenly messenger,* I thought. So much for humor leavening my mood.

Why me, you stupid bird? I thought. *On the one hand I have responsibility to my own feelings and desires, and on the other I have the acquired concerns for the rest of the people in the Land. I feel as if I'm being drawn and quartered!*

The eagle squawked a yet unintelligible reply. I sighed and

closed my eyes for a moment, wishing I were up there in the sky, high above the doings of men and Demons alike. I let my imagination drift, visualizing the scene beneath me as I circle the farmland, round and round. The barn was missing several roof shingles to the east of the peak; the top of the silo was dotted with nests of my eagle kin. The vision was so real that I even watched as Darius sauntered up beside me, answering my silent summons.

I sighed again, and opened my eyes, crashing back to the all-too real world around me. I looked at the scribe, who was smiling as congenially as ever.

"The time for asking "why?" is over, isn't it?"

"Yes, it is," Darius replied. "I hear that Clayton is dead."

"Yes, he is. Darius, how are we ever going to set things right again?"

He chuckled. "Good Gods boy, but sometimes I don't think you're very bright, not bright at all. Why, you *know* what must be done; I've heard you say it repeatedly: Find the dragon's blood and banish the Demons. The rest of the story is a mere formality."

"Where?" I whined. "Where do I find dragon's blood?"

"The time for asking "where?" is over," he said, and he wasn't so much mocking me as he was rephrasing an astute observation.

The scribe put a bony hand on my shoulder. "Remember Kyle, the Gods are with you." Darius grinned at that, exposing his yellow, scattered teeth.

Above, the eagle squealed. Contemplating the use of a bow and arrow, I looked up in disgust at the accursed animal.

*** *** ***

CHAPTER TEN: FLIGHT

Blood calls for blood,
Or so they say,
But spilling the red was not the Seer's way.
For he had come to bring lasting piece
And if blood was spilled it would be the least.
-The History of the Second Banderwallian War, verse 1034

Sleep would not come at a reasonable price on that dreadful night. I lay awake in my cot for some time, meditating on this and that. Clearly, banishment of the Demons would fulfill a major requirement for peace returning to the Land, but there was still the matter of how the Demons made it here to begin with, as well as the identity of Phyllaman's killer. And was Clayton guilty of conspiracy to dissolve the Council? I took pause to wonder if my questions would ever be answered.

Eventually, the farm fell silent about me as the knights settled in for sleep wherever they could find a place to recline. I tossed and turned on my cot; the weight of my destiny—or rather, the destiny that certain other parties wanted me to fulfill —would not allow me to escape from this world into that of sleep and dreams.

At last I could take no more; I felt as though I would go mad if I did not get out of bed and walk some of my anxiety off.

I put on my coat and boots and crept down the stairs as quietly as possible. Two lucky knights were sleeping at the foot of the stairs (lucky because they didn't have watch duty or weren't sleeping in the barn). I stepped over them cautiously, nearly losing my balance.

Outside the air was clear and cold. I was surprised that my breath did not freeze thick in my nostrils. Above, the stars shone without wavering, and if one of my superstitious elders had been with me, they would have said that it was under this kind of nightfall that the Gods visited our world.

I stuck my tongue out at the darkness just in case the Gods really were watching.

The decision to spend the night at the farm had been an uneasy one. Slakely and Dowry didn't seem to have any plans other than castrating or beheading Derek as a traitor. This lack of planning not only revealed to me that the knights viewed our current situation as hopeless and the magickal cure as abominable, but that they were expecting me to use my divine gift and chart the road to victory for them. How astute Darius was in weaving their beliefs to fit his ambitions!

It was some comfort to my concern about Slakely's and Dowry's competency as generals that I did not have to tell them to post a watch. Knights dotted the periphery of the farm compound, and Dowry even ordered two men up into the trees at the farm margin to look toward the city lest the Demons awake and start their fires anew. The fact that Dowry considered the possibility of the Demons awakening without my knowledge beforehand was most interesting. Was he being cautious, or did some unconscious part of him doubt my words? If the latter was true, then I cheer his solid, rational thinking.

I visited the silo to talk to Derek. I had my reasons.

The watchmen were kind enough to step outside and close the door behind them to give us some privacy.

"You've got to get me out of this," Derek said.

I regarded him closely. Without his armor the bulges of his physique were more apparent. He could easily break the bonds that lashed him to the chair and overcome the knights at the door. Luckily, that did not seem to be a part of his plans.

"I will see you released," I said, "though I can't say when. You've made your bed. If you had been watching Clayton instead of spinning tall tales—"

"Tall tales?" he said incredulously. "I've never lied to anyone."

"Come on! The bit about seeing one of the Nevermen was too much."

"I've seen one."

"And I've got a magic wand that turns stone into gold. Look, I don't mean to sound nasty, but the affair is displeasing. Just sit and wait for me to convince the knights to let you go. Don't do anything rash, is that clear?"

Derek sighed. "Yes, it's clear."

"Good. Now excuse me."

I stepped back out into the night. That Derek continued to insist his ridiculous tales were true made me even more troubled. I should have stayed out in the peaceful night.

The peace of the night was not the tonic that I had hoped it would be, and so I sought out the company of the perimeter watchmen, hoping for conversation, not the ludicrous tribute I received earlier.

I scanned the darkened fields for movement, but there was none. I caught the men between shifts, I thought, and moved onward toward the hill and trees that bore view of the city.

As I passed the barn, the silence of the night settled in around me. Why was there no dialogue between the watchmen? I told myself that the knights were being courteous to those who were sleeping, wishing I could believe that something so outrageous was possible. Alas, when I reached the trees designated as a watch post, I could no longer deny that something was amiss. It did not take an owl's vision to see that branches overhead were devoid of everything but leaves. Terror suddenly gripped my chest; with dread as thick as my prose I slowly moved my eyes from side to side, while my ears strained to hear the rasp of demonic gills in the underbrush.

Nothing. I was greeted with the sight of the dark wood and the silence of a trap about to be sprung.

Rather than alert our foe to my discovery, I nervously

began to whistle and walk slowly down the hill, toward the farmhouse. The distance between pitiful sanctuary and myself seemed stretched in the most terrible way; what had been a hundred paces away was now several thousand. Even more terrifying was the absolute lack of indication as to where the Demonic army lay hidden. All I had as evidence was the absence of the guards and-

There! At the base of the hill a wisp of odor reached my nostrils, and it was none other than the unmistakably asperous smell of singed hair. No part of me needed any further evidence that doom was hanging over the farm just as black smoke still hung over Rind.

Strangely enough, I was not concerned for my own welfare that night, for if I had been I would have realized the great peril I was in out there in the open air, which surely would have led to me fainting dead away. In reflection I see that dreadful night as a turning point in my "history": My thoughts had begun to run completely within the framework of concern for "my" men, my own safety be dammed.

At long last I reached the farmhouse. There was no time to speculate as to why the Demons had not attacked me nor mounted their campaign of death yet.

I stepped over the knights (none of whom woke when I inadvertently kicked them) on the floor of the main room, making my way to the bench on which Sir Dowry had sought escape from the matters at hand. I shook him by the shoulders (and violently at that).

"Sir Dowry!" I whispered loudly. "Sir Dowry, wake up!"

Dowry turned his head toward the wall. "I closed the drawbridge hours ago," he mumbled.

"This is no time to be dreaming!" I hissed. "The Demons are preparing to attack us!"

Dowry's bloodshot eyes snapped open. He sat up so quickly that our heads almost collided. "*Demons?*" he cried, and then jumped to his feet. "*The Demons are about to attack!*" he shouted, waking those men on the floor.

"*Shh!*" I begged. "If they hear us, they'll be upon us all the sooner."

Dowry clenched his eyes shut in a mortified cringe, indicating that I should not have had to warn him to be silent. He grabbed the nearest knight by the arm and whispered into his ear: "Get to the other men in the barn and kitchen and quarters—and bring Slakely here."

The knight nodded and started for the door; apprehension clearly smeared on his face.

"Oh, and Cedric," Dowry added, "Be *quiet.*"

Cedric nodded anew and disappeared into the night.

Now what?

Without a word Dowry turned and stared at me, waiting to be told what to do.

"We'll have to split up, just as we discussed," I said. "Either you or Slakely must take some men and lure the Demons into the forest."

"What if the Demons split up, too? If they're awake, then they've given birth and there's twice as many now."

"It's a chance we'll have to take," I said. "We've got to buy some time with which to search the other kingdoms for dragon's blood."

I watched as Dowry's eye shifted from my own to some unknown point behind me. I turned around and saw Sariah standing at the top of the stairs that led to the loft.

"Kyle?" she asked, rubbing her eyes. "What's wrong? What's happening?"

Dowry answered for me. "The Seer has had a vision of the Demon's impending attack."

The dread that dawned on Sariah's face was deep enough to match my own. And Sissy was upstairs, too!

"Wake Sissy," I instructed her, "and put on traveling clothes and find Erdo. Quickly!"

Fear of death overcame my earlier spat with Sariah. She spun and disappeared into the loft; in a moment I heard a shocked intake of breath, which was surely Sissy's reaction to the current situation. In that moment my heart grew heavy as stone in my chest. The women had insisted on staying and I had let them. If misfortune befell either of them, I knew I would never forgive myself. (Though I was certainly not to blame—far be it from me to tell women what to do. It's a waste of breath, my son.) I wished I was a Seer and had the knowledge that Sissy and Sariah would escape unscathed.

Slakely came bursting in not long after that, with Cedric in tow. "Where are the sentries?" Slakely queried.

"Gone without a trace," I said.

"I didn't see any of those green monsters out there," Slakely insisted.

"Neither did I—but can't you *smell* them?" I asked.

All three of the knights sniffed the sir, looking at one another in worriment.

"We have to move now," I insisted. "The Demons have surely noticed our activity."

Dowry interrupted. "Then why haven't they attacked?"

In frustration I wanted to shout, *"How am I supposed to know?"* but bit my tongue. "Perhaps they're lying in wait," I suggested. "Their tactics are beyond the point. Their awakening is cause enough to act."

Dowry sighed. "Then it's settled. I'll take my men into the forest-"

"No you won't," Slakely said. "I'll take *my* men into the forest."

"You?" Dowry asked incredulously. "What do you know of these woods?"

"There's no time to argue!" I snapped. "When the attack comes, I want you to divert the horde, Sir Dowry."

It was an arbitrary choice, though I was influenced by Dowry's familiarity with the kingdom. Dowry took the order as a blessing; he sneered at Slakely.

"Roust your men and meet me in front of the barn," I said.

My stomach churned and gnawed at itself as I waited in front of the barn for the men to gather. Sissy and Sariah were right there beside me, blanketed against the cold night air. Things were going to grow very hot very quickly, to be sure, but though we kept intense watch into the darkened farmlands, we did not see hide nor hair of our enemies.

"Where are they?" Sariah whispered to no one in particular. "The way they wait—they're mocking us. It's driving me crazy."

She was probably right on both counts. I had entertained the notion that the sentries had run out to get drunk and the burnt smell I noticed at the top of the hill had come from the dying embers of the night's meal preparation, but such a scenario was surely a fantasy. I knew—categorically, absolutely, irrefutably *knew*—that the Demons were nearby.

Darius came wandering by in his usual fashion; he was so wide-awake that I wondered if he had been asleep in the first place.

"Quite an operation," he noted of the current scramble to depart. "I hear the sentries had vanished."

"As far as we can tell," I said.

"And?"

"And what?" I asked.

Even in the dark of the night I could see his thin frown. "What are you going to *do?*" he asked like an impatient father.

"We're leaving," I said emphatically.

"I see. You're leaving. That is, if the Demons *let* you leave."

Knowing full well that he had just driven a spike of cold fear into my heart, Darius strode away into the growing crowd, calmly whistling to himself. I thought that if ever I understood the maelstrom of thought and plot that went on in the scribes' head that it would be only by divine intervention. Alas, now I know all too well what went on in his skull and it is more of a demonic curse rather than heavenly gift.

My anxiety grew with proportion to the number of knights that assembled near the barn. At last, when I thought I could take no more before my head exploded, Dowry and Slakely pushed their way toward me.

"We're all here," Slakely said.

Dowry nodded in agreement.

"Then we'll be off," I said, and began to walk away.

Behind me, Dowry cleared his throat. "Excuse me, Lord Seer," he asked, "but where are you going?"

Gods, I hadn't thought of that either.

"To the Third Kingdom. We still have to ask Clayton's Chamberlin about his involvement in this horrid mess of an affair."

"Oh." Dowry furrowed his brow and stared into nothingness; confusion reigned in his simple brain. "Well...I mean—when do we head into the forest?"

I was completely dumbfounded by his question. Wasn't Dowry heading for the forest? What sort of soldiers were these men?

"Flee into the forest when the Demons attack," I said, trying to sound as if I wasn't concerned that our miserable strategy would fail. "You'll have to wait until you can get their attention and then pray that they'll follow you."

"Oh."

While I was counseling Slakely, Dowry tapped his foot. His armor made a rhythmic clink-clank, taking out his impatience on the damp ground. "Are we ready *yet?*" he groused. "All this standing around—we're only giving those fiends the time they need to organize!"

The Demons have all the time they want, I almost said, but if Dowry wasn't aware of their battle-worthiness by now, it was too late for him to ever learn.

I looked about me in anguish, not wanting to give the orders that would either buy us time or set ourselves up for annihilation.

"Yes, we're ready," I sighed at long last.

Slakely had enough sense to designate a small band of warriors to lead the way to the second kingdom. Darius, Erdo, the women and I followed behind, flanked by knights to the side and rear. As for Derek, well, a decision had to be made about his fate, and soon. I fully intended to release him as soon as the dissentful knights and lords left the area.

We started out across the fields toward the road that led back to Rind and points east. No one uttered a sound as we cautiously made our way across the farm and toward the silo; I hesitate to say that it would not have made much of a difference if we had sung drinking songs at the top of our lungs, for we had surely generated enough noise making our preparations to warn even the hardest of hearing villains as to our intentions.

The moon hung low in the night sky, bleaching the vivid colors of the countryside to a sickly gray. Every shred of movement in the landscape—the flutter of leaves in the trees, the sway of grain stalks to the tempo of the night breeze, all yanked my worried attention this way and that until I thought that I would go completely insane with anxious expectation. Alas, my sanity was saved when someone in the lead stopped and shouted:

"Look!"

They came down from the trees, flowed around the bases and over the crests of the hills, springing from every available pore of the landscape. The monsters sprang from their hiding places, surprising us not with their attack but with their diversity of form: shapes almost to terrible to describe. Our pregnant foes had given birth to a grotesque brood indeed.

A short, bloated, fish-like thing with four legs led the onslaught. "Food!" it bleated, lips curling back over its slather-glazed teeth.

For a moment we were too stunned to act, and then all semblance of order within our march immediately gave way to chaos as the knights panicked and scattered into the night. The Demons did not seem to care about this breach in war protocol. Theirs was no organized conquest; they were simply acting in response to their most base instinct: hunger. Clearly this was why Lord Banderwall had failed: his weapon was as wanton, random, and heedless to human desires as fire.

"*Kyle!*" a thin, female voice screamed.

I was suddenly all-too aware that I had *not* run, but that I had foolishly/unconsciously held my ground. Curiously enough, most of the Demons had scattered after the fleeing knights, leaving me to face but several flopping, fan-shaped monsters that shambled towards me. The horrible sound those devils made as they contracted and expanded, inching themselves towards their prey! It was sort of wet sucking noise, and coupled with the slap of their quivering, soft flesh as it smacked the ground it was enough to make any man flee in horror.

Yet I was beyond horror, for I was surely to bear witness that night to the destruction of the army that was supposed to free the Land from its demonic plague, and furthermore, I was to be done in by the same villains. I slowly turned away from the oncoming horror, pivoting in place in a catatonic stupor.

I cannot surmise what forces were at work inside of me, causing me to calmly turn away from the fan-things and limp into the night. Around me came the rush and crackle of the Demons' fire belches, the shouts of the stunned knights, the cries of the captured.

The blackness closed in, blackness like that I experienced in my fall from the cart into that dread ditch. And yet now I am sure that this is no utter darkness, but a twilight, a lingering on the edge between sleep and death and as inexplicable as both. Now this journey to that place was voluntary (more or less). I consciously closed the doors of my mind in order to avoid bearing witness to the destruction of the Land's last hope for redemption.

Sariah and Sissy would the next day fill me in on what I missed. They say my faced glazed over as I stumbled towards them (it was Sariah's voice, of course, that was reeling me in) and then suddenly became animated. "*To the mineral flats!*" I bellowed, giving the signal that Slakely hadn't the sense to know instinctively. Suddenly the disorganization that had been present at the onslaught became *directed* disorganization as the knights were sparked to dash into the fields. And all this time the Demons and their kin shambled *past* me, seemingly avoiding my flesh as if it were not suitable for their consumption. Perhaps I should be offended in some strange fashion, but I am not.

As I mentioned earlier, the Demons' attack was not of the methodical type, and as soon as the knights scattered into the fields so did the Demons, as if we had planned it. Apparently, it took quite a bit of time for the more misshapen of the brood (the fan-things are included in this category) to deploy them, and therefore there was still something of a threat present.

In the distance I heard the mineral crystals being trampled by panicked feet. I too reached the flats, and a most remarkable thing happened: small pinpoints of colored lights rose from the earth, lights like those that guided me in my fever dream to the Oracle's shrine. But this time the lights were accompanied by a most noxious of smells.

The Demons rushed our way, but as soon as they reached the edges of the flats they stumbled backwards, wrinkling what I assumed were their noses. Those with legs paced about the edge of the flats, looking for a way to enter and devour us. It was an incredible moment. The Demons paced and paced, but their attention span was short. After a while they turned and ran off into the night.

Oh, but I felt the thrill of victory! I heard the screams of those who had not made the retreat, and I knew that the night would have a dear human cost. We were safe—for now.

*** *** ***

A hot wedge of sunlight slicing across the horizon woke me. For a moment I was disoriented, mineral flats were the last place I would have made a retreat to.

I raised my head from the crust ground to see Sissy and Sariah still asleep, curled together in a protective knot beside me. Sissy began to stir, as if sensing my gaze through the wall sleep. "Are we in the Hells?" she asked, rubbing her eyes.

"No," I replied. "Not yet."

Sissy smiled. "Good." She gently shook Sariah. "Wake up," she urged, "It's morning."

Sariah's blue eyes opened to let in just a sliver of light, for she too had not been sure if she would wake in this world or be digested during the night. "Oh Kyle, you saved us," she said, in a tone I hadn't heard since Derek appeared.

"I guess I did," I replied. "However, I can't remember exactly how I did it."

"The Gods are certainly smiling upon you," Sissy said with warmth. I wanted to ask her how our current situation was indicative of heavenly benevolence but didn't. "You might have well been invisible to those Demons. And I honestly don't know how you managed to face such terror and still be able to command the men! What a general you make!"

First a peasant, then a Seer, and now a general. What was next? Sainthood? Martyrdom?

"Thank you," I recall blurting.

The knights were stirring all around me. I estimated that forty men were left of the original one hundred, including Darius. There was no sign of Derek or Erdo. Derek surely would have broken the bonds that confined him at the first sense of an ambush. Erdo would have extreme difficulty with the stench the Soda People produced. It left me wondering if he had become Demon fodder or died by asphyxiation.

I investigated the fields, and the landscape that greeted my eyes was a dismal sight. The hills and fields of the farm were singed black. Scattered about were the ashen stumps of plants or trees (many still smoking) and the occasional scorched bone or heat-warped armor of the Demon-victims. The farmhouse had been completely gutted; only a blackened ghost of it remained. Horror had sunken into me, the horror of war. War was bad enough, but the terror of the Demons made the situation even more terrible. What were we going to do?

"Are those things still out there?" Sariah asked over my shoulder.

"None that I can see."

"Oh, whatever are we to do?" Sissy moaned. I heard a soft thump behind me as she let herself go, falling back against her bed of dirt.

"For one thing, we're not staying here. I see no other choice than to head for the Second Kingdom, as I instructed before. The Demons seem quite busy here; perhaps we can buy some time."

"Time for what?" Sariah wailed, and too loudly for my taste. "Time to fatten ourselves for the Demons' pleasure? It's hopeless. We can't fight them and there's no way to send them back."

"No, there *is* a way," I insisted. "Lord Banderwall found it and we can, too. I see no other course of action than to familiarize ourselves with magick and try whatever we can to win out over this situation. Once the Demons are banished, then we can begin to sort out the rest of this mess we're in."

Sariah withdrew quietly inside of herself, silenced by my words. "We don't know what happened to Dowry. He dashed into the forest, and that the last time he was seen."

I prayed that Dowry and him men were still alive.
It occurred to me that Darius had formidable obstacles to overcome should he wish to guide me in saving the day and righting the wrongs in the Land.

I do not know what Sissy's or Sariah's reaction to the destruction was, for I could not bring myself to turn and face them with tears in my eyes. Everything my family and theirs had worked for was completely ruined, and from the way things stood, it would apparently stay that way for quite some time, if not forever.

Enough. I rose, and everyone watched as I stepped off the edge of the flats and headed for what had been a grassy hill. From that vantage point I could see that all around us were sleeping, bloated Demons, ready to give birth to another and surely even uglier brood. Even the fan things were bloated, breath rasping in their gills as they slept.

"It's all so horrible," I heard Sissy sob behind me as I crested the hill. It was a good thing too, for I had not peeked over my shoulder to see if they were still with me. "Look what those monsters have done! All is but ashes now: the barn, the house, the silo-"

Behind me came the sharp intake of breath, sharp enough to lop the head off any man that stood in the breather's way. Suddenly Sariah was bounding past me, the singed hem of her skirt rasping and popping as it cracked in the wind.

Even if I was able to run, I would not have done so, and neither did nor would Sissy, I surmise. Instead, she calmly (and I jealously) made our way past the barn to the silo, or rather the place the silo had been. Now there was nothing but a ring of ashes with a black heap in the middle—presumably the remains of the chair in which Derek had been confined. About this Sariah was alternately pacing, stomping, and stammering with imagined agony.

"You fiend!" Sariah spat, and Sissy need not tell me that the words were meant for me and not the soil nor the Demon Commander. "You *knew* this was going to happen! You *knew* that those monsters would torch poor, helpless Derek and eat him even before the flames died out!" She stomped at the ground with such ferocity that I thought she was in danger of stomping a hole straight to the Hells that Sissy so dreaded. "I'll never forgive you, Kyle! Never!"

A braver soul than I, Sissy moved toward the girl, head cocked in sympathy. "Now Sariah, we don't know that Derek is dead."

Eyes burning with hatred, Sariah's head whipped around to face the old woman. "Of course he's dead! Just ask that stupid seer over there. Derek's dead, and Kyle knew it would happen!"

Anger boiled up within me; anger so hot and so foul that the Demon's breath was a wisp of sweet perfume in comparison. Jealous? Me? Ridiculous. I was the Lord Seer, Claimed of the Golden Oracle. And Sariah was accusing me of so mortal an emotion as jealousy?

"Don't be foolish," I said, not being able to conjure up a wittier or biting retort. "Derek isn't dead; why, he escaped with scores of knights. We'll be reunited soon."

Sissy took on a satisfied, motherly look. "There, you see,

Sariah? The Seer has spoken." She wrapped her scrawny arm around Sariah's agonized shoulders. "You mustn't be so rash."

Ye Gods, but if anyone shouldn't have been rash then, it shouldn't have been me. So long had Darius been urging me to lie my way into the history books that I was beginning to don the prophet's mantle without his prompting. And what if we *didn't* see Derek again? What if the Demons had made quite the savory dish out of the brash fool, smacking their tough lips at the prospect of sinking their teeth into their prey's sweet vital organs?

"If ever you've trusted me, trust me now," I insisted. "There's no time to mire ourselves in argument. Who knows when the Demons will wake and give birth? We've got to get someplace safe and study the magick."

The vicious wrinkles around Sariah's eyes softened. She sniffled once, and then looked at the ground. "Well...all right-" and suddenly her eyes shot to meet mine, "but if Derek is dead, I swear you'll be sorry."

I saw Sissy smile at the girl's submission. "Let's organize and begin our flight."

We all collected Soda into our garments and rubbed it on our skin. It itched something awful, but it seemed to be the key to repelling the Demons. I instructed some of the knights to find whatever vessels they could and fill them with the white-flecked earth. Perhaps we would then be safe.

After that, the knights, all whom I cannot name, fell in line and we headed to the road.

The smoke that filtered and wove through the trees made the long journey to the Second Kingdom agonizing. As we walked, I thought of Erdo and that fateful trip of just a few days ago when we first encountered Derek. Now the full impact of what I had said to Sariah bored its unfortunate way into my skull. Derek was the *competition*, for the sake of the Gods. I had longed for him to take his leave of us, but not in this fashion. I was doomed. If Derek were alive, then Sariah would surely remain out of my grasp. And if Derek were dead, the girl would probably smother me with a pillow while I slept. What a predicament.

I looked over my shoulder to see that Sariah was lagging a few paces behind Sissy and me. She was obviously dallying in her worried grief, for Sissy and I were the slowest walkers I knew.

"Perhaps you should keep up with us, Sariah," I suggested.

"I'm fine back here," she said. "These brave knights will protect me." Ash clung to her singed dress, enough ash to blacken the cloth to a color appropriate for mourning.

My eyes returned to the road that stretched out before me. I did not think it possible that we would make the Second Kingdom before dark but did not express my concern to the women for being the practical type, they would invariably ask me what I planned to do once night fell. There was little in the way of shelter for some distance, even past Gallman's Bridge.

Sissy interrupted my tormented thoughts. "Should we really be walking on the road? What if the Demons spy us?"

"The Demons are dormant."

"Dormant?"

I frowned to myself. Sissy hadn't heard the uncomfortable news. "It appears that our foes fall into a deep slumber after gorging themselves, only to reproduce in their sleep."

Sissy emitted a sound of such debased, mortal agony that I can scarce describe it. The last thing I needed was for her to fall apart, for long she had been the sturdy tree upon which all of us at the farm leaned against for encouragement, and I could use all I could get.

"Really, the Demon's breeding habits are to our advantage," I said, trying to sound as upbeat as possible in the face of total disaster. "These intermittent periods of dormancy provide the time we need in order to seek out the spell which banishes them."

"Oh," Sissy said.

The dejection in my nursemaid's voice told me that I had

not been successful in allaying her fears. What was I to do? Tell her that there was going to be a brighter side to all the misery we had been plunged into? I wasn't going to prophesy that the Golden Oracle had shown me the end of the story and we would prevail. That was a lie I could not bring myself to tell.

Sissy glanced over her shoulder at Sariah. "Do keep up with us, girl," she said.

I will spare you the details of our trek, but by the time we reached Gallman's Bridge, the moon-drenched night had fallen upon us, weighing heavy on the soles of our aching feet.

"Can't we stop for the night?" Sariah whined. "I honestly don't think I can take another step."

Sissy answered her for me: "Have you lost all sense of reason? We must keep moving lest the Demons fall upon us in our sleep."

Sariah heaved a thin, whiny sigh. What was she complaining about? There I was, a cripple, and Sissy was so old that I could hear the clatter of her joints as she walked, and Sariah was complaining of being tired and in pain.

And so onward we trudged. As morning began to peek over the horizon it cast its glow on the ramparts of the capitol of the Second Kingdom. Thin wisps of smoke curled from the parapets, and at first, I thought we were too late. I realized, however, that fires lit as signals to knights and peasants still roaming the kingdom probably produced the smoke. Clayton had said he had taken defensive measures before marching on Rind, presumably to save it from the monstrous invasion.

We must have been quite a sight to the guard that sat at his post high above the road in a niche in the city walls. No sooner than we could resolve his figure framed in his watch-window did he shout commands to an unknown party. Metal squealed and wood groaned as the colossal city gates opened a sliver and out stepped two cautious knights in full armor. All I had to do was raise my scarred hand and then they rushed toward our weary band. I collapsed as soon as they reached us; I believe Sissy and Sariah did the same, but I can't be certain.

*** *** ***

CHAPTER ELEVEN: THE SECOND KINGDOM REVISITED

It seemed that Soda was the key
And armed with it the same
But the Demons still shall haunt thee
Until banished, in His name.
-The History of the Second Banderwallian War, verse 12,000

From somewhere inside the blackness came the sound of dripping water. My eyelids fluttered. What horrors they revealed! I had unfortunately regained consciousness.

"Rest, dear Kyle," the woman said as she blotted my sweating brow with a cool damp cloth. "Darius has told me everything. My life, my land, my people—they are yours, O Claimed of the Golden Oracle."

"Darius!" I sat up suddenly in bed, mad with fever. "Is Darius here?"

"Yes, O noble one—but rest!" She placed her perfumed hands on my bare chest and gently pushed me back, returning my head to a pillow. "Rest and recover your strength. Tomorrow we will wage war against the Demons and write the final chapter in this unfortunate history."

I swooned again, falling, down into a hellish nightmare. Darius' wrinkled face loomed large and bright like the sun before me; I tried to avert my dream eyes from the glare but could not.

Darius' voice boomed across the dark dreamscape. "Don't

act so surprised, O noble one." He grinned, and what an awful sight those yellow teeth were, towering above me. "What was I supposed to do? Tell Elwynna that you had ordered your men to pursue her dear, fleeing brother—dear, fleeing *unarmed* brother, that is—and that one of the knights *accidentally* killed him? The last thing you need is Elwynna calling for your head."

Darius' countenance loomed closer, as if to whisper in my too small for scale ear. "Besides, I think Elwynna likes you, boy. And I doubt she's ever taken a fancy to anyone—or that anyone has ever taken a fancy to her, for that matter. She is a valuable ally."

My dream imagination ran wild. A vision of Elwynna and I—frumpy, sour, *old* Elwynna and I—married and with children began to take shape.

"NO!"

I sat bolt upright in bed, cold sweat pouring down my forehead.

"Good heavens boy, do you have to shout so?"

Darius was sitting on a chair to the left of the bed. A scowl was planted on his face; a finger was planted in his left ear, soothing it.

"Where did you come from?" I asked, panting.

"I've been here since before you last woke. I was talking to you until you so rudely shouted in my ear."

My head fell back, clunking against the carved paneling that ornamented the wall. I hadn't been dreaming after all, just semi-conscious. "What are we going to do?" I said. "We can't banish the demons without the blood of a dragon, and everyone knows that those monsters were hunted down and slaughtered so many years ago."

"Oh pish," Darius said. "Even I know that's not true. After all, the demons were banished once before, and so there must be fresh dragon's blood out there somewhere."

I thought about his words and realized that he was right. "But where, Darius? We could use some help."

Darius did not respond. Instead, he just smiled and

shrugged. He didn't know either. It was a terrible predicament.

There came a knock at the door.

"Enter," I said.

Oh Gods, it was Elwynna. She was bearing a tray with a bowl of soup and some local fruits. She smiled broadly as she brought it to my bedside. Her gaping smile revealed rotten, yellowed teeth.

I took the tray into my lap as Elwynna sat on the bed beside me. The soup did smell wonderful, and it had been a few days since I had eaten well.

Elwynna and Darius remained silent as I ate, each gazing at me, albeit for different reasons. Finally, I confessed to Elwynna that it was perhaps the best soup I had ever eaten. She said, "Thank you, My Lord. It is my own recipe."

Silence fell again. I wanted to run out of the chamber, or at least scream. "We've got to get to work," I said. "Princess, if you will excuse me…"

"Certainly!" Elwynna said with a smile. Before rising from the bed, she patted me on the knee. I was repulsed. She exited the chamber, smiling as she went. The smile did nothing to hide her raw ugliness.

I turned my attention to Darius. "Where are Sariah and Sissy?" I asked.

"Safe in the castle's upper chambers."

"And have you heard anything of the knights who fled into the forest?"

"Not a word."

I rested my head against the wall in thought. I said, "How does the demon banishing spell work?"

"How should I know?" Darius responded. "I'm sure the mechanism will be apparent once we attain the dragon's blood."

"You mean *if* we attain the dragon's blood."

Darius frowned and shook his head. "Oh, but you give up so easily! It's just a matter of time before—"

"We don't have time, dammit!" I shouted. "The demons are multiplying in number, and our numbers are dwindling."

"Yes, you're correct on both counts. So what do you propose to do, wise one?"

"I don't know yet."

*** *** ***

I got dressed in fresh clothes that had been provided for me, and left Darius' company to wander the castle. Deep inside of me my feet were propelled by a chance of visiting with Sariah and Sissy.

The castle buzzed with activity, the servants going about their chores, peacefully oblivious to the real terror.

I stopped to gaze out of a window into a formal garden. Everything was still green, flowering, and lush there, but I knew that it was only a matter of time before the demon-scourge blackened it as they had done my home. It seemed that the weight of the Land's troubles rested upon my shoulders, and at that I sighed heavily.

"Why do you sigh so, My Lord?"

I turned around to see Elwynna standing behind me, hands clasped at her portly belly in a gesture of honor.

"I was just contemplating our predicament," I said.

Elwynna advanced on me, resting a hand on my shoulder. Gods, but she was ugly! She had a flat nose with a wart on the end of it that had sprouted hair. Her eyes were beady and gleamed of some distasteful light. She truly had a face that only a Trog could love.

She paused there for a moment while giving me a loving gaze, and then turned her attention to the scene outside the window. "Isn't it lovely?" she said, looking over the garden.

"Yes."

"And to think that the Gods made it from force of will." Her attention shifted to me. "And the Gods made us, Lord Seer. And we, in turn, broke the barrier between the Demons and our world. The Gods put them behind that veil for a reason."

I didn't have the heart to tell her that a man created the demons. In her fanaticism she wouldn't have believed me anyway.

She continued: "Are we to perish under this plague? Will everything be righted in The Land? I know this is a presumptuous question for me to ask, but what do you see?"

She backed me into a prophetic corner. If I promised victory and we met with defeat, I would be persecuted. Then again, if the Demons overran The Land, I would be grilled alive and devoured. I wouldn't suffer too long.

"I see strife," I finally said. "As for how this affair will end, I haven't a vision."

"Oh," Elwynna said, disappointed. "Could you—I mean, would it be right to pray for one?"

"I suppose."

She lifted her skirt and began to kneel. "Then let us fall to our knees and ask for guidance from the Golden Oracle."

I began to kneel, but obviously couldn't. It was bad enough that I had been given a dreadful label, but to pray in public to something that I knew didn't exist was ludicrous.

Confused, Elwynna looked up at me. I fished for words. "No, Princess, not here," I said. "I must get to a shrine."

She blinked, and then stood. She said, "Then we must hasten to one. I shall muster a carriage."

With astonishing speed she dashed down the hallway and out of sight. I knew, and I knew that she knew that her kingdom was dedicated to the Mistress of Mysterion, and that the closest Oracle shrine was at the village in the kingdom where I was reared—that is, if the Demons had not torched the shrine as they did everything else. And yet returning home seemed like going in harm's way. Still, it was better than waiting in a decrepit castle for the Demons to attack. Who knew? Maybe I would find the answers I was looking for along the way. And as for praying at the shrine, well, at that point I figured such a gesture would please the crowds, and that it wouldn't hurt me.

I was left with the realization that if I were to ensure Sissy and Sariah's safety, they would have to journey with us. And of course, Darius would come along as well. I only hoped I could coax Elwynna into staying behind. And as far as Dowry and

Slakely were concerned, no one had a clue as to where they were. Or Derek's whereabouts or fate, for that matter.

"Return to the village?" Sariah exclaimed.

"Yes. I think it would be safer for you to be at my side. And besides—" Oh Gods, here it came! "We might find Derek again, or at least lay him to rest."

Sariah half smiled, half sobbed. "Oh yes!" she said. "That would please me."

Darius was pleased as well. "Goody!" he squealed. "More action for the history!"

Sissy refused to leave the castle.

I said to her, "Sissy, it might be safer."

"How?" she asked. "I suspect it will be a while before the Demons invade this kingdom, and by then I expect you to have banished them. No, I'm too old. I'm staying here."

Elwynna put her arm around Sissy's bony shoulders. "I'll watch after her," she said.

What could I do or say?

Sariah, Darius, and I boarded the coach. The driver tipped his cap, at me. "I am Densi, and at your service, my Lord.

"Thank you," I said flatly.

I settled into the coach, Densi cracked his whip, and we were off.

*** *** ***

CHAPTER TWELVE: A REUNION, AND A FATEFUL FLIGHT

To return to his home seemed a foolish thing,
But the seer saw the all and all
No one felt a pang of fear,
Assured that the Demons would fall.
–The History of the Second Banderwallian war, verse 16,500

    We spent most of the short trip in silence, each of us contemplating our fates. Well, to be honest *I* was contemplating my fate, and I'm sure that Sariah was hoping to find Derek alive, or at least to honor him. And Darius? The Gods only knew what he was thinking.

    By the time we reached Gallman's Bridge the landscape had turned from lush forest to scorched earth. There was no sign of the Demons. In fact, there was no signs of life at all. I was sure that the Demons were at rest, gestating a new brood.

    We passed through what was left of the city of Rind and wound our way back into the countryside. I spied the path that led to the shrine and signaled for the driver to halt.

    "Why are we stopping?" Sariah asked.

    I looked at Darius nervously, and then spoke: "I need a few moments to commune with the Oracle."

    Darius grinned, and I imagined that it was difficult for him to keep from bursting out in laughter. That was what he wanted. He wanted me to play his silly game, and so I did.

I climbed out of the carriage and hobbled my way down that path that led to the shrine. The vegetation was burned away, and there was no cover. I was going to have to kneel before the idol in order to complete the ruse.

The shrine had come through unscathed, and I hoped that was a good omen. I bowed before the shrine, wondering what to do. I looked at the scar on the back of my hand, which seemed to have precipitated these terrible events. I wondered if this mess would have come to pass if I had not stumbled down the same path a few days ago. Surely they would have. I was simply in the wrong place at the right time.

Or was I?

There, in that moment, I once again considered the possibility that the Gods really existed and that I was the pawn of an ethereal mistress.

Suddenly I heard a rustling sound, and knew it was a Demon in the brush. I jumped to my feet and came eye to eye with an eagle that was perched atop the shrine. It flapped its wings, producing the sound I had heard.

The bird cocked its head, as if waiting for me to say something.

"Don't tell me this is real," I said.

It is.

"Then I'm—?"

Yes, you are.

"Shoo!" I said, waving my arms at the creature. The bird remained on its perch.

"This is too much," I replied, and returned to the carriage. I convinced myself once again that what was happening with the Oracle was nothing but coincidence. The voice came from inside my head, not from the eagle's beak. Yes, the whole thing was a coincidence.

I returned to the carriage.

Leaning out the window, Darius said, "Well?"

"Well what?"

"What did the Oracle have to say?"

I gave him a scornful look and climbed back into the carriage. I said, "I want to take a last look at the farm."

Across from me, Sariah's interest piqued. "What will we find there?" she asked.

I confessed that I was unsure.

The farm was in a condition far worse than I had perceived just the day before. To put it succinctly, everything—the fields, barn, silo, and housing—was reduced to a pile of ash. I wept openly at the sight, and so did Sariah.

Darius sauntered up to me as I stood in the sooty remains of what had been my home. "Oh, it's not so bad," he said.

I whirled around to face him. "Not so bad?" I spat. "There is nothing left all the way to the edge of the forest."

"Yes, but you can always rebuild when you—" and then he cut the comment short and began to walk away.

"Don't avoid me," I said. "What were you going to say?"

He continued his retreat, saying, "Oh, it's nothing."

Rarely has my bad leg allowed me to move so swiftly. I stomped to him, and then in front of him, kicking up a cloud of ash. "You know something you're not telling."

He looked at me with those mischievous, old eyes and said, "I know a lot of things I'm not telling."

I remember wanting to hit him over the head with my cane. I opted to voice reason. "Darius, if you know something that could help us out of this mess, I suggest you spit it out."

"What would be the fun in that?"

And then I *did* hit him on the head with my cane. Not too hard, but enough to indicate that I was angry. And at that, Sariah and the driver came running.

"Kyle!" Sariah exclaimed. "What has gotten into you? How dare you strike a defenseless old man!"

And Darius just smiled, rubbing the crown of his skull a little. "It's all right, my dear," he said, "but I appreciate your concern."

Sariah glared at me while the driver checked Darius' scalp. She said, "Honestly Kyle. You have become so self-important in the last few days."

I rolled my eyes. What was the use?

Something else was drawing my attention from the scene. I looked over Darius' shoulder into the scorched forest and saw a figure stumbling out of the residue the Demons left behind. The sun glint off his armor, and as he drew closer, I recognized the gray head of Lord Dowry. The others must have recognized the look on my face, for they turned to see him as he shambled closer. In a moment we ran (well, some of us ran) to meet him.

Dowry stumbled and fell into Sariah's arms. His face was red and blistered; in some places it appeared that his armor had partially melted. His sword was missing. "Demons!" he cried, looking into Sariah's sweet face. "Demons! Demons everywhere!" His eyes were wild and reddened, and I suspected that he might have gone mad.

As I reached the quartet, Dowry broke from Sariah's embrace and stumbled on his knees toward me. "Oh, Seer!" he said, grasping at my garments. "Seer, tell me that this will come to a peaceful end soon. Tell me!"

What could I say? I didn't know anything of the sort, but I found myself saying, "It's alright, Lord Dowry. Everything will work out in the end. Where are the others?"

He collapsed to the ground, nearly dragging me with him. "The others are dead. They're *all* dead. They—they were roasted alive and devoured by the Demons!" He began to let out heaving sobs. "All of them! The farmers, the knights, all of them!"

I caught a glimpse of Sariah, who turned away so that we would not see her tears. Her obsession with Derek was truly deep.

I knelt and put my hand on one of Dowry's quivering shoulders. "Where are the Demons now, Lord Dowry?"

He continued to sob. "Oh, it was horrible, horrible."

"Yes, I know, but where are the Demons now?"

"I do not know, Lord," he said, still crying into the ash. "I —I think they have formed two groups. There are so many of them now! Some of them appeared to be heading for the Second Kingdom, while the others—oh, I don't know! I don't know!"

I looked at Darius, who answered my gaze with another one of his shrugs.

I was desperate. Apparently, there was nothing I could do to save The Land. And yet, Darius' behavior had puzzled me. I began to get the feeling that he really *did* know something he wasn't telling, or that he was feeding me information in convenient pieces in order to cultivate the history he so desired to write.

I decided that I would try a ruse to squeeze information out of him. I said, "Darius, could you step over here for a moment?"

"Surely."

I led him away from the fidgeting driver and the others.

I took a deep breath and said, "I need to consult with you about the matter at hand."

His eyes bulged, much like Erdo's. Oh Gods, Erdo! That poor Trog. To think that he was incinerated...

"*You* want to consult *me?*" Darius said.

"Don't act so surprised," I replied. "You've read the book of spells that summoned the Demons. Is there anything else useful in it, beside the banishing spell?"

"Oh, well, not really. It barely mentions their breeding habits—they were a shock to me. The only other item of significance is that they loathe the cold."

I chewed his words. The only cold habitat in The Land was the mountains, of which we were standing at the base of. Was it possible to arrange a mass evacuation in order to save lives? Surely there was no time for that, for the Demons were spreading like the hardiest of weeds. But I *could* save Dowry, the driver and Sariah's lives.

"Thank you, Darius," I said, and joined the group.

"What?" Sariah asked flatly.

"I've got to get you and these men to safety. Cold temperatures affect the Demons. We're going to flee into the mountains."

"*What?*" the three evacuees exclaimed in unison.

"Are you mad?" Sariah said. "The mountains are the home of the Nevermen!"

"She's right," Darius quipped. I wanted to strike him again.

I tried to control the ridiculous rumor. "Good people, I speak with authority when I say that the Nevermen are just a fable designed to scare children into good behavior. After all, have you ever personally met anyone who has even seen a trace of them?"

"Derek saw one," Sariah said.

"Maybe he did, maybe he didn't."

"Are suggesting he lied?"

"I'm not suggesting anything. There is simply no hard evidence."

"Just because you haven't seen it doesn't mean it doesn't exist," Dowry explained.

"I see. Then would you rather be eaten alive?"

Everyone looked at the ground.

I tried to appeal to their senses. "Look, I am so sure of this that I will personally lead you to safety. It's barely a day's journey from here. As I see it, we have no choice. As soon as we find a safe haven, I will return to The Land and evacuate as many people to the mountains as possible."

We *all* looked at each other then. By their silence I knew I had prevailed.

And so Darius, Lord Dowry, Densi the driver, Sariah and I began our trek.

The wheels of the wagon hardly turned three times before I heard the most terrific bellowing I have ever heard. It sounded like a man's voice, but its booming quality was strange to me. It sounded like it was saying something. I listened closely, and then the words found resolution in my ears: *"Sariah! Beloved Sariah! Oh my darling Sariah!"*

It was Derek! Damn it all to whatever Hells existed, it was

Derek.

I popped my head out of one side of the carriage as Sariah did the other. As soon as she saw his sooty countenance headed for us, she leaped from the moving carriage, tumbling headfirst into the dirt banks at the side of the road. She righted herself, smoothed her skirt, and ran to him.

"Derek! Derek! You're alive!"

The two reached each other and embraced. They entwined in a passionate kiss that made my blood boil and my heart sink. Beautiful maidens preferred strapping, whole men like Derek, not slight, broken ones like me.

I retreated into the carriage, sick with grief.

Derek, of course, had to sit in the carriage with us. He and Sariah sat next to each other, holding hands, and cooing in a most distasteful fashion. If this was love, it was a foolish thing indeed.

"So," Darius asked, "how did you escape the Demons?" Darius was obviously writing more fiction.

"Well, they hate those little lights," he said.

"The Soda People," I spat.

"I didn't see any people."

"That's what they're called."

Sariah gave me a stern look for my tone.

"We figured that out too," I added, not that a barb would penetrate his thick skull.

Derek went on to relate how the demons simply torched the forest as they went, flushing out the knights and devouring them in mid stride. He acknowledged Dowry and professed that he knew of no other survivors.

"I ran," he said. "I ran in circles until I walked on the mineral flats. Then the Demons wanted nothing to do with me. Lord Seer, are you sure the mountains are safe?"

"Certainly," I said. "The Demons loathe the cold and the soda they would have to cross to reach them. We should be quite safe."

This, I hoped, *was* a prophecy.

*** *** ***

CHAPTER THIRTEEN: THE MOUNTAINS

Into the mountains they bravely fled
Into the Nevermen's land
Hearts full of woe and dread
A ragged, brave band.
-The History of the Second Banderwallian War, verse 20,630

Eventually, we had to abandon our horses and cart and walk up the slopes on foot. There were no roads here, for everyone was so afraid of the Nevermen that roads or paths had never been cut.

"But it's true," Derek kept insisting of the myth. "I've seen one."

Sure. And I had been Claimed of the Golden Oracle.

"What were you doing in the mountains at the time of this encounter?" I asked.

"Prospecting."

A likely story.

The mind is an amazingly resilient thing. As we began our trek into the mountains it appeared that Lord Dowry grew more capable and more rational with each step. He felt better enough to launch into endless chatter and storytelling that was almost as excruciating as Erdo's.

Densi began to bemoan our fate. "We're doomed," he said. "Everyone knows that the reason there are no reports about the Nevermen is because everyone who encounters them doesn't live to tell of it."

"Everyone, but not our friend, Derek," I said with a caustic bite.

And Darius continued to play up my assertions. "Rubbish," he said over his shoulder. "You just haven't *met* anyone who has survived an encounter with the Nevermen—but now, since Derek is here, you have. That doesn't mean that there aren't any. Is my logic not correct, O learned Seer?"

"Whatever," I replied. I hated it when Darius sought confirmation of his theories from me. For myself to agree with the historian was for the Gods to affirm the same. If those poor wretches who listened to me only knew the truth!

"How far do we have to climb?" Sariah asked. I could tell by the sound of her voice that she was already tired.

"We have to get high enough that the ambient temperature drops to—say how cold does it have to get?"

"Very cold," Darius said. "We must at least be well into the snowpack."

"Huh, we'll freeze," Dowry said.

"We won't freeze," I insisted. "We'll be just fine."

I hoped no one would bring up the issue of food,

We trudged, we rested. We trudged, we rested. Funny, but from our vantage point the mountains did not seem as high as I had previously thought they were. I even saw a bird circling in the air that was apparently near the crest. I knew it was one of those damn eagles that taunted me so. I hoped it didn't spy us.

Night began to fall, a night so clear and crisp that it seemed supernatural. Without wood for a fire, we huddled close together. I hadn't realized how ill-prepared we were for the journey. Of course, Sariah and Derek made do by snuggling up to one another in a sickening manner. I was left to huddle close to Dowry, Darius and Densi, while the object of my desire was with someone else. How could I have been so misconstrued as to think that she could ever love me, or even dote on me the way Princess Elwynna did? Elwynna doted on me! Now *that* was frightening.

Everyone slept save me. I thought of the olden days, the

days of yore that were only a few short days ago. Everything was at least pleasant then. I was a pupil of the highest minds in the Land. I pined for a maiden who might someday see me as I saw her. I was sure of my future in the sense that I would never be anything other than a farmhand who worked with the women because he was crippled. I thought of my mother and father, and wondered where they were, or if they were even alive. I shed true tears that night. If only I had not fallen at that damn shrine. If only…

I tried to still my mind, to erase the troubling thoughts from it.

Believe, Kyle. Just believe, just this once…

I turned to silence Darius, but he was fast asleep.

You were chosen, Kyle. You were chosen for a destiny that Destiny herself had not dreamed of. She is angry, but there is war in Heaven as there is in the Land. You will bring balance and order. Believe, and stoke the fires of Destiny's ire…

"Why me?" I asked.

Why not?

I shook my head, trying to free it from the unearthly voice that rang inside it. I wanted to sleep. Instead, I watched the stars march across the night sky, and the sun rise in the east.

Yes, the sun rose, and we were back on our feet. We were tired, we were hungry, and we were scared. We needn't express this to one another, for each of us knew the other's heart.

Silence continued as we reached the edge of the snowpack. My cane was little help here and my bad leg little good. I did not complain as I dragged them both through the snow. This was by far the most fiendish predicament I had fallen into so far, for now we were trapped with inevitable death by Demon below and probable death above. Yes, there was a chance that the Nevermen were but a myth and that we would only freeze to death (a more agreeable fate than being twisted into a wraith) but uncertainty hung on my consciousness as the clouds hung about the jagged peaks above. A few short days ago I would have said that everything that had transpired since was impossible, but now I was coming to the realization that *everything* was and is indeed possible. Perhaps this was the most difficult lesson I had to learn. Opening one's mind to the myriad of possibilities this world offers is at once frightening and reassuring, for it implies that great good can occur, and great evil as well. And the most horrible possibility of all was that there wasn't anyone or anything standing outside of this mess we call our lives with the reins in his/her/its hands; that all was random, and the great evil was as probable as the great good.

My left foot suddenly plunged deep into the snow beneath it, deeper than I had been prepared for. I stumbled and fell face down into the snow.

"Lord Seer!" Dowry shouted. Hands fell upon me, lifting me from the wet ice beneath. As I regained my balance, I could not help but see the impression of my form in the snow beneath. One arm was above my head, its flailing position momentarily preserved. The outline of my right leg was warped, exaggerated. All at once the most terrible fear descended upon me; it was as if this mold in the snow was a sign from the Gods that read *"Foolish, impetuous boy! To think that for a moment you considered yourself the savior who would rid the Land of its pestilence! Destiny had other plans for you, dolt, and now her wrath at your rash doings will be felt by all those pitiful creatures who dwell in the Land."*

"Lord Seer, are you alright?"

Teeth chattering, I shook my head at my compatriots, who were holding me up. "No, I'm not all right," I confessed. How could I, a cripple, think of myself as a hero of the people, or a Seer, or anything at all but a liability? I wanted to climb to the highest peak and shout to the world that I was a fraud, and that putting faith in me was as useless as the plight for dragon's blood.

I saw the face of Darius, and his eyes spoke to me as if he was reading my mind: *It's too late, Kyle. If you told each and every creature in The Land that you were a liar, you would only reaffirm your position in their eyes, for they would see your confession as a humble act of modesty. Look at them! Every word you utter is prophecy to them. The entire population would gladly trudge into the wastelands above us if you asked them to. They'd die of thirst in the Great Desert if you told them to. My boy, we've succeeded. You're their messiah! Now all you must do is banish the Demons and you'll be a god.*

I wanted to vomit. Instead, I righted myself and moved on.

The ascent to a safe place on the snowpack was the most tortuous part of the journey. Since no one ever ventured into the mountains, we had no way of guiding our trek. I looked everywhere for a ledge, a smooth place—anywhere we could make camp. It drew more attention to the fact that we had nothing to make camp with. We had no supplies, no food or water, no blankets. Nothing. The quartet had followed me up into the desolate spaces blindly, as if provisions would rain down from the sky.

I paused in the snow, and my eyes turned to the crisp, blue sky. A bird circled overhead. I watched as the black silhouette sailed toward the mountains, and then *over* them.
"Did you see that?" I said.

"See what? Darius replied.

"Oh, nothing. I'm hallucinating."

We continued climbing.

After a while, Sariah asked the inevitable question: "Kyle, where are we going?"

"We're going…up." I replied.

"Yes, but how far? I'm tired and cold."

"So am I."

And still we climbed. Sariah suddenly stopped and pointed into the snow beside our path. "Look!" she explained. "Footprints!"

Darius, who was behind her, said, "Rubbish."

"But look! It's the imprint of a bare foot. It looks…it looks like a *child's* foot."

Densi and I reached the "print". I peered at it. In retrospect, it did look like a footprint, but I would not allow myself to entertain the possibilities. "It's too ragged to be a footprint," I proclaimed.

"Then what is it?" Darius asked. Leave it to him to ask the imponderable.

I thought for a moment, trying to come up with a logical explanation. I said, "I don't know what it is, but it's *not* a footprint."

Sariah looked at me with her soft eyes. Those eyes asked the question she dreaded: *Are you sure they're not footprints?* And how could she ask that question aloud? How could she doubt me, the infallible Claimed of the Golden Oracle?

Her eyes cast to the snowy ground, and we moved on.

A small stone came tumbling down the slope we stood on, landing in the snow with a crisp thud. I didn't have to explain that these stones were the cause of the marks in the snow. All we had to do was find a place to call camp, and then retrieve the evacuees.

As we continued to climb into oblivion, the strange "footprints" in the snow grew more and more common. No one said a word of them, for we had a plausible explanation.

Oh, but we were cold, wet and exhausted! I was certainly leading my comrades to certain death on the frozen slope of the mountains.

From the rear, Densi said, "Are we almost there?"

I stopped in my tracks, my eyes making an appeal to heaven. One of those strange birds was circling above us, darting in and out of the foamy clouds. "Yes," I said finally, hoping to give them hope. "We're almost there."

I shifted my eyes to the ground. There was no hope for us, and I knew it.

"Look!" Sariah cried suddenly. "Look up there! I see a ledge just a short way from us! Oh Kyle, you really *did* have a plan, didn't you? You really *are* a Seer!"

I said nothing in response. It was curious to me that I was dubbed Seer when it was convenient, and charlatan when it was not.

There was tacit agreement that we would head for the

ledge. It didn't seem far, but distances were deceiving in that realm.

Yes, distances were quite deceiving. It took us the better part of the day to reach the ledge, and when we had all climbed upon it and took stock of the landscape, our blood ran cold: there was a passageway into the mountain, the mouth of a great cave.

"I don't like the looks of this," Derek said.

"It looks like shelter to me," Darius responded. "Weren't we assured by the Lord Seer that it would be waiting for us?"

Everyone nodded in agreement. I needn't tell you how I felt. You know by now.

Derek pulled out his sword and headed for the cave. "I'll scout the place," he said. I had no objections.

Derek disappeared into the darkness of the cave. I saw Sariah chewing her lip in his absence, as if every moment he was away some imaginary pain increased.

A moment later, we heard Derek's boots on stone, and by the sound of it, he was running. He burst from the cave entrance, face white as the snow around us. "Get out of here!" he cried.

The rest of us stood frozen, of course, taken aback by his sudden and fearful appearance.

That was when the source of the horror appeared: dozens of squat, naked beings caked in white and with their genitalia swinging, came dashing from the cave entrance. Each was brandishing a dagger of gold with a jeweled hilt.

"Nevermen!" Dowry cried, and then turned and ran.

"Well, I'll be," Darius said, and remained fast in place.

There had to be at least twenty of them. I turned to run but more of the fiends were climbing up the ridges and mountainside. We were surrounded. We were trapped.

Derek's first instinct was to swing his mighty sword, but when it met a Neverman's blade it was cleaved in two.
And since Lord Dowry was not armed, we were at the creatures' mercy.

I made a sudden realization. These vicious entities were no larger than a child, and all males. The stories were true!

Unruly boys were snapped up to become one of these things with the glowing red eyes. They were just as Derek described them. He had been telling the truth about his exploits all along. That was the worst part of it all.

One of the Nevermen, presumably the leader, stepped forward and spat some words in an ancient tongue. As the cretins surrounded us, it was clear that they were forcing us into the dripping, cold and dark cave.

"Do as he says," I said to the others.

"But what did he say?" Dowry asked.

"They want us in the cave."

Sariah cleaved to Derek. The Nevermen closed the circle, ready to slice us with their horrible blades. We had to obey, and so into the darkness we were forced.

The entryway of the cave was cold and dark, but the deeper we were escorted into it, the warmer and brighter it became.

"Oh Derek, I'm frightened," I heard Sariah whisper. Derek mumbled something oozingly supportive back to her, and I was glad that I was unable to hear it.

"Isn't this exciting?" Darius piped up, and the little Nevermen growled and poked him with a dagger. I felt like screaming that no, this was not exciting. We were probably being led to our deaths. What was exciting about that?

I noticed that the air inside the tunnel was noticeably drier than the cold damp we had spent the previous night in. The mosses and lichens that we passed as we were driven in were dry, and then eventually disappeared from the walls of the cave. I may not have been excited, but I was at least curious about where we were being led.

As I said before, the tunnel grew brighter as we walked. Soon, a light at the end appeared, not the light of torches, but apparently the natural light of the sun. As we grew closer, I could see movement in the periodic change of light, of shadow spilling into the cavern.

The Nevermen stopped and congregated around us

before we were able to see what lay beyond the cavern exit. The one in the lead jabbered, instructing the others. They drew tight to us, and the leader disappeared into the light.

"They'll roast us and eat us," Dowry said.

"I don't think they mean us harm," I reassured.

"Harm? Can't you smell the fires and the meat? It's worse than the smoke of the Demons!"

I sniffed the air, but what I smelled was more akin to brimstone than burning flesh. "Keep hope," I said to Dowry and the others. "Perhaps they can be reasoned with."

"Do you understand their language?" the carriage driver asked.

I admitted that I didn't.

"Then we'll be roasted."

I frowned to myself. I looked down at the creatures that were standing watch over us, and though they were hideously ugly with their crusty bodies, nakedness, and glowing eyes, they did not seem overtly hostile. I think that we surprised them, for as far as I knew, no one had ever stumbled across them before. Then again, the tales of the Land were that no one who encountered them lived to tell the tale. There was nothing we could do but wait and see.

I heard garbled voices. Three Nevermen emerged from the light and came to face us. The one that stood in the center wore a queer adornment of a medallion of gold around its neck, a medallion with a strange and probably ancient symbol etched into it. I recognized the symbol; in my tutorials I was familiarized with a written language that was largely lost, but that symbol I knew: fire.

The two that flanked him drew their daggers, and all the Nevermen closed in on us. It was a tense moment as we humans were forced into a small group. Still, I reasoned that we wouldn't be killed in the tunnel. It just didn't seem logical.

The Nevermen formed a column on either side of us and led us into the orange glow of the light at the end of the tunnel.

I was blinded for a moment by the brightness of the

illumination. When my eyes adjusted, I could barely believe what I saw. There, hovering in the air above us seemed to be an artificial sun. Though small as the point of a sword, it gave off intense light, and more than that, a heat that my cold bones welcomed.

We stood before a great bowl of stone: a crater. It was immensely wide; the far walls were leagues away. The crater was verdant with fruit trees, grasses, flowers, and all manner of queer vegetation. Great birds circled it in the air, and I realized that these were the birds that I had seen earlier in our trek.

Three paths were laid out before us. To the left there was one of simple gravel, before us of some slick stone. The third path, the one to the right, was paved with blocks of gold. We were all astonished to see the precious metal in such quantity.

The Nevermen leader barked orders to his men, and we were forced to walk down the golden path, with me and Darius in the lead, Densi the carriage driver in the middle, and Dowry, Derek, and Sariah in the rear.

Our fears had melted and had been replaced by awe. The golden path followed the perimeter of the steeply walled caldera and was fringed with all manner of flora. Strange pink, ruffled flowers on thick, thorny stalks rose high into the air, blocking our view of the rest of the area. Intertwined with them were strange vines that bore purple buds that bore a slightly sickeningly sweet smell.

"I've never seen anything like this," Darius said quietly. "These plants must be indigenous to this environment and not that below in the valleys of the Land. I tell you, in my many spans I have never seen such incredible foliage."

I heard Sariah let out a little yelp behind us. She had reached out to touch one of the pink flowers and had been poked in the rear with a Neverman's dagger. If only there was someone to poke Derek every time he touched her.

The smell of brimstone became heavy in our nostrils as we walked. Furthermore, the golden pavement was slick, and it was difficult for me to keep balanced, for my cane kept slipping on the metal. The Nevermen didn't care; they ruthlessly marched us further and farther around the perimeter of that great bowl with its own sun.

What happened next nearly destroyed our minds. We reached the edge of a huge grassland, grass up to our waist and flowers of all manner. And there, lounging in the grass, their tails flopping back and forth in pleasure were several dragons. They were magnificent creatures, as large as our farmhouse. Their scales were gilded silver, from tail to the tip of their nose. Tails began with a point, and then gently tapered into their massive trunks. Even through the gilding it was clear that their bodies were incredibly muscular, and that flight springing from their elegant wings was inevitable. The trunk then tapered into a graceful neck and up to spiny heads. Each sported three spines above their eyes, and then barbs that followed their lips. Most curious were their noses, the aperture of which changed radically as they breathed.

Darius poked me in the side. "Ask them to take you to their leader."

"Yes!" a dragon said. "Let the King hear the absurdity!"

I realized that the first dragon fancied himself the leader but was not. Perhaps I could use that to my advantage.

"Oh, fine," the first dragon said with wisp of smoke wafting from the side of his mouth. He babbled to the Nevermen guarding us, and then they turned and were on their way with us to court.

I turned to see everyone's reaction and saw that everyone was moving save Sariah. It seemed strange because she would have followed Derek anywhere.

I fell back to the rear of the party. Sariah's eyes were glazed, and she had a dazed look on her face. I took her by the arm and tried to lead her away, but she wouldn't budge. "Sariah, what is wrong with you?" I asked.

"They're *beautiful*," she said in a tiny voice.

"Yes, they're lovely. However, we're on a mission, come on."

Sariah wouldn't budge.

"Sariah, I said, let's go!"

She began to walk, but in dreamy steps. If there were any way she could have floated above the golden pavement, she would have achieved it.

We didn't have to walk far. The grasses gave way to a huge, tiled arena lined with silver dragons. Each one of them screamed in turn when they saw us. "Humans!" one cried.

And there, lording over all was the King of the Dragons, a most remarkable and magnificent sight to see. He was lounging on a dais, stretched out to his full length. He was larger than the others, and it took many more Nevermen to polish his golden scales.

He raised his great head as we were led into the arena. Opening his green eyes, he shook his head. "Well, it was bound to happen sooner or later," he said. "Humans have found us."

The first dragon we met made a gesture with his head and wings, which I figured was a salute. I hoped he wouldn't do it again, for the force of wind nearly bowled us all over. "We have esteemed company, you highness," the first dragon said. "We have a Seer Claimed of the Golden Oracle."

The other dragons giggled.

The King of the Dragons sat up on his rear. "That's the most preposterous thing I've ever heard."

"Yes, and wait until you hear his prophecy."

More giggling.

The King Dragon surveyed us. "You look like vagabonds, not lords and ladies. Which one of you is the prophet?"

I nervously stepped to the front of the group. "I am Lord Kyle of the Third Kingdom, Claimed of the Golden Oracle."

The King rolled his eyes. "Leave it to the bitch bird to destroy our peace. What does She want now?

"Oh, just a little blood."

All the dragons were aghast. The King leaped/flew from the dais and came before me, forcing his great head down to level his eyes with mine. "Haven't we bled enough for your kind?" he asked. "You persecuted us to the point where we had to burn stone to form this, our fortress."

I was irritated. "And you never did anything to cause the strife with the race of men? You never scorched fields, leveled houses, and even ate our children? Don't tell me you didn't. I have read the Histories and know them to be true."

The dragon eased off a bit. "We have to eat too, you know."

"That's an excuse."

The dragon swept so close to me that his wet nostrils struck the bridge of my nose. "Watch your step, boy. We never ate your children. All we have done since being here for a hundred more peaceful years is to snatch up the babies you don't want—the boys that your mothers put on the stoop for us. And you! What did your people do? They attempted to destroy us. Can you not see the violence around you? Can you not understand why we gild ourselves with metal, to protect us from your blows? You are a foolish, impetuous boy."

He climbed back on his dais. "Destroy them."

The silver dragons swept in to surround us, ready to singe us with their fiery breath. This was surely it, the last moment that I would feel, sense, experience.

"WAIT!" Darius shouted. The cry was of such volume that I knew he was using a magickal voice. "YOU HAVE HEARD THE PROPHECY! IT WILL BE FULFILLED THIS DAY OR THE THREAD OF DESTINY WILL CLOSE AROUND YOUR NECKS!"

The mighty dragons took pause. Even the king seemed a bit leery of burning us to a cinder. "This is ridiculous!" he said. "That Oracle has hounded us since—oooooo!"

The golden king reared his head back, bejeweled talons scraping the stone dais. I didn't know what was happening until I saw that Sariah was below him rubbing his belly.

"Oh, so beautiful!" she said in loving tone I had never heard.

"Yes, yes," the king said, a bit annoyed, and then Sariah raked her pale, fragile hands across his gilded stomach once more.

"Ooo!" the dragon exclaimed. "Stop that this instant!"

Sariah was relentless. She stroked him until he rolled over on his back and shuddered in ecstasy with her every stroke.

The other dragons saw what was happening and got in line. "I'm next!" one said.

"Then me!" another cried.

The King of the Dragons rolled over and nuzzled the bewitched Sariah in the belly. The Nevermen scattered to avoid being crushed beneath the creature's body. "Where did you come from?" he purred. "What is your name, child?"

"My name is Sariah," she breathed in a manner that was almost sexual and seductive. "You are *so* beautiful!"

The grand dragon lowered his head, forcing it amongst us. "Can you not see our power? We can change stone to gem, metal to gold. There is, unfortunately, no manner for us to reproduce. When the dowager Queen Minmin left us…Bah! The Nevermen are a failed experiment because your kind only leaves boys for us to transmute.

"And so are you," the King said. He then looked at us, the rag tag band. "I'll make you a deal," he said. "I will bleed for you, but this lovely, delicate girl stays behind."

Derek strode to the front, drawing his sword. "She is mine!" he said.

Sariah did not look at him, but she said, "Oh shush, Derek."

"No deal," I said. I was trying to keep her close to me so she would see that Derek was a lout and that I was her savior.

"What do you want my blood for anyway?" the king spat. "What kind of evil do you have in mind?"

"We come to banish evil," I explained. "We are beset with a plague of Banderwallian Demons."

The majestic creature rolled his eyes. "I gave once for that."

"Well, they're back."

"Then some idiot deserves to pay," the king spat. "The deal is simple: dragon's blood for this lovely, fragile child that you have so thoughtfully brought to us."

He then turned to Sariah. "You will be eternally young and beautiful if you stay inside the caldera. And eventually—eventually—you will be our queen."

"I accept," she said, and took a seat on the dais next to the king.

"Well I don't," Derek spat angrily. "Sariah, you belong at my side."

The King chuckled. "Let her be the judge of that."

Sariah stood on the dais, her fair hair blowing in the breeze created by the breaths of the dragons. "What do you petty men know of beauty?" she began. "What do you know about love? Look at the beauty around you." She stroked the belly of the king, whose eyes half closed in ecstasy. "These dragons possess beauty beyond that of you surly folk. It is here I shall stay, and here I shall fulfill my destiny."

I cringed at the word "destiny." I could almost hear Darius speaking to me: *Let her go, boy. She was never yours and never will be. Take the blood and save the Land. That is what you love: the Land and its people.*

I was horrified, absolutely horrified. I mean, the choice was clear, wasn't it? Leave Sariah behind and let the dragons experiment with her organs or save the Land.

"It's a deal," I said hastily.

"*What?*" Derek exclaimed. "What gives you the right to determine the fate of others?"

"Destiny determines fate," I said, "and Sariah is destined to stay here."

He did not back down. "Why you sniveling—"

"The Oracle has spoken," I said loudly, and that was enough for everyone else involved.

Derek advanced on me, but Lord Dowry cut him off. "You have heard the will of the Gods," Dowry snapped. "Understand and deal with it."

That was when the King of the Dragons, an astute animal, chimed in. "Sheathe the stump of your sword," he said in a pleasing tone. "You will need it."

Derek stopped in his tracks. "What do you mean?"

"I know the potion you seek to make," the King said. "One drop on a sword, and the sword becomes an instrument of the Gods. It will slice through demon flesh like a blade through roast fowl. The Land will need a hero, and you surely will be it. As for the rest of the blood, well, you may use it as you see fit."

Derek's sword dropped from attack mode to his side. "Oh," he said. "Well, yes, I guess I'm it."

Hooray for the King of the Dragons! He had appealed to Derek's ego, and the ruse had worked.

Sariah clamored off the dais and walked up to Derek. "I will always love you," she said, and stroked his cheek. I could see him straighten up with fortitude and valor—and other feelings. She kissed him on the cheek and stroked his forehead with a finger. "I'll be all right here. The dragons need me, and the Land needs you."

"Of course," Derek said as she withdrew.

So much for the formalities. Now we needed dragon's blood.

I was trying to think of a subtle way to bring up the subject, but Darius caught me off guard by saying, "So, who's going to bleed for us?"

Everyone recoiled, dragon and man alike. I wanted to reach out and throttle Darius for his lack of tact, and then I thought of my father and how he had tried to choke me.

Sariah, who had climbed back onto the dais, bade the King to lower his head alongside hers. She whispered something in his ear, and it caused him to register displeasure. After a moment of thought the dragon spoke: "Fine. Let it be me. But be gentle, you cretins. I am not a lover of pain like you men are."

"Go on!" Darius urged me. He reached into his robe and produced the magickally shrunken bag. He expanded it (much to everyone's surprise) and produced a small bottle. "Here," he said, forcing it into my hands. "This much should do."

"But—"

He forced a small dagger into my left hand. "Oh, just stab the damn thing and let us be on our way. Who knows how many demons there are by now?"

He was right, but I was frightened. I approached the dais as if I had two bad legs. I mounted the steps the Nevermen use to reach their god, and then stood before him. The dragon regarded me curiously, as if I were making a blunder. I approached its belly.

"What are you doing?" it screeched. "Can't you see that our bellies are sensitive? The tail, you silly boy. Cut my tail!"

"Oh," I said weakly, and retraced my steps.

Scales guarded the tail, but they were finer than those that covered the rest of its body. I gently ruffled them aside to reveal flesh. I looked into the thing's eyes. "Get on with it!" it cried.

The skin was tough. I had to saw a bit to draw blood, and I could see the beast recoil in pain. The blood flowed; a black, stinking ichor that flowed into the bottle as if it knew where to go.

It seemed an eternity from when the blood flowed until the vial was full, an eternity to me and the dragon I bled. Its blood smoked slightly and had a heady smell that would surely make Erdo faint. It dribbled slowly, thickly into the vial. I heard the noble creature make a groaning sound, but Sariah continued to stroke its body, offsetting the pain.

As soon as the process had begun, it ended. I had what I needed, and I replaced the scales to their former position.

"Ouch," the dragon said vaguely, and then I withdrew.

There were several moments of silence as the dragon held its eyes closed, and then it said: "You have what you want. Now go!"

I looked at the men, and we began to retreat along the gold paved road. Derek stopped at the edge of the clearing, blew a kiss to Sariah, and said, "I will always love you."

Sariah blew a kiss back his direction but said nothing. Ha! Derek was defeated!

So was I.

As we were led around the edge of the crater, I shed a tear for Sariah. I had always known I would never have her, but here was a finality that had to be faced.

Two paces ahead of me, Derek kept looking down at the golden pavement. I knew what he was thinking but figured that he was not foolhardy enough to try to make off with one of the stones. It was then that I noticed the Lord Dowry's clothes had a heavy paunch at the back. He *was* foolish enough.

I caught up with him. "Put the gold back," I whispered into his ear.

"What gold, Lord?" he asked innocently. Yes, I saw that glint in his grizzled eyes. I knew what he was doing.

"The Nevermen will be angered if they catch you. Who knows what would happen?"

"The Nevermen will never know unless you tell them," he hissed. "This is not your business."

"You're putting us all in jeopardy,"

"Is that an official prophecy, you rogue, or is it another one of the games that you and that old coot Darius play?"

I was so angry that my jaws clenched tightly, tight enough to break one of my teeth. "It's on your head," I said, and then fell back in the column to distance myself from him.

Darius was in the rear. "Do not worry, young Seer," he said. "Lord Dowry will get what's coming to him."

"That's what I'm afraid of."

There was another time in our walk when I had to smack Derek's hand, for he was trying to pick a particularly beautiful flower from a vine that wound through the shrubbery. "Don't do that," I said angrily. "We don't know their customs."

"Well, excuse me," Derek said sourly.

We eventually came to the cavern we had entered by. The Nevermen escort formed two columns on either side of its opening and ushered us through. Immediately I felt the warmth of the dragon sun give way to the cold of the mountains. We were far from the rest of the Land. We had to make haste before the Demons lay waste to it.

There, on the ledge outside the cavern entrance, Lord Dowry began to laugh in a hoot so merry. "I'm a rich man!" he said and reached into his cloak to retrieve his prize. But what he produced was not gold, but a lump of hard, gray stone.

Darius hooted himself, laughing at the man.

"Shut up, old man," Dowry said, throwing the rock down in disgust.

"What did you expect?" Darius asked. "It was a different, magickal reality inside that crater. Nothing can pass but the Nevermen in and out without consequence. That's the way the spell works."

"Spells!" said Dowry. "I've had enough of evil spells and magick."

I chose not to tell him that the greatest spell, yet cast had not happened yet. I thought it best for him to cool down before we discussed dispelling the Demons.

As if reading my thoughts, Darius came to me and said, "We must get back to the magick laboratory in Rind. There are items I need—I mean *you* need—to complete the spell."

"Rind?" I said, loud enough to disturb the others. "Isn't that dangerous?"

"It will fulfill the prophecy," Darius said.

"What prophecy?"

"About the Second Banderwallian War. You made the prophecy yourself."

"I did nothing of the sort."

"Oh yes you did."

"Oh no I did not."

"Does it matter? Everyone believes in you and what you do. We must retrieve your friends who have made camp on the mineral flats and take it from there."

*** *** ***

CHAPTER FOURTEEN: GIRDING FOR WAR

Armed with the blood of the flying beasts,
The seer messiah came back to save
But before the party, before the feast,
A war would occur, to say the least.
-The History of the Second Banderwallian War, verse 24,509

And so we marched without rest, until we came down the mountain and to the edge of the mineral flats, guided by Derek and his knowledge of the mountains from his prospecting days. Funny, how it didn't help when we ascended.

In the distance we could see the fires of the refugees, all who were waiting for my return.

As we neared the crowds, my sore eyes saw that everyone was there: Erdo and a large assembly of farm people who had heard of sanctuary in the flats, all who brandished weapons. I prayed that Sissy was all right in the Second Kingdom, where there were no flats to flee to.

Erdo came rushing toward me, and then stopped several paces away. "Ye Gods, but you stink!" he said.

"Nice to see you too, Erdo," I said dryly.

My father and family, who had heard of the Soda People and rushed to the flats and retuned from the outlying areas, embraced me in a crushing hug, weeping and saying, "We knew you'd come through for us!"

My mother did the same. At the sight of my parents my heart soared, and for once I believed that perhaps Destiny was a kind goddess.

Soon I was surrounded by the desperate, wondering where I had been and what I had been doing. Yes, I could have explained to them exactly what had happened, but I chose to omit the choice parts. I said, "I have a solution to the Demon problem."

Oh, the cheers! Torches were raised high, as were pitchforks and shovels. The Soda People rose and fell, pinpoints of colored light that rejoiced in the fact that their homes would soon be rebuilt, and not stomped flat as they were.

"I have a mission," I said to the group. "I must go to Rind, and I will return with the magick that will free us from the Demon menace. Have no fear people, for the Oracle has shown this to me."

No! I had made another prophecy! I was beginning to believe my own words, and it was frightening me. But why not? Had not everything I had said come true? Why not this prophecy?

I had to choose my party wisely. I asked Erdo and Darius to accompany me. That was fine, for Derek and Dowry were more than happy to stay behind and defend the oppressed.

"Oh, not me!" Erdo whined. "Those Demons are out there."

"They will sleep through the night," I said, knowing that that was an outright lie and everyone knew it. Demons slept in the daytime, but there was no telling what the younger brood would do. "Besides, I need your nose."

His attitude changed when I said that. He was needed, and that was all anyone could hope to be.

And so we set off for the city. I was fearful the entire journey. The Demons were unpredictable. What if they had spawned some that *didn't* sleep during the day? I knew I was taking a risk, but it was a calculated one.

Erdo tried to remain as quiet as possible. He stepped around leaves and twigs in the wagon ruts, thinking perhaps the smallest sound would arouse the Demons.

And Darius? He strode beside me with a little smile playing on his lips, as if he was enjoying what was happening. I'm sure he was enjoying it! Here was a historian who was witnessing history as it happened. His tomes wouldn't be bland tales of the kings of yore, no, his books would be about the brief but intense Second Banderwallian war.

It seemed that an eternity had passed beneath our feet when we arrived at the gates to the city. We hadn't much time. We could only hope that the answers we sought were encased and entombed in the magickal laboratory.

Erdo tried not to breath as we waded into the moat, and then into the maw of the secret entrance. Unfortunately, he realized he had to breathe to live, and soon got a whiff of the laboratory.

"Oh Gods, why?" Erdo asked in the glow of the blue orb. "Why would anyone dabble in anything that smelled this awful?"

We stopped short of the entrance in order to hear Darius lecture. "There's a reason such things were banned, Sir Trog. Magick is a dirty, smelly, and thoroughly unpleasant affair. Don't expect a clean miracle."

"I'll take a dirty miracle," I said. "We must do whatever we can to rid the kingdoms of the Demons."

"Well said!" Darius exclaimed, and then ducked into the laboratory.

*** *** ***

The light of the orb seemed to be failing as we worked. I watched as Darius gave it a dirty look, and its glow intensified. Strange.

Darius gave each of us a book to search through for the proper spell. Erdo closed his quickly, and asked, "Why the hells am I doing this. I can't read anything but Trog!"

"I had no idea that Trogs have their own written language," Darius said, not looking up from the tome in his lap.

Erdo seemed defensive. "Well, then there's just a lot you don't know about Trogs. We have a very sophisticated culture."

"Oh really?"

"Yes, really."

Fortunately, I had been schooled in the elder tongues and could decipher the spells in the cursed tome I held under the blue light of the orb. However, I saw no spells concerning Demons.

"Oh, here's something interesting," Darius said, and pushed his smelly, yellow book under my nose. "It's a spell of protection from fire."

I looked at the spell, reading down the list of disgusting ingredients—ingredients that require Trog phlegm. My stomach churned.

The fire spell consisted of making a dreadful paste, and then anointing one's head with it. It was said to be effective for several hours. I wondered if that would be enough time to force the Demons back into their empty world.

"Give the book back, boy!" Darius exclaimed, and I hastily handed it to him.

I finished with my book, and took another from the shelf, and then another. I finally came to a curiously thin and newer-looking little tome. I opened it. The parchment it was written on was curiously orange, and the ink was dark brown, with red hues. I read the inscription on the front page: *Notes on Demons, Lord Banderwall.*

The revelation caused me to jump, scaring my companions. "Here!" I exclaimed and handed the open book to Darius.

"Aha!" he said. Now we're getting somewhere. I wonder whose blood this is inked in, and who dedicated the skin for the pages?"

"What?" I cried in horror.

Darius shook his head. "Look, boy! The page is hairy!"

I didn't want to look but did. There was a slight padding of hair on the page, and if one looked close enough, one could even see the veins in the pages.

Erdo fainted without complaining.

Darius recounted the highlights of the book as he perused

the pages. It was clear that Lord Banderwall did not know what he was doing when he created the Demons. He had no idea they would be capable of parthenogenesis and spawn a brood of even more hideous creatures every night. Most importantly, however, was that people had forgotten that it took a war to banish the Demons. Clearly, they would not just stand in line and jump into an empty dimension without considerable coercion.

Darius was looking for a more permanent solution. There had to be some way to destroy the Demons forever, and Darius was sure that the answers were encoded in Lord Banderwall's notes.

Erdo came around, took one look at the hairy book, and passed out again.

Finally, Darius closed the book. He looked me in the eye with the most serious gaze he had ever given me. "I have the answer: they must be cut in half, each and every one of them."

"Oh Gods, Darius," I begged. "Tell me there is some other way. Can't we just send them back where they came from?"

Darius stroked his beard. "Of course, and then someone summons them again, and we're back in the place we are. Listen to me, boy: Your destiny lies in the end of the Demons."

"Or is that just the history you're writing?"

"Watch your tongue. I had written hundreds of books before you were conceived. We have a spell to protect us from fire, and we know how to kill them. You see, I know a spell that makes everything bow to the blade—another benefit of dragon's blood, as those noble creatures said. We use it on our weapons, we protect ourselves from fire, and we destroy the terrible scourge that plagues the Land. We use Banderwall's odious dragon's blood spell to close the door to the empty dimension forever. Remember your family. Remember your friends. Think of the possibility that the Demons would multiply so greatly that—"

I raised my hand. "I understand," I said. "Do we have everything we need to cast the spells?"

Darius looked around the room. "It looks like it. And your

short friend has plenty of phlegm."

Erdo sat up. "Ye Gods!" he exclaimed. "I can help!"

*** *** ***

CHAPTER FIFTEEN: THREE SPELLS CAST

Magick breeds the need for magick
In the most appalling way
And so the Seer learned the trick
And showed us the glorious day.
-The History of the Second Banderwallian War, verse 23,704

Exactly how does one go about casting a spell? I certainly had no idea, but Darius did, and that worried me. True, he was old enough to be of the generation that habitually cast spells, but his prowess and manner gave me pause. He went about his merry way, collecting things from the dusty shelves, dumping them into cauldrons and grinding them in mortars. Erdo volunteered to wait in the outer passage until it was time to spit in the appropriate place. I knew he was suffering from the smells of the magickal materials, for I certainly was. Magick was smelly, indeed.

I sat in the light of the orb and thumbed through the various books, shuddering at the diagrams of anatomy and what the bits and pieces of various animals—including humans—were good for. Darius hummed an incessant tune; he seemed oddly in his element.

I grew bored and turned my attention to Darius and what he was doing. He pulled a crock down from the shelf, and when he opened it, the most terrible stench burst from it. Even Darius flinched; I could hear Erdo groan in the outer passage.

Darius even dared to sniff the contents. He reached into

the jar and produced a black *thing*—and organ of some kind—from inside. "Ah!" he exclaimed. "It smells as fresh as the day it was plucked from the belly of a beetlehog!" he exclaimed and tossed it into a cauldron with other ingredients.

"What the Hells is a beetlehog?" I asked, covering my mouth and nose with my tunic.

"It doesn't matter. They've long since been hunted into oblivion."

Darius went about setting up a rickety tripod he found in the corner of the chamber. He set the cauldron on it precariously. He then stepped back and stroked his long beard, thinking aloud: "Ye Gods, my magick words have escaped me." He raised his arms, hands above the cauldron, and uttered something so alien that I cannot transliterate it here.

A wall coldness swept through the room, causing the orb's light to dim.

"No, no, that's not it," Darius said and did some more pondering. I was witnessing magick firsthand, and it was frightening me.

Darius let his arms drop to his side as he muttered to himself. "Let's see, it's—" and then he mumbled something —"No, it's—Ah yes!" He raised his hands over the cauldron and uttered his words. Immediately a fire sprang up under the cauldron, and the contents began to simmer.

I was awed and fearful at the same time. "How did you do that?" I asked in wide-eyed amazement.

"The same way Lord Banderwall did it," he said. "You've been reading the books, boy. Surely there's something you can do."

"I don't want to."

"And that's the difference between you and me. Now shush and let me work."

Darius conjured. He stirred the pot, adding bits and bytes of unspeakable things here and there, until finally he asked for the dragon's blood. I gave him the vial, and he poured it into the vat. Immediately, a vast cloud formed above the cauldron, and the outlines of a face appeared in it; voids of smoke becoming eyes and nose and mouth. They twisted and transformed into faces of the Demons we had seen in the Land, and they with a wave of Darius' hand, were sucked back into the cauldron.

Darius turned to me in the corner I was cowering in. He said, "In this cauldron is the potion that, when poured at the gap, will seal the Demons' realm forever."

"Are you sure?" I asked.

"Quite sure," he said with a smile. He then put the mortar on the table and ground its contents a few times with the pestle. "Now, if you will please summon our Troglodyte friend."

I did so.

Erdo came in, pinching his nose shut. "Are you ready for me?" he asked.

"Yes," Darius replied. "I need you to sneeze in this mortar."

"More like vomit," he said.

"A sneeze will do."

Erdo removed his fingers from his nose, and they flew back just as quickly. "Oh Gods," he said in that nasaly tone one has with their nose plugged. "I'm going to be sick."

"I know what will do the trick," Darius said. He plucked a small jar from the shelves and opened it. "Smell this, my friend."

Erdo gave him a suspicious look, and slowly opened his nasal passages. With one whiff he grew alarmed. Darius deftly put the mortar under his mouth and nose, and Erdo sneezed into it. Darius investigated the mortar and said, "Excellent! You are excused."

Clutching his stomach and his nose at the same time, Erdo rushed out of the room.

Darius mixed his—well, whatever it was he was mixing. "Look at this, Lord Seer," he said.

I cautiously peered into the stone bowl. I saw a red-brown paste that looked and smelled harmless enough.

"One dab of this on the forehead, and you will be impervious to fire."

"Are you sure?"

Darius grabbed the bowl away from me. "Of course I'm sure," he said indignantly. "Now I must give power to our swords."

*** *** ***

I fell asleep at some point while Darius was working his magick. I had a dream...

In the dream I was flying over the land on the wings of a great eagle. The land was blackened and scorched, and I knew it was by the Demon's handiwork. But then as we circled round, I saw the Land grow green again, and its people flourish. I heard a voice, a female voice, the voice of the Golden Oracle: *Free the Land, Kyle. Free the Land and restore it to its former glory. Only you, the Chosen, the Chosen of the Golden Oracle, can. It is beyond saying that you must do this. You will do this. It is your destiny, as Destiny herself has decided...*

I woke with a start. Darius was holding a vial under my nose; a vile that smelled so bad that it woke me from my sleep.

"Back in the land of the living?" he taunted. He held a jug in his gnarled hands. "One drop of this on a blade and it will cut stone."

"Then let's cut Demons," I said.

*** *** ***

CHAPTER SIXTEEN: THE LAND GOES TO WAR

Fortified by magick
The seer did seek
To make the Demons die in death
And cause them to shriek.
-The History of the Second Banderwallian War, verse 30,353

Eventually, the magick had been worked and it was time to return to the farmhouse and wage war.

When we came to the end of the tunnel, Darius came to a terrible realization: we had spent the night in the tunnels. He anointed us against fire, but we had no weapons to defend ourselves with. It was daylight, and we had to find our way back hoping that the Demons would not challenge us.

Before leaving the moat, Darius smudged a little more of the fire protection balm on my forehead as a precaution against losing the Claimed. The balm smelled terrible and produced a strange cold and tingling sensation in my limbs. He did the same to Erdo, who protested, and them to himself. We were safe—for a while.

Well, we crossed the moat without incident. We trudged into the city, finding nothing but the burned-out relics that we had seen before. The Demons, it seemed, had gone elsewhere in search of food, and that was the worst part of it. If they had been confined to the Second and Third kingdoms, we would be lucky.

If not…

Nothing moved around us as we made our way back to the farm. How could it? The goings were singed, dead, devoid of life. I hoped and prayed that the evil had not spread to the other kingdoms.

We neared the farm. I smelled brimstone, and so did Erdo and Darius. It seemed to be coming from the direction of the farm, which caused me anxiety. What was happening?

We continued to walk, and although everything was burnt all around us, there was no sign of the Demons.

As we came close to the farm, the reality set in: A line of hungry Demons had blocked those in the mineral flats from leaving. Without food and water, those held captive would die.

We stopped well out of the presumed earshot of the Demons.

"What are we going to do?" I asked no one in particular.

Darius chose to answer me. "We must fight."

Erdo ran behind me.

"But we have no weapons!" I said.

"You have your dagger."

"Oh, sure," I said. "Like I could run up on a fire-spitting demon and cut him in half with the dagger."

Darius masticated my words. He turned his head and spied the burned-out farmhouse. "Have you got an ax in there?"

"What has that got to do with it?"

"We have the fire protection balm. You could cleave a few of them in two, I can rush into the flats and treat the swords of those armed. It's a simple plan, really."

"That's insane."

"Of course it is."

We sneaked across the farm to what was left of the barn. There in the middle of the burnt space, was an axe sunk into a stump. It seemed unreal, prearranged.

I watched as Darius dribbled a few drops of his preparation on the ax blade. It glowed a terrible blue. "Now, take the ax," he said.

I tugged at the ax, but it was well-sunk. I had to put the foot of my good leg onto the stump in order to brace and release the ax. I stumbled backwards onto my bad leg and almost fell.

"This will never work," I said dejectedly. "I'm a cripple."

"Oh stop," Darius. "It is distasteful for a hero to whine."

"I'm not a hero," I insisted.

"You will be, you will be."

There was nothing left to do but approach the literal line of fire.

"Look!" someone shouted. "It's the Lord Seer! Gods be praised, we're saved!"

I only wished I shared their confidence.

The Demons took notice of us. First it was just one, and then he alerted his "companions." "Food!" it said, which I understand is the only word the bulk of them can speak or understand.

Slowly the Demons—and there were scores of them—took notice. Slowly they advanced on us. I chose a solid piece of ground to take my stand as Darius and Erdo hid behind me.

These were barbarous moments. I had to wait until I saw the yellow of their eyes to strike.

No matter, they struck first. Two of the Demons spat fire at us. I felt it bathe me with no pain; there was just an intensification of the tingling sensation I felt in my limbs.

The Demons seemed not to take notice their fire wasn't having the desired effect until they were upon us. A terrible, bipedal monster with billowing gills, red eyes and horns drew near, and I raised my ax. I brought it down upon the thing's head as with as much force as I could muster. To my surprise, it cut through the thing like butter. Its body split in two, spilling ugly, black organs on the ground.

The other Demons stopped in their tracks, and I began swinging. They were all well within my reach, and three of them felt the weight of my ax. I split them across their midsection, and now the stench of their organs was rising into the air. The Demons in the background responded by flinging fire into the mineral flats, but luckily everyone was out of their range—and cheering in glee.

Confidence swelled in me. Not realizing that I did not have my cane, I stepped toward the flats, swinging at anything with green scales. Darius was behind me, and dashed into the flats, followed closely by Erdo.

The Demons began to understand and retreated into the singed forest.

Covered in ichor, I stepped into the flats. The accolades I received were welcome, but ridiculous. Everyone—Dowry, Derek, and my parents—felt the need to hug me and get their clothes mussed. But I was most stunned when Chamberlin Bule appeared, lauding me in a manner similar to the others.

Not satisfied with a mere embrace, Dowry threw himself at my feet. "Blessed savior!" he said. "How did you do it?"

"Magick," I confessed.

Everyone took a sharp intake of breath.

"Listen to me!" I shouted. "Listen to me, all you. Magick started this whole affair, and so magick can only end it. Come, anoint yourselves and your swords. We have a war to fight."

More cheers.

Darius treated each man and his blade with the paste and the oil.

*** *** ***

We had plenty of balm and oil left once Darius performed his rituals. And then, naturally, they all looked to me for direction.

Derek lifted me upon the stump in the barn. I was facing about a hundred people who had Demon's blood in their mouths. It was all I could do to release them.

I began my speech, a speech more carefully worded than any of those that came before: "The Demons have fled into the forest and are undoubtedly headed for the Second Kingdom. We must intercept them and destroy them before they are able to pillage."

More cheers.

"Then I charge you to kill as many as you can. I don't know how many there are, but they cannot withstand our swords. Follow Dowry's lead!"

They continued to stand before me, waiting for another word.

"GO!"

My army took into the forest. Gods help me, but I had become a general, as prophesied.

Where was my cane?

It was leaning against the stump, where I left it when I pulled the ax from the stump. I suddenly realized that I was disabled, not crippled. Somehow, someway, *that* cane had found its way back to me. It was the one my father had fashioned for me, and it had been freshly polished. I never figured how it got there. I simply took the cane and the ax in the other. I felt balanced and satisfied.

*** *** ***

As I strode through the forest, the foliage was greener as one neared the Second Kingdom. That is not to say that there was a dearth of demon bodies; no, their split corpses lay everywhere. My army was doing their job. Nothing moved under the canopy of trees save those creatures nature had put there.

The walk took the entire day, but eventually I fell under the shadow of the Second Kingdom's run-down castle. There, at the base was my army, slathered in black goo and cheering victoriously.

Dowry advanced toward me, arms clasped. "Victory!" he cried.

"Not yet," I said.

Lord Dowry said, "We have slain the Demons! The Land is free!"

I adopted my General tone. "Not yet. I have to close the gap they came through."

The men looked at each other. "Then what shall we do?" Dowry asked.

"Stay vigilant," I warned. "Split anything with green

scales."

"Yessir!" he shouted, and then gave the traditional salute of three extended fingers to the forehead.

This was bad, to be assured, but got worse as Princess Elwynna bored through the crowd and threw her arms around my neck. "Bless you, Lord Seer!" she exclaimed. "You are a hero among heroes!" She planted her bubbly lips against mine and kissed me in a way that I had envisioned for Sariah and me.

I did my best to shove her away in a manner that was not too obvious. "The work is not over," I said. "That you were spared by the Demons is good news; they were confined to the Third Kingdom. I still have to—"

She kissed me again, and I felt my gorge rise.

I practically shoved her away. "I must go," I said, and walked away, trying to hide my disgust.

In the distance, I thought I heard Darius laughing.

*** *** ***

CHAPTER SEVENTEEN: CLOSING THE GAP

With Demons slashed to and fro
The Seer made haste to Rind
Perhaps he should have gone there first, foremost
A surprise sure to find.
-*The History of the Second Banderwallian War, verse 38,924*

So many questions riddled my mind as we made our way back to Rind. It seemed as if someone was trying to direct my attentions from other matters at hand, namely the murder of Phyllaman the Foolish and the identity of the one that brought the demons across the barrier. And who put the poison in the food at the Council meeting? There were no real suspects, and no real reasons. Peace had been maintained, even if the ten rogue kingdoms were dabbling in magick.

If someone was trying to distract me, they were doing a good job. I realized that I would have to take care of one problem at a time, and first and foremost, it was the Demons.

So back to Rind we went. Darius had anointed me again and the same with my ax. He even anointed the cane, but I could hardly see it slicing a Demon.

We were not alone. Dowry, who obviously felt it was his birthright to ascend the throne of the Kingdom, accompanied us. Thirty or forty followed him, mostly knights but some civilians. All wanted to see me perform the task that would put an end to this entire miserable affair.

We kept our weapons ready, for we never knew if we

would encounter a Demon. As a matter of fact, we did, but it was frightened and ran at the blue glow of Dowry's sword. Lord Dowry went charging off into the forest after it and retuned shortly covered in black glop. His perfect teeth shined white in his blackened smile. Everyone cheered.

In the distance, Rind's gilded stones shone like stars in the night—well, the stones that weren't blackened with soot shone. I was tired, hungry, and irritated. If my acts could bring about the end of this foolishness, I would be glad. All I could think about was Sissy's stews, her pies, and delicious dumplings. My belly was empty, damn it. That was all I could think about.

When we reached Rind, Darius realized that he was at a relative impasse. The drawbridge was up, and he didn't want everyone winding through the guts of the castle—and nowhere near Lord Banderwall's laboratory.

Darius sized his group and realized that he had left the strongest—Derek—behind, and was lost.

"Excuse me," Darius said, and waded into the moat.

I watched as Dowry shook his head. "Serpents," he said under his breath. Good old Dowry, still clinging to the bizarre rumors of watery death.

We waited.

Finally, the drawbridge began to lower, and then stopped when it was halfway lowered. I heard the chattering of gears and realized that the thing was stuck.

Darius called for men to help by trying to pull the drawbridge down, but everyone believed in the serpents.

"It's safe," I asserted, but the men were still reticent. And so I said, in all authority that was not mine, that the Golden Oracle bade their crossing the moat. There were no serpents, and their bite would bear no venom.

That was enough. Men spilled into the murky waters that weren't so deep, and they all grabbed the drawbridge. With concerted effort, the bridge was pulled down.

We spilled into Rind's blackened court. No one was afraid, that is, save me. The singing of the metal frightened me enough, but what lay inside frightened me further.

We made our way to the thrones room, the court where the gap had been opened. It was as I remembered it; a room with a gaping hole on one rock wall. The gap did not reveal what was outside, but what was *inside*, inside the so-called empty dimension from which the Demons came.

So there I was, the savior of the Land, standing before the gap. Now what?

Darius sneaked up beside me and dropped a vial into my hand. "Do it," he said.

"Do what?" I asked.

"Close the gap, boy! Close it now before more of the Demons find their way into our world!"

Gads, what a thought! I thought all of them had come through.

As usual, Darius provided me with no explanation of what I was supposed to do. Vial in hand, I approached the gap. I thought of Darius' anointings, so I began to smear the edges of the gap with the odorific contents of the vial.

There was immediate movement in the black hole of the gap. I could see scores of demons rushing toward me, roused by the stench of the magick. I continued my spreading, working as fast as I could.

The Demons were fleet indeed. I could hear those behind me drawing swords, but I knew that even with Darius' spells they would have trouble dispatching the multitude that were now drawing near to the gap.

I finished spreading the oily mess and stepped back quickly, but nothing happened.

"Speak the words!" Darius urged me.

"What words?" I asked in terror.

"Good Gods boy, did you read the Litany, or did you not? Speak the words!"

The Litany? I read that years before! How was I to recall the proper passage?

It was then that I heard a high screech; the screech of an

eagle. The words fell from my lips: *"And those that were conjured shall be remanded to the empty dimension forever."*

The stones of the wall began to rebuild and reposition themselves. The Demons charged for the gap, but the wall continued to build, making a weird sucking noise. Finally, the gap closed itself, and a Demon with a raised claw was sealed into the wall, its claw protruding through the sealed wall.

Dowry raised a sword and was about to sever the claw. "No, Dowry, leave it," I said. "Leave it, and let it serve as a reminder to those who follow."

Dowry replaced his sword in its hilt, albeit reluctantly.

The drama was over.

Or was it?

*** *** ***

CHAPTER EIGHTEEN: THE COUNCIL'S DECISION.

Back in the castle shiny and high
The Kings decided to meet
The time of Destiny was nigh
And it is a hard yoke to beat.
-The History of the Second Banderwallian War, verse 54,987

The city of Rind was given a quick polish, for the Council was about to convene. I felt some happiness at last, for now the task would be removed from my shoulders and placed somewhere else.

My fate was up for the highest bidder.

I did not attend the Council meeting, and this infuriated Bule. "You can at least advise the council should the Demons reappear."

"They won't unless someone tries to open the gap., but I believe that the gap is closed for good."

"Goodness!" Bule exclaimed. The sleeves of his poofy, Priory-provided blouse were too long for his arms. Even without Phyllaman the Foolish the stupidity continued.

I heard a voice in the hallway, and it sounded as if someone was calling my name. I followed the sound around the corner to see King Delwyn, supported by Darius, coming toward me. The hair stood up on the back of my neck.

"Lord Seer," Delwyn said, "the council has made a

decision, and we need you to seal it."

"Oh," I said absently. "Surely."

I followed the two men down the hall. King Delwyn, the most wise of the thirteen—I mean eleven—and he had taken the time to summon me himself without sending an errand boy. Trouble was brewing.

We reached the doors of the room. I deferred to Delwyn to enter, and Darius took his place behind him. No sooner did we enter the chamber did Darius shout, "HAIL KYLE, LORD SEER! CLAIMED OF THE GOLDEN ORACLE! LOFTY OF PLUMES! CHOSEN OF THE GODS! HIGH OF POSITION IN THE HEAVENS! UNITER OF THE TWO LANDS, CAUSING THE GODS TO BE PACIFIED! SMITER OF DEMONS! CLOSER OF THE GAP!"

I was horrified. All the kings, princes and knights had raised their swords, and at the end of Darius overblown introduction, the knights and kings, walked up to me and laid their swords at my feet in the traditional gesture of submission.

I was at a loss for words, awash in sickness and grief. Maybe I did some heroic things, but not enough to have the most powerful men in the Land to lay their swords at my feet.

"Well!" I said, trying to find words. I had to direct attention away from myself. "I'm honored but let us not forget that that Golden Oracle made this possible."

"She worked through you; you are the hero," someone said. If I'd known who it was, I would have slapped him.

I stepped further into the room, nearly tripping on the swords. I was trying to think of something to say, but King Delwyn beat me to it: "There are two kingdoms without kings, and no heirs. It is our desire to form one kingdom of the First and the Second. One land, one king. We just need your blessing to seal the deal."

"Who are you nominating for the throne?"

"*You.*"

I blinked. The blood in my veins chilled. Words came quickly. "I'm sorry, but I must insist that there is a better candidate."

Everyone else blinked.

Suddenly, I felt something very sharp poking me in the small my back. Darius was standing behind me and had a knife. "Take the position," he hissed. "This is your destiny, but moreover it is *my* destiny. Take the position and fulfill your destiny."

What was the use? I agreed.

"Excellent!' Delwyn said. "You will wed Elwynna tomorrow."

All hail the farm boy king. I was the wisest of all. A goddess blessed me. I was a hero. I fit the position.

The knights and kings collected their swords and bowed to me. I was the most powerful man in the Land. All I had to do was claim prophecy, and everyone would follow my lead.

There were proceedings that day, to be sure. I sat at the kings' table, and other things were discussed. Magick was banned once more, and it seemed that everything was in its place.

*** *** ***

CHAPTER NINETEEN: ANSWERS AT LAST

The gap was closed with surest bet
And the Land was now at peace
But the biggest battle was not fought yet
But answers abound, as sure at least.
-The History of the Second Banderwallian War, verse 60,202

Eventually, the Council broke for the evening. I wanted to run away, but I didn't want to disappoint the kings when they realized what a terrible ruler I was.

One would think that a king elect would be well guarded, but I suppose that since everyone thought I was chosen of the Gods that I needed no protection. And so I strolled beyond the castle walls and into the courtyard before the drawbridge. It was a flawless night, and as my eyes adjusted to the moonless starlight, I saw a figure reclining next to a flowering bush.

"You disappoint me," Darius said, approaching me.

"I'm not up for your foolishness right now," I said.

"Foolishness?" he chortled. "O my Lord King of the United Kingdoms and Claimed of the Golden Oracle, I am never foolish. Rash perhaps, but *never* foolish."

King? Bah! I was as unfit to rule as any farm boy. I sighed and said, "Then speak your piece and then leave His Majesty."

Darius looked at the ground in a coy gesture. "Well, your Highness, you still don't know who summoned the Demons, or who poisoned the food at the Council meeting, or who put the wax pin in the carriage."

"No, I don't. But I'll pursue the matter."

He smiled. "Yes, well, there's just one problem."

"What?"

"I'm dying."

I was stunned.

"No, no, it's all right. Don't say you're sorry. The magic of the Goren root has taken its toll. It prolongs, but it kills. The real problem is that my history of your affairs is not finished and that pains me. I had thought that with all your education you might have deduced the answers by now, but I now see you haven't. Since I don't have the luxury of time, I shall tell you what you need to know."

I began to feel sick to my stomach. I said, "Don't tell me that you knew the answers all along, and that you were waiting for me to light upon them on my own."

He smiled again. "Well, that's what it all amounts to..."

"Darius, you *idiot!* You would compromise the safety of—"

"Don't lecture me," he snapped. "I told you a few days ago that I was writing my most fabulous work. What kind of a story would it be if it concluded with the scribe seeing for the Seer? I expect you to do as you ought."

"What? To march into the castle and announce that I have received a revelation?"

"Don't interrupt. I expect you to *earn* the truth. You and you alone must fight one last battle."

Suddenly the hair on the back of my neck stood on end. The night seemed to grow brighter, and I realized that Darius' personage had begun to shimmer and glow. "You never asked, 'Why now?'" he said, his voice becoming deeper and throaty. "The Litanies are correct: the universe is a study in opposites. The Black Oracle has claimed his own, too."

With that he began to swell and grow before my eyes, becoming impossibly tall and massive in form. He began to cackle, and then to laugh in a booming voice that shook the very ground.

I heard a shout of alarm from the parapets of the castle, and suddenly the armaments were filled with revelers and knights, gazing in the horrible spectacle.

Darius was taller than the castle, towering over the gilt stone. Everyone cowered except for me; I was frozen in terrible awe. *"I KILLED KING THEODORE THE FIRST!"* Darius boomed. *"I POISONED THE COUNCIL OF THIRTEEN! I SUMMONED THE DEMONS AND PLOTTED FOR THE LAND TO BECOME CONTENTIOUS AND BARREN,*

FOR I AM HE, CLAIMED OF THE BLACK ORACLE!"

I didn't know what to do. I suppose I could have run, but one stride of the giant Darius was equal to a hundred of mine. And then a thought struck me: in order to fulfill the destiny that Darius had written for me, I had to defeat him. He *wanted* me to defeat him. I decided to stay put and see what happened next.

From the parapets came the cries and moans of my subjects. Darius certainly knew how to put on a show.

"Destroy him, Chosen One!" someone shouted (I think it was Elwynna.)

My decision to buy time paid off. Darius extended an impossibly long arm into the night. His fingertips shimmered, and in them appeared what was apparently a spear with a black shaft and a glowing silver head. It was but a twig in his hands, but I knew that if it pierced me, it would mean my death. *"DO YOU SEE THIS, SEER?"* he bellowed. *"THIS IS THE SPEAR OF DESTINY! YOU HAVE AROUSED HER IRE BY FORETELLING THE FUTURE, AND ONLY THIS WEAPON CAN STILL THE HEART THAT BEATS AS CLAIMED BY THE GOLDEN ORACLE! PREPARE TO DIE!"*

Spear in hand, he reared back to throw a mighty blow. And then he hesitated, as if waiting for a cue.

"I SAID, PREPARE TO DIE, SEER!"

And still he hesitated. Suddenly I heard the high screech of an eagle.

"Look!" someone shouted.

I looked up and skimming the surface of the night was a golden eagle. I was awe-stuck and horrified at the same time, for *this* was my Mistress, the embodiment of the Golden Oracle herself.

"NOOOOO!" Darius shouted melodramatically and dropped the spear. He covered his eyes with his huge hands, terrified by the sight of such goodness.

The spear (which I had paid no attention to) fell to the ground, piercing the stones at my feet. I later realized that if I had taken one step forward during the affair, the sharp end would have entered my skull.

And so I took the spear into my hands. It seemed fragile, but it throbbed with some mystical power. I reasoned that if it was enough to kill my Goldenness, it could kill his Blackness. However, it seemed ludicrous that such a small implement could do him harm.

I looked up to see Darius flailing with his arms, trying to shoo the bird that circled his head. Suddenly the Eagle swooped down toward me, meeting my eyes with hers, as if to say, "What are you waiting for?"

I looked at her and shrugged. What I was about to do was no more ludicrous than anything else I had done. And so I hefted the spear and threw it at the giant. In its trajectory the spear grew larger and larger, and finally Darius-sized as it pierced him in the chest.

"NOOOOOOOOOOO!"

The giant reeled backwards, then forwards, then turned its face into the night. *"GODS, FORGIVE ME!"* he cried, and fell to his knees.

Good old Darius, melodramatic to the last.

He clutched his wound as his body returned to normal size. There was no blood, thankfully, for it there had been the giant's liquor would have filled the moat. He reached up and grabbed me by my blouse, pulling me close. "You play a good game, boy," he said. "The history is under the throne. IT's enchanted, so it cannot be torn, burned or otherwise. *Everyone* will know. There is naught, as I, and there is not, as you. What happens next? It's in your hands."

"But—how did you know the eagle would come?" I asked.

He smiled then, the last smile he would make. "Eagle?" he said. "It was all done with mirrors."

And then Darius collapsed to the ground and died.

I was barely aware of the throng that flooded the courtyard, bowing and kneeling, praising me for saving The Land. I had been had, duped, and used by the greatest charlatan ever to walk The Land. And now? Now he was still writing my destiny, for I held the fate of two kingdoms in my hands.

"Hail King Kyle, Claimed of the Golden Oracle!"

Claimed? Oh yes, I think so, but not by a golden eagle.

*** *** ***

EPILOGUE

...and so, my son, understand this: so great was Darius' desire to make a mark that he risked the safety of the Land and everything that dwells in it. Why poison, you ask? Why summon the Demons? Why kill King Phyllaman? It was all part of his plot to work history to his likening. I don't know how or when he hatched the plot. It's immaterial. All he saw was a farm boy that he would raise to greatness; a farm boy who couldn't even farm and is now a king.

Still, there is one fact that bothers me, namely Phyllaman's death. He was in the carriage with Chamberlin Bule *and* me. How did he know Phyllaman would die? How did he manage that trick? Well, I don't think he knew what the outcome of the event would be. He saw three important people in a carriage and plotted to injure us. That Phyllaman died was gravy.

Oh, but Darius left so many questions behind! How did he manage to sneak the poison into the Council's food? I think that he indicated that to me when we discussed the possibility of a magical disguise. Sometimes I think that Darius hadn't written the entire history yet, that he waited to see what developed and played his game with whatever material suited him. And yes, his history of the Second Banderwallian War is regarded as a classic. It makes me nauseous just thinking about it.

You know the rest of the story. There is no sense in recounting my marriage or ascension; all these are a matter of public record, and just as false as Darius was. Chamberlin Bule was indispensable to me as I ascended the throne; he served me well into your fifth year when he succumbed to a fever. I never thought I'd miss that prissy man so much. Erdo, a hundred years old and counting, is by my side. He deserves that much, you know. He still has another hundred years left; I will not know whom to consult when a crisis arises after his death. And as for me, well, I married hideous Elwynna to secure the two kingdoms into a united one. I have suffered ever since. If only she knew the truth about her brother!

In closing, I pray that you have learned one thing: the Gods do not write our destinies. They are in our hands. Some of us are clever like Darius and can manipulate the future, while others suffer whatever comes our way. I guess that what I'm really trying to say is this: Remember my story, my son, and don't let your life be dictated by others. Don't let this happen to you, too.
Love,

Your Father

*** *** ***

CONCLUSION

Elwynna closed the book. Her blood boiled. Someone was going to pay...

The Black Oracle would have his day...

...for naught produces naught, and together the universe deigns the right to be.

THE END

ABOUT THE AUTHOR

Howard Scott Shuford is a Pug-loving, eclectic strangeperson who shed his schooling in Geology in order to write and cartoon. He is the author of the novel *The Nine Circles: Adventures Across Conflicting Realities,* the compilation *Professional Sports and the Decline of Western Civilization,* and numerous shorter weird works.

Made in the USA
Columbia, SC
27 June 2023

340ca12c-1f49-4b27-a8b5-d78cc015e4d3R01